LIZ DELTON

Paperback ISBN: 978-1954663206

Cover design by JV Arts
Map by Angeline Trevena

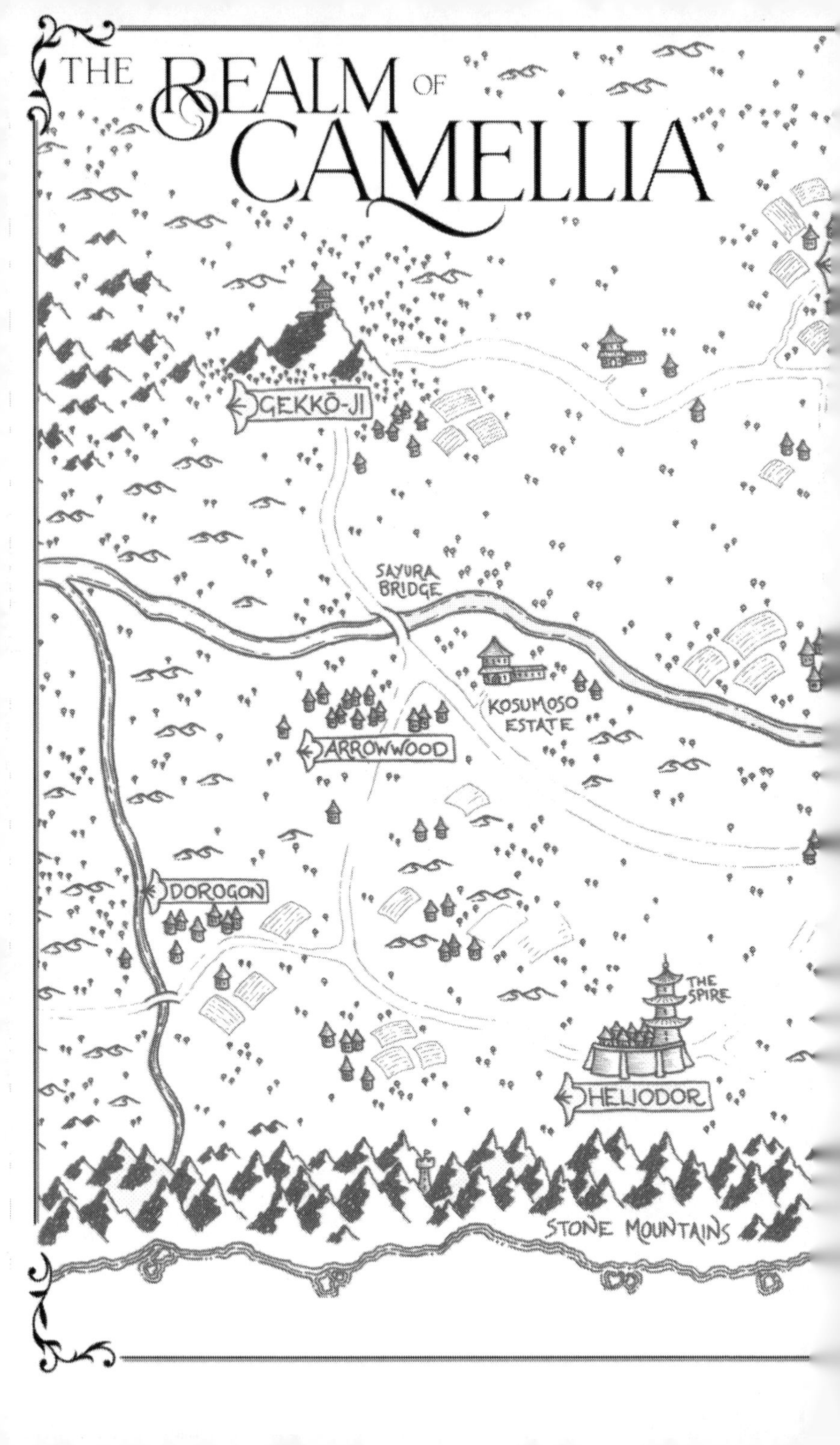
THE REALM OF CAMELLIA
GEKKŌ-JI
SAYURA BRIDGE
KOSUMOSO ESTATE
ARROWWOOD
DOROGON
THE SPIRE
HELIODOR
STONE MOUNTAINS

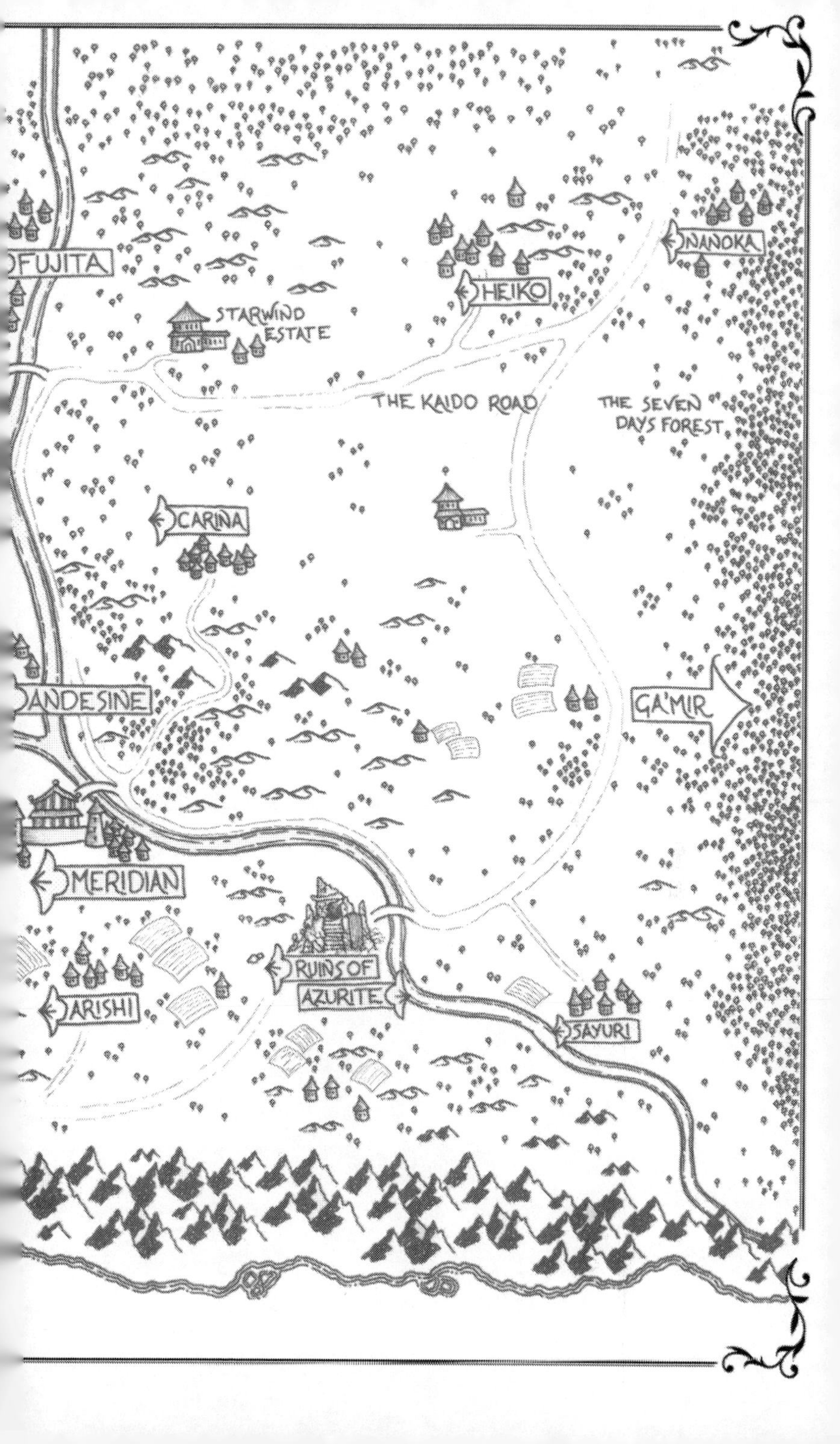
FUJITA
NANOKA
HEIKO
STARWIND ESTATE
THE KAIDO ROAD
THE SEVEN DAYS FOREST
CARINA
ANDESINE
GA'MIR
MERIDIAN
RUINS OF AZURITE
ARISHI
SAYURI

Chapter 1

Broken

Kira Savage was broken.

No matter how hard she tried, she couldn't get her Shadow magic to work.

Of course, she wasn't supposed to be using it. But who would really know, anyway? Shadow magic was the unseen, intangible side of magic, the opposite of her physical Light magic.

She sat on her small bed in the dorm house, gazing into the trunk she was supposed to be packing with her meagre belongings. This morning she was leaving Gekkō-ji, which had been her home here in the Realm of Camellia for almost two years now, to go to the Spire.

Kira would be staying in Heliodor for a whole year to train at the Spire, so she could become a Gray Knight—one of only eight people in the realm to be blessed with both Light and Shadow magic.

It was finally time, and she couldn't even conjure a Shadow wind to pick up the paper crane her friend Nesma had made for her, which sat atop her open trunk. She bunched her hand into a fist, trying to remember the paltry lessons Lord Raiden had taught her about Shadow magic. Maybe she just forgot how to do it.

Someone hammered on her door, and she jolted off the bed, her bare feet landing on the wooden floor.

"Yes?" she called, padding across the room then sliding the wooden door open along its track.

Jun Kosumoso stood there, his hand still raised to bang on the door again. His face cracked into a wide grin when he saw her, and he brushed a few strands of his gold-tinged black hair out of his eyes. "You ready?"

Kira slouched back over to her trunk and picked up the paper crane. "Basically. What are you doing here so early?"

He shrugged and casually leaned against the door frame, but Kira noticed his toe tapping.

She tucked the crane inside the small wooden box still sitting on her bed, the only thing she hadn't packed. Inside it was a simple leather bracelet that had belonged to her father, a few of his drawings, and a slim piece of plastic that was almost as out of place in this world as she was.

It was a library card, from the *real world*—or, as everyone here called it, the Starless Realm. Yet both worlds were very real to Kira. The Realm of Camellia had seemed like a fantasy when she had first arrived here, but now she knew her parents had been raised here. And last year she found out that she was the daughter of departed Gray Knight Rokuro Starwind, and everything changed.

Ever since last spring when she discovered she also had Shadow magic, she had been banned from even trying to use it until she started her official training at the Spire. But the leaders of the Light temple of Gekkō-ji wouldn't let her and Jun—who also discovered he had inherited Shadow magic—go to the Spire until they had honed their Light skills enough to advance to the level of squire. After close to a year's hard training, yesterday they both completed their advancement trials.

After months and months with nothing but combat training and learning more and more complex Light magic, Kira hadn't worried about her trip to the Spire—until she received the message from Lord Raiden two weeks ago.

Kira had promised the Storm King she would train at the Spire to learn more about her Shadow magic. Now that she was finally a squire, it was time to go.

But she was broken.

How could she conceal her lack of Shadow magic from everyone at the Spire? From the Storm King himself? Had it all been some sort of fluke? Could her magic just *go away*? Her Light magic worked as well as always; she had even impressed Master Tenchi at her combat trial with her speed and accuracy with throwing knives.

Last spring, she had been able to tap into Shadow magic and move things with the wind, control vines, and even move water. She had even figured out how to hear things from far away using Shadow—a fairly useful skill she had been quite proud of. As Lord Raiden had told her, the possibilities of Shadow magic were endless; a mage could do any kind of magic they had the proficiency for. Yet Kira couldn't so much as move a slip of paper anymore.

She packed her keepsake box into her trunk, then closed the lid. As she and Jun bent down to lift her trunk by its ornate silver handles, she blurted, "I can't get my Shadow magic to work."

Jun's side of the trunk slipped, but he caught it up again. "You're probably just out of practice."

"I'm not," she said quietly as they heaved the trunk from the dorm room and into the hallway. "I've been trying all year."

A half-smile brought up the corner of Jun's mouth. "Even though we're not supposed to?" he whispered conspiratorially as they wound their way through the labyrinth of corridors of the one-floor dorm house.

She scoffed. "Oh, please, Kosumoso," she said, grimacing at him, "don't pretend like you haven't been practicing. I know you. When you first came to train at Gekkō-ji you knew more about Light magic than half the novices who'd been here for months."

Jun snorted, looking over his shoulder while he walked backwards into the morning sunlight. They reached the outside gallery that ran along the front of the dorm house and set the trunk down beside the railing. She and Jun glanced around at the temple square, the pleasant glow of early summer sunshine warming their skin.

A few pages were milling around outside the kitchen house, where most of Gekkō-ji's trainees were finishing breakfast. Kira had gone early for some tea and steaming sweet buns before she finished packing.

She glanced left toward the enormous three-columned gate that led down the mountain, where two Light Knights with their pristine white belt-sashes stood guard. It was so strange that she would be leaving the temple so soon.

"Fine, I've been practicing," Jun admitted. "But I can't do much of anything yet."

"Uh huh."

As the son of one of the realm's six trained Gray Knights, Jun had not only inherited his magical talents but also grown up seeing his father use them. Kira had grown up not knowing about Camellia, magic, or even knowing anything about her father.

"I'm sure you just need proper training," Jun went on.

"But last year I was able to do all kinds of stuff!" Kira said, hating how whiny she sounded. She hopped up to sit on the gallery railing. "And I *started* training with Raiden when he was here for last year's festival."

Jun joined her on the railing. "Come on, you trained with him, what? Twice? His visit during the spring festival wasn't exactly optimal training conditions."

Kira chuckled, tucking a stray stand of hair behind her ear. "I guess."

"And if I recall, Lord Raiden was arrested, and the temple was overrun by commoners bent on breaking the peace between Light and Shadow," he mocked. "Yeah, great time to train in extremely difficult magic, I'd say."

"Yeah, yeah, yeah. That's all over now though." The commoners had settled down after the so-called Lord of Between had disappeared, the mysterious person who could not only create portals between realms, but magically change their own appearance, too.

"But I really thought I had some skill at it," Kira went on, "and ever since we caught the Lord of Between and he escaped, everything I thought I could do with Shadow just feels like it's slipping away. And now I can't so much as lift a piece of paper with it."

"I'm sure it'll be fine," Jun said, leaning over to bump her shoulder with his. "Lord Raiden and all of his mages can help you figure it out again."

She chewed the inside of her lip. "Yeah, I guess." She knew there was no getting around Jun's excitement, so there was no point in continuing to complain.

"We're finally going to the Spire!" Jun said, causing her to smirk; she knew him well. "We're the first new Gray Knights in two decades! The best Shadow mages will be teaching us; I'm sure they'll be able to help you figure it out again. Besides, you'll probably have your own private tutor, anyway, right?"

"Oh, come on," Kira griped, "You've got Gray magic too now; I think we're both on even footing. And everyone knows I'm really from Camellia now."

"Yeah, but everyone still thinks of you as being from the Starless Realm. I mean, you did grow up there."

"Yeah, yeah."

Jun sat up straighter. Kira followed his gaze toward the middle of the sunlit square, where a tall man wearing a black cloak was striding toward them. His wavy, shoulder-length hair was inky black, and his face was set in a scowl.

"Aren't you two ready yet?" Zowan called.

They both hopped down from the railing. Lord Zowan Koi, also known as The Defector, was one of the most powerful Shadow mages in all of Camellia, and he was one of Kira's closest friends. He was also the nephew of the Storm King. Much like an older brother or uncle, he had looked out for her when she first arrived in this realm, and had even given her her own horse.

Kira straightened the silver crescent moon buckle at her waist as he approached. "I thought we were meeting you at the stables later?"

"Change of plans," Zowan grunted. "I just met with Master Starwind." He leaned against the front of the railing, looking out at the square with his arms crossed over his chest. "I never thought your grandfather would agree with the Storm King," he muttered.

"What do you mean?" Kira asked. "What did Ichiro say?" Her lips curled up in a smile, having only last year found out that Master Starwind, one of the leaders of Gekkō-ji, was her grandfather.

"I can't help escort you to the Spire," Zowan said. "My uncle took advantage of my return visit to Heliodor and decided to appoint me as his personal liaison to the Imperial Palace. I have to report to the palace first and meet with the Empress' advisors. Who knows when I'll be able to join you in Heliodor."

"Can't you say no?" Jun said.

"I did. But Master Starwind and Mistress Nari both want me to accept. They think I can keep better watch over you if I have access to all of my uncle's affairs, which, if the palace advisors are concerned, I'll need full disclosure on."

Kira bit her lip. It did make sense, but she wasn't going to say anything. Zowan's animosity toward his uncle was longstanding, and completely warranted—over twenty years ago when everyone thought the Storm King destroyed the Light temple of Azurite, Zowan denounced him, but in turn, the Storm King wouldn't let Zowan's wife and daughter leave Heliodor. They then succumbed to a fatal illness that swept through the Spire. Though Raiden had apologized endlessly once the feud between Light and Shadow abated, Zowan still refused to spend more time than was necessary with his uncle.

Zowan uncrossed his arms. "The other issue is that I'll probably have to travel back and forth from Heliodor to Meridian a lot. The Empress and the advisors want personal updates on this experiment. Most of them are worried about you, Starless girl."

"But it's not like this is new," Kira said, furrowing her brow. "All the Gray Knights had to train at both temples."

"Yes, yes," Zowan said, half a grin bringing up the corner of his mouth, "But you're the first two in a long time—the first in Empress Mei's reign, I might add. They're worried they're sending you into Shadow territory never to be seen again. And you're their precious Starless girl."

Kira rolled her eyes. "I'm not precious, and I'm not *theirs*. I can take care of myself."

Jun snorted. "Tell that to them at your next fancy palace tea," he muttered under his breath.

Kira shot him a dirty look, but then spotted someone approaching them from across the square. It was her grandfather, Master Ichiro Starwind.

Master Starwind moved quickly for someone she was learning to call *grandfather*, though the liberal gray strands in the long black hair he kept tied back showed his age. He wore a simple but elegant dark gray overcoat that went down to his knees with matching wide-legged trousers. The silver sash at his waist pronounced his status as a Master, and the crescent moon buckle they all wore represented Gekkō-ji temple.

"Ah, good you're ready early," Ichiro said as he reached them, a tight smile forming at his lips. It didn't reach his eyes, and Kira wondered if something was wrong.

Kira and Jun both stood up straighter, then gave him a slight bow.

"We're changing the travel plans," Ichiro began.

Zowan muttered, "Yes, I was just telling them."

"Ah, no, actually there has been yet another change since we spoke."

Ichiro turned to Kira and Jun. "Lady Anzu and the rest of your escort are needed elsewhere today. They'll join you later on."

Kira frowned. She had really been looking forward to spending the day's ride to Heliodor with Anzu. She didn't get to see the knight very often, since she was always busy with quests all across Camellia, and she only stopped in Gekkō-ji every other month or so. But there would be plenty of time to see Anzu in Heliodor—she hoped, anyway.

"Lord Zowan will accompany you to Heliodor after all," Ichiro said. "He will be sufficient guard. The advisors can wait."

Zowan grunted and nodded an appreciative thanks at the compliment that he was worth the strength of five Light Knights. "Where's Lady Anzu and the rest heading?"

Ichiro hesitated for a second, pursed his lips, then admitted, "There has been word of a strange group of people disturbing Andesine village. Mistress Nari and I thought it best to dispatch a group of knights right away, and those are the only ones in residence at the moment."

Kira's heart sank to her stomach. "Is it the Lord of Between? Is he back?"

The Master shook his head. "The reports don't infer that, no. Hopefully, it's just raiders from Ga'Mir that have gotten wildly off course. We thought it best for the two of you to make haste for Heliodor in any case. I've heard whisperings from the palace that they're forming a small contingent of common soldiers to help protect the realm. They might not want you two traveling if these raiders get out of hand." Ichiro bowed his head at Zowan. "We'd like you to leave this morning—as soon as possible, in fact—instead of this afternoon."

Kira's jaw dropped, "But—" then she quickly shut her mouth. Even though he was her grandfather, she knew better than to talk back to the head of the temple.

"Your luggage will be sent on separately," Ichiro said, glancing down at Kira's trunk. "Lord Zowan, I want you to take them straight up to the stables and make ready. But first—" he pulled two small scrolls from inside his wide sleeves and handed one to each Kira and Jun.

Kira accepted hers, looking at the special seal that she knew was made from Light magic—it would be made so that only she could open it. She had only seen this magic once before and knew it was something special that Ichiro could do.

"Even though you will be training at the Spire," he told them, "You will still need to fulfill your requirements as squires. As you know, all squires must complete one year in the service of a Light Knight—or, Shadow mage, I suppose. I cannot restrict you in your choice between a Light or Shadow superior, since you have both."

Out of the corner of her eye, Kira saw Jun grinning. She idly picked at one edge of her scroll, wondering how in the world she was supposed to choose someone to serve under for an entire year. "When do we have to decide?" she asked.

"It is up to you, just as your training is up to how quickly you master your skills. The quicker you decide, the sooner you can advance to knight."

Kira and Jun nodded. She slipped her scroll into her deep pants pocket.

"Now," Ichiro said, bringing his hands together, "You must get moving. No doubt I shall see you back in this region soon, Zowan. Kira, Jun, be careful at the Spire and make Gekkō-ji proud. Zowan, I want you all on the road within half an hour, and I want a message sent the moment you arrive. I don't like what I'm hearing about these raiders—I don't actually know whether they're from Ga'Mir or not, and for once, that's troubling."

Ichiro bowed deeply to them, smiled at Kira, and hastened back toward the Moonstone, the small castle-like building at the north end of the square.

When Ichiro was out of earshot, Jun asked Zowan, "What's going on with these raiders? Why do we have to leave so early if they're only over in Andesine?"

Zowan shrugged, staring at the retreating form of Ichiro. Then he shook his head and said, "I don't know. But we better get up to the stables if we're to be gone so soon."

Kira followed reluctantly as Zowan started across the square.

"Wait," she called, and dashed back to her trunk. Opening the latch, she retrieved her keepsake box with her father's belongings. She couldn't just leave it here waiting to be sent to the Spire. They were her most prized possessions in the entire realm. All of her other belongings had been donated to her—clothes and other essentials—so she didn't particularly care if something happened to them.

Across the square, they passed the blooming cherry tree in the center, its blossoms ever-glowing with Light magic. Each blossom had been made by a Light Knight who had trained here, as part of their advancement ceremony. Kira couldn't believe that she might become a knight in a year at minimum—now that she had advanced to squire, all that was left of her training was the year of service. She would have a chance to put a blossom on that tree.

"So, who are you going to apprentice under, Kira?" Jun asked as they passed the tree, his mind clearly in the same place as hers.

Kira's gaze darted to Zowan's back as they followed him out the small gate and up the stone stairs to the stables. "I don't know yet. What about you?"

"I'm not sure. I'll definitely have to consult my father. Since we're going to be in Heliodor for a year, I think I'd like to do the squireship while I'm there. If I want to set a record for the fastest advancement to knight, I can't waste all that time, you know? So I guess I'll have to choose one of the knights Master Starwind is sending."

"Or you could pick a Shadow mage," Zowan chimed in as they reached the lookout over the temple square.

Kira paused and rested her hand on the ornate black railing at the edge of the lookout point, taking a moment to soak in the view of the temple that had been her only home here in Camellia. The walled temple square lay nestled in a dip between two rises at the top of Mount Gekkō, the glowing cherry tree a beacon in the center. The two L-shaped dorm houses were situated in the corners beside the main gate, their black ceramic tile roofs soaking up the morning light as the sun began to shine down on the mountain. In the northern corners stood the bath house and kitchen house, and between them, the large stone edifice of the Moonstone, named for the large clock it boasted, its gemstone face winking and shimmering in hues of gold and blue as the sun hit it. She would miss this place.

Not only because it was familiar to her, but because she knew what she was doing here. She knew how to do Light magic. She even thought she was pretty good at it.

What would happen when she arrived at the Spire and couldn't even do Shadow magic?

Would they make her wait until the knights could be spared to send her home?

"Come on Kira," Jun called, jerking her out of her trance. She slid her hand off the railing and followed.

Before she stepped away from the railing, she spotted something small and bright dashing into the grounds and heading toward the Moonstone. Lithe and glowing, one of Mistress Nari's messenger foxes lit up the entrance of the Moonstone as it entered, then winked out of sight. "I hope it's not more changes," Kira muttered, wishing she were skilled enough to create a messenger like Nari's foxes, able to travel across Camellia and relay messages back and forth between the temple and its knights.

Zowan was already out of sight, but he shouted, "Let's go Starless girl!"

Kira's face warmed and she jogged up the rest of the stairs to catch up.

Chapter 2

Goodbyes and Secrets

Up at the stables, they headed through the large open door, and Kira found her dapple-gray mare Naga standing in the middle of the aisle, already bridled and saddled.

Kira smiled, coming forward to pat Naga's cheek when someone bumped right into her.

"Oh, Kira! I'm so sorry!"

Kira reached out to steady herself on the shoulders of the girl. "Nesma! What are you doing here? Don't you have calligraphy lessons right now?"

Kira smiled automatically, and then she realized—now was the time when she would have to say goodbye.

Nesma beamed at her, her narrow face lighting up. "Master Starwind asked me and Hikaru to get your mounts ready and bring up some supplies. He ran into us at the kitchen house before breakfast." She lifted a small sack in explanation, and Kira could see some bundles of food through the opening at the top.

"That's great," Kira said. "I didn't know if I was going to get a chance to say goodbye to you after Master Starwind changed our plans so last minute."

Nesma's gaze flickered away and settled on Naga's bridle. She adjusted a buckle that had already been done. "I can't believe you're going to be gone for so long."

Kira's chest tightened, and she put an arm around Nesma's shoulders. Even though Nesma was a few years younger than her, the girl was Kira's mentor here at the temple, because Kira had arrived here after her.

"I know," Kira said, "I hate to leave you and Hikaru and everyone, but Jun and I made an agreement with the Storm King..." she trailed off. She wished she didn't have to leave Nesma—especially now, after everything that had happened with the Lord of Between.

When the commoners had started kidnapping mages and knights, Kira had discovered that there were spies inside Gekkō-ji—and it turned out to be two girls who came with the Storm King's retinue. The girls were Nesma's estranged sisters.

Though Nesma had never spoken of them before, the girls had powerful Shadow magic, and the unique ability to manipulate other peoples' minds. That magic had kept

Nesma from telling anyone about the sisters' power until it was too late, and the sisters had already been discovered. That was finally when Nesma told Kira about her childhood and Nia Mari and Nikoletta's abuse, their mind control tricks.

After seeing them here in Gekkō-ji, and experiencing the devastating mind control all over again, Nesma hadn't been the same. Normally a rather shy girl to begin with, Nesma became closed off, focusing mainly on her Light magic. Kira even had to remind Nesma to eat enough sometimes when they shared meals at the kitchen house, when the girl just picked at her food and only drank tea.

Kira forced herself to smile. "You and Hikaru will have plenty to keep you busy while we're gone."

Nesma stared at Naga, then reached out and scratched the mare's ear. "You're right. Maybe I'll even advance to squire while you're gone." Nesma's smile looked about as forced as Kira's.

"I'll send letters," Kira promised, pulling the small girl into a hug. "Maybe I can get Zowan to teach me how to send letters with the wind using Shadow magic." And then she remembered about her Shadow problem. "Or something," she muttered.

Nesma pulled away and tucked a long strand of dark hair behind her ear. She turned away quickly, but not before Kira noticed how glossy her eyes were with tears. Nesma began busying herself by stowing the provisions in one of Kira's saddlebags.

Kira opened her mouth, but she didn't know what else to say.

"Time to go," Zowan announced. His black gelding Briar was saddled and ready by the open door. "Master Starwind wants us on the road."

Jun came over to say goodbye to Nesma, and Kira took Naga's reins and led the mare over to the door. While she waited for Jun, Kira slipped her keepsake box and her scroll from Ichiro into one of her saddlebags.

Just as they had all mounted their horses, the clear metallic sound of the temple's large bronze bell rang out over the mountainside, and with it came the sound of footsteps approaching the stables.

"We better get out of here," Zowan said, brushing his hair out of his face as he turned to look back at the stairs where trainees would soon be approaching from.

Kira nodded, glancing down at where Nesma stood by the open door. She gave her mentor a sad smile. "Take care, Nesma."

Nesma pressed her lips shut tight, but raised a hand in farewell.

Zowan had already urged Briar down one of the dirt paths that led down the mountain when a tall squire ran up to them from the stairs. It was Hikaru, Nesma's mentor.

"Oh good, you're still here," he said, panting. He clutched a stitch in his side with one hand, and with his other, pulled a scroll from his pocket. "For you, Lord Zowan. Master Starwind just received word—"

"Thank you," Zowan said, accepting it from where he sat atop his horse. He touched the seal and it dissolved into thin air, recognizing him. His eyes scanned the message, and he frowned. Glancing at Jun and Kira, he cocked his head to the trail. "Let's go."

Kira looked down at Hikaru, then jerked her head toward Nesma. Hikaru nodded in understanding, placing a hand over his heart. He strode over to Nesma and put a brotherly arm around her shoulders and led her to a quiet corner of the stables, which was now filling up with trainees readying for horse care lessons.

With a light tap of her heel, Kira urged Naga to follow Zowan and Jun down the trail, leaving life as she knew it at Gekkō-ji behind.

She took a deep breath of the early summer air as they began their descent down the mountain. Regardless of whether or not her Shadow magic worked, she was finally *going*. She would fulfill her promise to Raiden by coming to the Spire. What did it matter if she had Shadow magic or not?

But the thought of the keepsake box in her saddlebag and her father's legacy as a Gray Knight made her heart sink. If she didn't have Shadow magic, she wouldn't be like her father at all. He had been the leader of the Gray Knights until he was killed by raiders in the town of Sayuri, only a month before Kira's arrival in Camellia. Knowing she also had the same blend of Light and Shadow magic like him had made her feel *some* connection to the man she had never known.

She closed her eyes for a second, took a deep breath, and tried to focus her energy on rustling up a breeze to move the dry leaves at the side of the trail with her Shadow magic.

Nothing.

She sank into her saddle and sighed. What was wrong with her?

"What was that message about?" she finally asked Zowan as they reached the bottom of the mountain. "More changes?"

"It's nothing to be concerned about," he said in a would-be casual tone.

Kira glanced down at the leaves on the side of the path and frowned. It looked like she wasn't the only one keeping secrets.

Chapter 3

Standing Ground

At the bottom of the mountain trail, they passed through a tall gate and left Mount Gekkō and its forest behind. Ahead lay the imperial Kaidō road that wound all over Camellia.

Just as they started down the road, Kira spotted an old man standing under the shadow of a black pine tree. She gasped. He hadn't been there a moment ago when they had come out of the woods. And that meant it must be—

"Gekkō?"

It was the spirit of the mountain. The old man peered up at them. Zowan, Jun, and Kira halted their horses, and each of them bowed to him from their saddles.

Leaning against the tree, his back didn't look as hunched as it had the first time Kira had met him, back when he had appeared to her in Gekkō-ji's garden, and urged her to unite Light and Shadow. He still wore the same sandals, carried the same gnarled walking stick, and his short white hair stuck up like dandelion fluff.

A fat gray and white flying squirrel sat on Gekkō's shoulder. Thistle's big black eyes were wide, as—Kira imagined—he fought the urge to say something snarky.

"You three carry momentous change with you today," the old man remarked, as if he were commenting on what they carried in their saddlebags.

"And though you are leaving my mountain," he continued, "I still harbor concern over your actions, for they will greatly affect the tenuous balance of the Realm. The spirits of Camellia are still in turmoil over the actions of one human, the one who has mastered vile power beyond decency."

Kira's stomach twisted as she thought of the Lord of Between and what he had done to a knight and a mage—what he had almost done to her.

In addition to knowing how to open portals between realms and subsequently turning the local spirits mad, the Lord of Between knew how to extract the soul from another person. He had almost killed Ichiro this way before Kira had intervened, and it had been a close call when it almost happened to her, too.

Gekkō went on. "I am sending Thistle with you when you go to the Shadow region. Camellia's spirits are still vulnerable until this threat can be removed. You would do well to uncover as much truth as you can about this violator. Thistle will keep me informed."

Thistle chirped, and swooped from the old man's shoulder to land on the pommel of Kira's saddle.

The fluffy squirrel gazed up at Kira with a toothy grin, and Kira wondered if he was remembering the last time he had accompanied Kira to the Spire, when she had gone to convince the Storm King into brokering peace.

"But, sir," Kira began timidly, "last time Thistle came to the Spire, he wasn't..." she trailed off, unsure whether it was polite to speak of the spirit's magic.

Gekkō nodded solemnly. "Yes, at the time, Thistle had never been so far from me and he didn't have sufficient capabilities to use magic. We have rectified that problem; he will retain all his magic no matter how far he is from the mountain."

Thistle chittered in agreement, then hopped up onto Naga's head where he steadied himself by holding onto the tuft of gray hair. He looked at Kira expectantly with his big black eyes.

"Oh," she said.

Zowan bobbed forward in another bow, "Thank you for your blessing," he murmured.

"Th-thank you, sir," Kira said, "for sending Thistle with us. I'm sure his company will be—"

But where Gekkō had stood, there was only a dim haze of purple light, which wafted on a delicate breeze away from the tree.

"—useful," Kira breathed, turning to look back at Mount Gekkō.

Jun whistled appreciatively. "I've never spoken to the spirit of the mountain before."

"Nor I," Zowan said. "But we should really move on. Are you ready?" he addressed this last part to Thistle.

The flying squirrel nodded, clutching Naga's forelock tighter with his tiny claws. "I have no love for these uncomfortably jostling rides, but I'll survive."

Kira snorted. She remembered all too well Thistle's complaints the last time he had ridden with her.

Zowan clicked his tongue and urged Briar into motion down the Kaidō road, the others following in his wake.

* * *

They rode at a fast pace, and passed through Arrowwood around midday. They didn't stop. Zowan claimed he wanted to get to Heliodor as quickly as possible, but Kira wasn't so sure that was the reason. She thought it might have something to do with the fact that Zowan had once been held captive in one of the estate houses nearby, so she kept her lips pressed tight as they rode on.

Her stomach grumbled as they passed, the smell of food wafting from nearly every house. The early summer sun grew warmer by the hour; Kira was sweating a little with the effort of their pace.

Finally, when they were passing through empty countryside, did Zowan allow the horses to slow to a walk so they could eat. They entered the cool shade of some trees alongside the road as they came upon a small wooded area at the base of a hill.

Zowan had been quiet ever since they left Mount Gekkō. So while they opened up the food parcel Nesma had given them, Jun chatted with Kira about the Spire.

"It's going to be fantastic, Kira, trust me. They haven't had visitors from the Light region in decades."

"Yeah, and they were only at war with Gekkō-ji until about a year and a half ago. Don't you think they're going to resent us a little?"

"Of course not," Jun said, waving the idea aside with the dried date he held, his mouth full. "It's an honor to have the newest trainees with Gray magic—right, Zowan?"

"Hmm?" Zowan glanced back, then furrowed his eyebrows. "I don't know, Jun. You might want to rein back your excitement; don't you remember what happened when Kira came to the Spire last time?"

The shriek of the dying lake spirit that used to reside at the Spire seemed to echo in Kira's memory.

"But that wasn't my fault," she said, her shoulders drawing up toward her ears. "The lake spirit went mad because of the portal—and we know that the Lord of Between must have summoned it. *And* I didn't ask the Gray Knights to show up and attack Raiden and his mages—"

A shriek went up through the air.

For a wild second, Kira wondered if it was the memory of the lake spirit haunting her—but no, Zowan's horse Briar was rearing up in terror, nearly throwing him off.

Zowan held on as Briar danced backwards on his hind legs, then dropped back to all fours. Kira could see an arrow sticking out of Briar's shoulder. Eyes white with terror, Briar reared again. It was a wonder Zowan managed to stay on. Kira felt a drop in the air pressure around her, and thought she saw Zowan steady himself with a blast of Shadow magic.

With a flash, Kira summoned a polearm with Light magic, the long staff with a sharp curved blade atop winking into existence in her hand. She stared around, searching the woods beside them.

Briar continued shrieking, and Kira reached out a thought to pull more Light magic from her surroundings. With a steady exhale to will strength into her magic, she summoned a shield in place on her left forearm, fearing more arrows.

"There!" Jun cried, pointing with the blade he had summoned.

Kira saw something moving in the woods, and the next second, an arrow slammed into her shield as she raised it.

Still dealing with his panicked horse, Zowan sent a violent force of Shadow wind into the woods where they had seen movement.

"You two, go!" Zowan called. "Get to the clearing ahead!"

Kira stood her ground, banishing her polearm and instead summoning a small throwing knife. Knife after knife she summoned as she threw them into the woods, still unable to see their attackers.

Jun hadn't left either. Now he held a longbow at his side. As he shot each arrow, he summoned a new one onto the bow, with no need for a quiver.

"That was an order!" Zowan barked, and with a clap like thunder, both Kira and Jun's horses bolted toward the clearing ahead, urged onward by some Shadow magic of Zowan's.

"Zowan!" Kira called, grasping desperately for her reins, unable to turn back as she fought to regain her balance while Naga cantered forward. Thistle clung to Naga's forelock with a death grip.

Her heart hammered in her chest as she and Jun burst out of the trees. She finally got control over Naga and reined her in. They had emerged onto the edge of a wide field, where a canal ran alongside the Kaidō road. The small woods where Zowan now stood ground was nestled at the bottom of a hill.

Kira tried to think back to all that she had studied in Master Eizan's battle strategy lessons. Which way should they go to mount an attack? Was the higher ground better, or should she and Jun lay in wait hidden in the canal? She couldn't think straight. Zowan was in trouble.

She banished her shield and dismounted, again summoning one of her favored weapons, the polearm. She looped Naga's reins over the mare's neck, and the obedient horse stood still, Thistle perched atop her head like a comical furry hat.

"I wouldn't," Thistle advised.

Jun dismounted right as Kira began to stride back toward the woods. But instead of marching alongside her, he caught her with a hand to her shoulder.

"Don't."

Kira whirled around, blood rushing in her ears. "We have to! Zowan's in trouble."

Jun let out a weary sigh. "He can handle himself."

"I—I know he can," she said, throwing her arm up in the air. "But we should still go help him. Who were those people? You don't think it's commoners again, do you? And we're way too far from the border of Ga'Mir for it to be raiders. I know Ichiro was really worried about the people who attacked Andesine village. It could be them."

Jun shook his head, frowning. "I don't know. But Zowan ordered us to go." He said the words as if it were the end of the argument. Kira pressed on.

"I don't care." She took another step forward, and Jun followed, yanking her arm this time. "Hey!"

"Zowan won't thank you for going back in. He's just trying to keep us safe. He's here to protect *us*."

"Leave off it, Kosumoso!" she shouted. Then her fury cooled as she voiced a new thought, "Shouldn't he be here by now? What if he's hurt?"

She would never forget when Zowan was kidnapped by the Lord of Between's rough commoners; beaten and suffering head wounds, he could have been killed just like two of the others who had been kidnapped. What if he had been taken again?

But last time, the commoners had a secret weapon: a mage who could prevent others from using Light or Shadow magic. That was how they had kidnapped so many skilled mages and knights. Kira knew for a fact that the mage in question was in a high-security anti-magic cell along with the other insurrectionists.

She paced away from Jun, leaning on her polearm and gazing into the woods. The place where they had been attacked was around a slight curve in the road, so they couldn't see anything but the empty road. She strained her ears, but she couldn't hear anything over the babbling of the canal.

"He's fine," Jun assured her. "Look, I've known Zowan for a long time. He's probably the most powerful Shadow mage in Camellia—after the Storm King anyway. Are you really going to disobey an order from him now, when we're supposed to be picking a mage or knight to squire under?"

Kira's eyes bulged. "I don't care about that right now," she snapped, but made no further moves toward the wood. She banished the polearm and crossed her arms tightly across her chest. Fuming, she stalked back to Naga and buried her face in the mare's mane.

A light weight on her right shoulder told her Thistle had hopped down. "I'll go check on him," the musical voice said in her ear.

Kira's head whipped up. She craned her neck to look at Thistle. "Could you?"

Thistle cocked his head to the side.

"Please?" she added.

He chittered and swooped away toward the wood, somehow gaining height as if he were a bird on the wind, perhaps with the help of Gekkō's borrowed magic.

Jun led his horse over to the canal, and Kira followed suit, if only just to get Naga out of the open. Down the short grassy embankment, Naga went straight over to gulp out of the lazily moving water. Kira turned her back on Jun and watched the trees for any sign of movement.

Finally, after what felt like an eternity, the small gray form of Thistle came swooping toward them. Before the flying squirrel could say anything, Kira also spotted a single form limping toward them down the road.

"Zowan," Kira burst, and rushed toward him, leaving Naga to sample the grass beside the canal.

Dirt and sweat marred Zowan's face, but he looked unharmed, though something must be hurting to make him limp. "Are you all right?" Kira asked. "Where's Briar?"

"He's fine. Safe back in the woods, though, with that wound. I never was any good at Shadow healing. Maybe one of you could patch him up temporarily? I wanted to come check on you two before trying anything."

Jun had come up behind Kira. "I have some salve in my bags." He turned and went back to his horse.

"Who were they? What happened?" Kira asked Zowan.

He shook his head. "I have no idea. There were maybe a half-dozen of them, but I couldn't get close enough to any of them with all of their arrows. No sign of magic though, so it could be commoners again. It seems likely that it's the raiders Master Starwind was worried about."

Kira's stomach plummeted. "How do we know it's not the Lord of Between's people though? He convinced commoners to follow him last time."

Zowan shrugged. "If they were, they're acting a lot differently. They were shooting to kill this time—and even the Lord of Between's commoners had mages with them. No, I think it's something else."

Kira thought back to that note Zowan had gotten this morning. But before she could ask Zowan about it, Jun returned with a healing salve he had gotten from the apothecary at Gekkō-ji. In his other hand, he had summoned several lengths of bandages with Light magic.

"Let's get Briar patched up," Zowan said. "We need to get to Heliodor right away. I'll feel better when you two are behind their walls."

Chapter 4

The Spire

An hour outside of Heliodor, a contingent of seven Shadow mages rode up to greet Zowan, Jun, and Kira. Zowan had sent a letter ahead on the wind describing the attack, and the mages had ridden quickly to help escort them the rest of the way. After working some hasty Shadow healing on Briar's wound, Zowan's horse was as good as new.

"We're lucky it was such a shallow wound," Zowan told the mages.

It was a quiet and tense ride to Heliodor after that. Surrounded by the terse Shadow Guard, Kira and Jun did little talking. Kira wished it had been the Third Guard that had responded to the message; she had met them a few times before, and they were an amicable lot. This was the Second Guard, and they were all business.

The city of Heliodor wasn't hard to spot once they emerged from a shallow valley between two hills. They could see the pinnacle of the Spire rising up in the sky like a black beacon, the walled city at its base. Kira gasped at witnessing the height of the Spire. Even having visited Heliodor once before, it was still a phenomenal sight.

She looked up at the walls of Heliodor as they passed through the ornate wooden gate, the doors which would close behind them at least a foot thick. She felt her shoulders relax a little once they dismounted and led their horses down the crowded main street. There was no fear of raiders *here* anyway.

Jun's eyes were wide as he took in all of the variety of weapons vendors, so prevalent here in Heliodor since Shadow mages couldn't summon weapons like Light Knights could. Kira found herself eyeing a set of throwing knives at one vendor's stall that they passed, but she wasn't going to waste what little coin she had. Ever since Ichiro had learned she was his granddaughter, he had provided her with a small allowance so she could enjoy the local market with the other trainees on the rare occasion they had enough free time to frequent it. She had saved up as much as she could for her trip to Heliodor though, knowing she'd be training here for a whole year.

And besides, she could summon an infinite number of weapons with Light magic. That is, unless someone like that darkener mage was around who could stop you from using magic.

She shuddered at the thought, then absently touched the hilt of the steel dagger tucked into her belt sash. It had been a gift from Zowan ages ago, and wouldn't fail her if she lost her magic. It had saved her life on one such occasion.

It wasn't safe to just rely on magic.

They led their horses up the main street, the Second Shadow Guard still escorting them. Kira couldn't help but flick her gaze up to look at the Spire every so often. Impossibly tall, the dark tiered tower with its countless levels rose up high over the city. Kira suspected magic held it up, it was so tall.

Zowan had a closed look on his face, staring straight ahead, while Jun couldn't get enough of the new sights of the city.

"We finally made it! We're here," he said to her.

Kira smiled uneasily back at him and readjusted her grip on Naga's reins, which had become slick with her sweat. The mare bobbed easily along behind her.

"I don't know why you're so worried, Kira," Jun went on, gazing up at the tiered tower. "This is going to be *wicked* great," he said, eyeing her slyly. "Am I using that correctly?"

She snorted. "Yes. And I'm sure your use of Starless Realm lingo from New England will really impress the mages and masters."

Chuckling, he continued, "But seriously, you'll be fine. This will be great for us. Just think, after a year, we'll be ready to become Gray Knights!"

Kira didn't say anything. It was hard to get her hopes up when she couldn't summon the slightest whisper of Shadow magic. The thought of Jun becoming a Gray Knight without her sent her frowning down at the cobblestones. They had trained together for so long it was depressing thinking of him moving on without her. They competed with each other during combat lessons, and they helped each other learn more complex Light magic. She had never had a closer friend—even in the Starless Realm. She couldn't imagine leaving him here to train in Shadow magic without her for a whole year when they realized she didn't have Shadow anymore. Then she would just have to go back to Gekkō-ji to train in Light, with no one to challenge her or egg her on.

Finally, they reached the bridge that led over a deep canal to the temple grounds. All the while, the Spire towered over them, stark black against the light blue sky. Now a lush green lawn spread out before them, with various shrubbery set in calculated designs, most of it blooming with early summer flowers. Beside a small lake stood a beautiful open pavilion, the stone-tiled roof arching up artfully at the corners.

The Shadow Guard said their goodbyes to Zowan at the bridge, affording respectful nods to Kira and Jun before they turned their horses back down the busy street, no doubt to return to their patrol outside the city.

"Well, here we are," Zowan said, gazing at the grounds of the Spire, his jaw clenched. With what appeared to be some effort, he took a step forward into the place that had been his home so long ago.

Kira frowned watching Zowan's retreating form, but pulled Naga along nonetheless. She knew this was going to be hard for Zowan, returning to where his family had lived and died, but he could have declined the posting—she had made sure of it several times. She was just grateful he had wanted to be at her and Jun's side as they began their training.

As the three of them crested a short rise, they finally spotted the castle that stood at the bottom of the Spire. Steep stone walls at its base raised the castle up high with only one visible entrance, a narrow tunnel opening at the front.

The white wooden castle itself was enormous, nearly the size of the entire temple of Gekkō-ji, covered with elaborate gray gabled roofs, their corners decorated in gold filigree. And from the center of the castle, the impossible Spire rose high into the sky, the endless tiers nearly piercing the clouds as they rose up like a black dagger.

Kira drew in a sharp breath upon seeing it all up close. Thistle whistled from where he sat perched on Naga's head, then hopped over to land on Kira's shoulder.

Just as she was wondering where they should go, a small group of people came out of the castle, emerging from the dark entrance at the base of the stone fortification. The tall woman at the front beelined straight for them. She wore a tight-fitting robe of dark blue, closed up the front but clasped with a silver pin at her throat: an inverted-V, in the shape of the Spire, the symbol of the temple. Her pin-straight black hair was cut short, a style Kira hadn't seen on a woman since leaving the Starless Realm. Her sharp chin jutted out as she surveyed Kira and Jun.

"You are the new trainees?" she asked without preamble.

Kira nodded swiftly, then bowed at the waist.

The woman looked down her short nose at them. "You're later than we were expecting after the... *messenger* we received this morning." Kira sniffed, wondering the reaction of everyone else to one of Mistress Nari's Light fox messengers.

Zowan took a step forward, "We were attacked on the road—"

The woman cut him off as if he hadn't spoken, and she continued to address Kira and Jun, "My name is Kusari Kashjian; I'm the Keeper of the Spire. I will be assigning your training schedules, chores, and quarters while you reside here."

She glanced curiously at Thistle perched on Kira's shoulder, but she pursed her lips and apparently chose not to say anything about the flying squirrel's presence.

Kusari then gestured to the two people behind her, a boy and girl dressed in the same fitted Spire robes, but in black and gray. They stepped forward towards Kira and Jun.

"Normally you will be responsible for your own mounts," she said, "but Yuki and Tolson will take your horses to the stables for you on this one occasion. You are supposed to be meeting with the Storm King right now, and Kamellia help me if his schedule isn't the hardest to manage."

Kira remained silent as the boy took Naga's reins, until she remembered her possessions in the saddle bag. "Wait a second," she said, and retrieved her keepsake box and scroll. She hadn't expected to be rushed on like this, and she wasn't sure she liked this woman Kusari.

It wasn't until the two acolytes had walked away that Kira realized they hadn't taken Zowan's horse for him.

Zowan stood with his arms crossed staring down Kusari. But the woman continued to ignore him. Kira winced as she remembered Zowan's reputation here in the Shadow region wasn't exactly in good standing. Of course, they all thought *he* was a traitor after the Fall of Azurite.

But the Storm King had been framed, and it wasn't until last year that the shaky peace had been established between the two factions. The Storm King had forgiven Zowan for defecting, but it appeared that his people hadn't.

"Come," said Kusari, "It is a long walk up to the top of the Spire."

The bottom dropped out of Kira's stomach as she looked up at the tiered tower. Jun nudged her forward, and she realized Kusari had already turned back toward the castle entrance. Were they really going to have to climb all the way to the top?

Kira looked back at Zowan.

"I'll find you later," he said, seemingly unphased by Kusari's behavior. "I'll make sure they treat Naga well while I'm settling Briar in." He turned and led his gelding in the direction of the stables.

Thistle chittered. "I think I'll go with Zowan. Though I like the height of trees, I've no interest in going as high as *that*," he said with a disgusted look up at the Spire. He leaped off her shoulder and soared over to land on Briar's saddle.

With one last glance up at the impossibly tall tower, Kira followed Kusari into the dark stone passage into the castle, Jun behind her.

She had come this way once before. At the end of the tunnel lay a long hallway, with alcoves on both sides containing statue after statue. It was the Hall of Spirits; each statue modeled after one of Camellia's many local spirits.

Kusari didn't slow down, so they didn't have time to look much. Kira got a glimpse of one statue that looked like a miniature dragon, with a plaque reading, *Spirit of Fortune, Dorogon region*. Another was a beautiful woman with long hair covering most of her face, who had talons instead of fingers. She made a mental note to come back when she had more time to inspect the hall fully.

As Kira spotted the statue of an old man with a flying squirrel on her shoulder, she snorted and said quietly to Jun, "Thistle should have come in this way; we'll have to show him his statue later."

Jun grinned. Kira noticed Kusari glancing back at them, so she picked up her pace.

Finally, they reached the end of the hall and emerged into a wide-open foyer. Kira's eyes were immediately drawn upward, and she found herself looking up at the inside of the Spire tower. She felt like an ant at the bottom of a well.

Unlike the last time she had visited the temple, there were other people about. Two mages walked along one of the open galleries above them, and a group of girls sat in the middle of the foyer on the edge of the fountain in the center, their backs to the enormous jade sphere at the center of the fountain.

Various hallways and staircases led off the foyer, including a covered walkway that led out the back of the castle into the grounds. The faint scent of incense hung in the air, and the gentle sounds of water coming from the fountain brought a sense of peace that surprised Kira.

Kusari glanced up at the inside of the Spire and placed her hand on the corner of the wall beside them. Her eyes closed briefly. Then she scrunched up her face and frowned at Kira and Jun. "Well, Lord Raiden had to go to another meeting. You'll have to meet with him another time."

Kira's gaze flickered toward Kusari's hand on the castle wall and wondered just how the woman knew that.

Kusari let out an almost inaudible huff. "Very well, I'll take you to your chambers then. You can spend the rest of the day settling in. I can't go rearranging schedules all day. You will both meet with Lord Raiden tomorrow to determine the direction of your training."

She beckoned them toward a narrow passage off the foyer to the right. This one had a neglected look to it, and as they walked down it, Kira's nose wrinkled at the smell of dusty stone that was never completely dry.

"The Gray Knight quarters haven't been used in quite some time," Kusari said as she led them down a short staircase. "But tradition dictates that these quarters are to be used by Gray mages—and Gray mages only—so you must reside here during your stay.

"All trainees, regardless of what magic they possess, are expected to clean and maintain their own quarters, so I expect you to abide by this rule. You can't very well expect to achieve peace of mind with an untidy living space."

They came to a set of wooden double doors, with black wrought iron handles, and Kusari opened one side, leading them in. They emerged into a large common room with a threadbare colorless carpet covering dark wood floors. Rice-papered sliding doors on the far wall had been pushed aside to reveal an open balcony, so that the light breeze wafting in stirred up the dust all around the room. The thick layer of dust coated the low tables and floor cushions grouped in the center of the room. A large abstract painting done in black hung on the interior wall, but Kira couldn't tell what it was supposed to be.

"I opened the doors earlier to let in some air," Kusari said, crossing her arms and glancing about the place.

As Kira and Jun stepped further into the common room, little dirt clouds rose up from the thin carpet at their feet.

"Individual quarters are down that hallway," Kusari said, pointing down one of two corridors leading off the main room. "You're lucky; trainees normally have to share rooms with others, but the Gray Wing has plenty of private rooms, and you even have a private training room too."

Kira said nothing, pressing her lips tight. A sinking feeling grew in her gut the more she looked around the common room. An imposing slate fireplace held a few crumbling blackened logs, with cobwebs draped over them like streamers. Dusty lanterns hung from the ceiling and side walls, their iron fixtures gilded in rust. She avoided Jun's gaze, not wanting to see disappointment mirrored there as she knew it would be reflected in her own face.

"I'll send word when Lord Raiden is ready to meet with you," Kusari continued. "While you wait for your belongings to arrive, you'll want to start cleaning. Everything you need is in here." She slid open a door on the wall beside the entrance, revealing buckets, rags, a broom, and a mop that looked like they had been put there recently. They weren't covered in dust anyway.

Kira nodded at Kusari, crossing her arms around her middle. She felt almost sick.

After Kusari turned around and left through the double doors, Kira dropped her shoulders from where they had crept up.

"They couldn't have cleaned the place up for us?" she muttered to Jun as she went over to the cleaning supplies and inspected the worn broom. Its bristles stuck out at odd angles from where they were tied around the handle with a frayed string.

"Oh, who cares," Jun said. "They probably make everybody clean when they get here."

Kira was about to point out that the other trainees' quarters probably hadn't sat unoccupied for two decades, but she didn't say anything. Instead, she dropped the old broom back in the cupboard and pulled on her Light magic. As she let out a breath, a pristine new broom appeared in her outstretched hand, bristles stiff and attached tightly to the handle.

She was no stranger to cleaning, but being able to summon a broom with so many bristles was actually one of the more difficult objects she had learned to create from Light magic. More than once she'd made a broom that had fallen apart as soon as she tried to use it. She tested this one out a little, but the bristles held as they swiped a stripe through the dust on the dark floor.

"I mean, come on, we're *here* Kira!" Jun was saying, stepping further into the common room. "The Gray Wing is all ours. My father told me all about it in his recent letters. He stayed here when he trained in Shadow magic of course—and *your* father stayed here too."

Kira gasped, leaning on her broom. "You're right; I'd almost forgotten," she said, the beginnings of a smile coming to her face.

"We better start cleaning," she said. "This is going to take a while, and who knows when Kusari will come to check and make sure it's pristine enough for her peace of mind or whatever."

Jun chuckled. "I'll go look for a water tap."

She summoned a few cloths for dusting and a large bucket.

Jun froze on his way toward the other corridor leading off the common room. "Kira, come look at this."

He had paused beside the open doors leading onto the balcony, and Kira went to join him as he drifted outside, drawn by whatever force he was looking at. She blinked as she came out into the sunlight.

The Gray Wing had a view of the center of the castle, the base of the Spire. The tiers with their decorative tiled roofs, each tier smaller than the one below it, rising higher and higher into the early afternoon sky.

Kira craned her neck up to look at the point, like a needle at the top of a skyscraper.

"This is going to be an interesting year," she said.

Chapter 5

The Gray Wing

After they located a small kitchen down the hall beside the balcony, they loaded up some buckets with water from the pump and began cleaning the common room.

Kira didn't mind the menial labor. It made it easy to forget about her Shadow magic—or lack thereof—and the upcoming meeting with the Storm King. Despite having gone on a rescue mission with him and even flying on the wind with him, the man was still quite intimidating. He could summon a storm in an instant, raining down water and thunder and lightning if he so chose. He led the Spire and all its mages, giving him control over the entire Shadow region.

She dreaded finding out what he would say when he realized she had lost her Shadow magic.

After several hours of getting their hands dirty, a knock came at their door. Kira wiped her forehead with the back of her hand. Jun was on his hands and knees cleaning out the immense fireplace, so Kira dropped the dusty rag she was cleaning a lantern with and went over to see who it was.

A knock came again, and Kira pulled the door open. Warmth flooded her chest when she spotted Zowan with Thistle on his shoulder.

"Here, take this," Zowan said, pushing a sack into her arms as he juggled a second sack into a more favorable position.

Kira looked down and saw a bunch of radishes and potatoes, a few apples, and small sacks of rice and barley. Her mouth watered, and she stepped back to let Zowan inside.

"Wow, is this all for us? Thank you. I'm starving."

"I thought you might be hungry. I figured I'd come by and see your quarters."

Jun came forward, wiping his hands with a wet cloth. He took the second bag from Zowan and put it on the large low table in the center of the room with the other bag Kira had taken.

Zowan stared around the room, hands on his hips. "So this is the Gray Wing, huh? You know, I've never been in here before. The Gray Knights would visit occasionally when I was training here, but we were forbidden from even coming down the hallway, especially when they were in residence."

Kira smiled, imagining Zowan as a teenager here at the Spire. She wondered what the Spirekeeper would say about him coming here now, but Kira didn't care. She didn't think the traditions of the Gray Wing were stingy enough to keep out visitors.

She sunk down onto a floor cushion beside the table, and the others followed suit. She and Jun had already beaten most of the dust out of the cushions, and they were pleasantly and surprisingly soft with their red and gold fabric still in good condition.

"Where are the Gray Knights anyway?" Zowan asked Jun, bringing up one knee to put his elbow on. "I thought your father would have wanted to be here, if not just for the historical significance of the new Gray trainees, but maybe to threaten my uncle a little bit about keeping you two safe."

Jun and Kira chuckled. Thistle laughed his musical laugh as he swooped off Zowan's shoulder and onto Kira's. She raised her hand to pet his soft gray fur, and he chittered happily. His warm weight on her shoulder was oddly comforting.

Jun said, "Most of them are on an expedition in the Seven Days Forest, and Lady Sasha is dealing with a blight in her home village. But my father plans to come to Heliodor when he can. And yes, probably just to threaten Lord Raiden."

Kira snorted.

Thistle hopped down from Kira's shoulder and went to explore the bags of food on the table. He perched on the edge of the stiff cloth bag and stuck his twitching nose inside, sniffing.

"All of that's for us?" Jun asked, glancing at the food too.

"Of course. You do have a kitchen somewhere in here, right?"

"Through there," Kira said, pointing at the short corridor leading off the common room.

"Well, let's get these away, and we can make some tea or something," Zowan said, getting up off his floor cushion and reaching for a bag.

Thistle scrambled off the bag and hopped back onto Kira's shoulder. She grinned and grabbed the other bag, and they all followed Jun to the kitchen.

The corridor was bright, with windows on one side facing the Spire. On the other wall, there were several paintings done on parchment hanging from bamboo scroll frames. They didn't look at all faded from the sunlight, and Kira squinted at them, wondering whether some magic was involved. One painting was of the Spire, another of an immense waterfall, and one of a sweet little pond amid a forest of bamboo.

Inside the small but cozy kitchen stood a black stove in the center of the far wall, with an iron pot atop it. In the corner by the windows, a few droplets of water fell from the mouth of the water pump into a large wooden basin underneath it. The floor was stone, the walls dark wood, and little cabinets covered the back wall. There were a few more small paintings hanging in here too.

Kira and Zowan set down the sacks on the counter beside the pump. She went over to wash her hands in the basin and summoned a clean cloth with Light magic to dry her hands on. She wiped her sweaty face before letting the magic disperse back into the world around her.

"This should get you through a few days," Zowan was saying as he took out a sack of barley.

"A few days?" Jun repeated. "What do we need so much food for?"

Zowan looked at him quizzically, then smirked. "What? No one's told you? You have to cook for yourself here."

Kira peered into the bags with a new interest, and Thistle chirped when Zowan pulled out a small sack of dried cherries. "Kusari neglected to mention it," she said.

Ever since living at Gekkō-ji, Kira had benefited from three meals a day from the temple's kitchen house, but back in the Starless Realm, she had often cooked for herself while her mother was busy working. She glanced at the unfamiliar stove with apprehension.

Zowan unpacked the food, and the three of them found places to store everything in the small kitchen's black cupboards.

"No meat, huh?" Jun said when they were done.

"Don't tell me your father didn't tell you about that—" Zowan began.

Jun shook his head and laughed without heart. "I had hoped it wasn't true. I don't know how they can expect us to learn magic and train to fight as vegetarians."

Zowan shrugged. "Well, I think you'll find that learning Shadow magic isn't just about fighting—despite what's happened between the two regions up until recently," he added in response to Jun's scoff of disbelief. "At its heart, it's a magic based in purity of mind, body, and soul."

Kira reached to the back of the counter where Zowan had left a bag of apples. "So we have to cook our own food; what else do we need to know?" She took a bite of her apple and her stomach rumbled as if it couldn't wait any longer. "Where'd you get the food anyway?"

Confusion then annoyance crossed Zowan's face as he leaned back against the counter next to Kira. "I got it from the Spire's kitchens. They haven't given you a tour of the temple yet? I can show you two around if you like."

Kira's face lit up. "That sounds great! Maybe you can show me where the Apothecarium is. That's where Spectra and Micah work, I told them I was finally coming to train here, and Spectra wanted me to come say hello as soon as I got here."

She found her face growing warm, and quickly took another bite of her apple. Spectra wasn't the only one excited for the meeting. When Micah had visited Gekkō-ji with his sister last year, he and Kira had shared a kiss or two. They had been exchanging letters every month since, but it had been over a year since they had seen each other in person.

"Sure," Zowan said, pushing himself off the counter, "it's not far from the Gray Wing actually. And maybe when we're done, I'll take you out into Heliodor to get a proper dinner to celebrate your arrival."

Jun whooped and grabbed his own apple to tide himself over. After they had finished, and Thistle had convinced Kira to give him some cherries, Kira went to find somewhere to tidy herself up a bit. She didn't want to be covered in dust and grime for her first meeting with Micah in over a year.

Back in the newly cleaned common room, Kira poked her head down the other hallway that led to the private quarters, which they hadn't explored yet. She almost felt like she was intruding. How long had it been since any of the Gray Knights had been in residence here?

Her father had stayed here when he trained in Shadow magic, and any time he visited the temple afterward. The thought made her heart leap. She stepped forward, wondering which room had been his.

But then a hasty knock came at the front door.

Kira whirled around and went to go answer it. She ran her fingers through her hair and straightened her belt sash, which displayed her crescent moon buckle from Gekkō-ji. She still felt grimy, but at least her hands and face were clean.

Upon opening the door, she came face to face with a girl her own age. She filled out her fitted robes with plump curves, and she wore an anxious smile on her round face. Her straight black hair was cut just below her ears, framing her face under long bangs.

"Hi," the girl said breathlessly. Then she bowed her head a little. "I mean, hello. You're Lady Starwind, aren't you?" Before Kira could answer, the girl went on, "I'm Yuki. The Spirekeeper sent me to tell you and Lord Kosumoso about your meeting with Lord Raiden for your Scrying. Lord Raiden is ready to meet you for your ascent."

"Oh, all right," Kira said, nodding vaguely and wondering what the girl was talking about. "Would you like to come in while I go get Jun?"

Yuki's eyes grew wide, and she gaped at Kira. Then she looked down at the ground. "Thank you, Lady Starwind, but I couldn't possibly—"

"Call me Kira," she said uncomfortably. "Give me a minute then, all right?"

Yuki nodded and took a step back from the open door, folding her hands in front of her.

Kira brushed her hands down the sides of her trousers as she rushed across the common room, trying to swat away any remaining dirt.

Jun and Zowan were laughing when she entered the cozy kitchen.

"What is it?" Jun asked upon seeing her face.

"Our meeting with the Storm King; apparently he's ready," she told them, and her heart inexplicably began racing. "Someone's here to take us to meet him. She mentioned a Scrying?" Kira glanced over at Zowan who was studying the painting of plum blossoms hanging across from the stove.

His face broke into a grin. "Oh I wish I could see that. It's been ages since I've been up to the top of the tower. But I think I'll head on into the city and get a few things. You'll be occupied with my uncle for a while, no doubt, discussing your training outlooks. Perhaps I'll meet you two back here later?"

Kira forced a smile as they all left the kitchen and joined Yuki at the front doors to the wing.

Yuki let out a little gasp at the sight of Zowan, and turned her eyes toward the ground.

Zowan gallantly ignored this, said, "I'll check in on you two later," and made his way past Yuki and down the corridor. Thistle swooped after him, muttering about obscene heights.

Kira's heart sank as she watched them go, and not just because they would likely be missing their planned excursion into the city with Zowan.

It was finally time to go and face the Storm King.

Chapter 6

The Dragon Crystal

Yuki beamed and bowed upon meeting Jun, and the three of them set off down the narrow hallway leading away from the Gray Wing.

"Lord Raiden is waiting in the Jade Foyer," Yuki said, "So you may ascend together."

She said the words with such awe that Kira had to ask, "What does that mean, exactly?"

Yuki gasped a little and said, "Oh, well, the Spire is the most magical part of the temple; it's full of Shadow magic, ancient artifacts, and treasures. Several of the highest tiers are also dedicated to some very powerful spirits. It's rather revered by the mages, so it's an honor to ascend to the top, you see."

"And why are we going up there with Lord Raiden?" Jun asked.

"Well, all the Shadow acolytes ascend for their first Scrying—" Yuki stopped speaking as they emerged into the foyer and spotted Lord Raiden.

Yuki halted and bowed low at the sight of him, bending at the waist with her hands sliding down her thighs. Kira and Jun followed suit, though Kira felt a little silly showing such formalities after her adventures with Raiden last year. But it wouldn't do to be disrespectful to him here in the Spire.

"Kira," Raiden boomed, opening his arms out wide and welcoming them. He stood in front of the fountain with the large jade stone at his back. Much like his nephew, Raiden had wavy black hair that reached his shoulders, though the Storm King stood much taller, and with his stiff collar and broad shoulders, he cut an imposing figure. His mage's robes were the finest Kira had ever seen, the black fitted fabric embroidered with fine silver threads, clasped together under his throat with the inverted-V pin of the Spire. At the bottom of the robes, subtly woven in the fabric, were golden storm clouds.

"Come, come," he motioned them forward.

Yuki muttered a goodbye to Kira and Jun and seemingly melted away down the next hallway.

"Well, I've finally got you two all to myself," Raiden said as they came closer. "I thought Master Starwind and Mistress Nari would never let you out of their sight!"

"We had to advance to squire first," Kira said.

Raiden waved his hand. "I know, I know. I'm merely glad there weren't any further stipulations in you two coming here—especially from the palace advisors. Tigran Tashjian has been breathing down my neck ever since last year, constantly wanting updates on the terms of the peace treaty we all signed. But now that my nephew has returned to the temple, he can deal with the Empress' cronies."

He clapped his hands then rubbed them together. "But enough about that—we must begin our climb. Lady Kesshō is waiting for us at the top of the Spire."

At that, Kira and Jun both looked up. Kira turned her gaze back down after an unpleasant swoop of vertigo ran through her middle.

Raiden headed to a wide staircase directly across from the Hall of Spirits, and Kira and Jun hastened to follow. The stairs were smooth gray stone, worn from use. Kira put her hand on the dark wooden handrail and began to climb, trying not to think about how long this was going to take. Why did they have to have their meeting up at the very top?

The next level had wooden floors, the kind that reminded Kira of the palace in Meridian—the floorboards chirped like birds when they walked. Far from a defect, it was actually a security measure that would alert anyone nearby of an intruder.

Along the outer walls in the open gallery were doors leading to what Kira assumed were classrooms. Wooden stairs lined the hollow center of the Spire, leading up countless floors of the square structure.

Kira stopped glancing over the side after the first few floors as the ground got further and further away.

She peered curiously into the classrooms. Some were filled with groups of acolytes or even a single person. Kira didn't see any actual magic until what she thought was the tenth floor when she spotted a young boy kneeling on a mat inside a room. He held his hands out in front of him, concentrating on levitating a large wooden sphere. Behind him on a low shelf were more spheres of various sizes. As they passed by him on the stairs, he never moved, just sat there with all of his attention focused on the sphere.

Finally, when they got to perhaps the twentieth floor, Raiden spoke. With the tiers getting smaller the higher up they went, the rooms on each level began to dissipate. Some of these higher levels only held statues and what looked like shrines along the open galleries beside the stairs. And there were far less people the higher they went.

"It's been a few weeks since I've received an update from Master Ichiro. Has there been any word on the Lord of Between?" Raiden asked, turning back to look at Kira and Jun as they continued climbing. "Or of their spy inside the imperial palace?"

"No," Kira said, pleased that she wasn't out of breath yet. Her thighs had begun to complain, but she could power through it. In their combat training classes back at Gekkō-ji, Master Tenchi sometimes made them run up and down the stairs to the temple for hours on end.

"Mistress Nari has been visiting the palace more," Kira informed Raiden, "But she's no closer to finding out who the Lord of Between's spy is there than I was."

"Well, you didn't make a very good spy yourself," Jun said under his breath.

She rolled her eyes as they turned another corner on the stairs.

"I'm not surprised there's been nothing," Raiden said. "*Shapeshifting*. We've no idea how long they've been inside the palace."

"That would make identifying them all the harder," Kira said, shaking her head. Ever since they had discovered the imperial ring as evidence beside one of the portal doors, they had come no closer to discovering the culprit. "We're never going to discover who it is."

"Oh, I'm sure they'll reveal their true intentions soon enough," Raiden said. "This Lord of Between has powers beyond reason, that sort of thing is difficult to hide forever. We know he was working to extract souls from the mages and knights, but he seems to have stopped doing that for now. Surely he's not done with whatever nefarious work he began in the first place."

"You mean with the portals to the Starless Realm?" Jun said.

Kira frowned. "Technically he's been working on that for decades though. He summoned the portal that my mother fell through—when she disappeared while she was pregnant with me."

Raiden nodded but didn't turn around. "True, but these disturbances he's been making these past few years have been increasing. He's experimenting with *wrong* magic. He has to be up to something bigger. Something worse."

Stifling a shudder, Kira said nothing. The Lord of Between had almost stolen her soul. Sometimes she woke up in the middle of the night after dreams of being chained to the ground, a sick fever-like chill running through her entire body.

She brought a hand to the back of her neck, almost feeling the chill sensation creeping up again at the mere thought of it.

"But enough about all that," Raiden said bracingly. "We'll meet that challenge when it comes banging down our door. What we need to focus on now is your Shadow training. A year is such a short time to get you two trained, but you both come from such gifted families, so I have no doubt you will soar in your studies."

Kira remained silent.

On and on they climbed, each level getting smaller, the stairs shallower. At one point, Kira let her gaze wander over the side of the railing, and she almost threw up.

The enormous jade sphere in the fountain at the bottom was the size of a coin. She wrenched her gaze back to the narrow stairs in front of her and grit her teeth.

At last, they stopped climbing. They reached the smallest level—about the size of the kitchen down in the Gray Wing—but there was nothing there. Just the wooden railing that lined the edges. Kira kept to the back wall, wondering why in the world they had climbed all the way up here for an empty space. Jun edged over to the railing to peer down.

"Careful," Raiden warned. "You might want to learn how to fly on the wind before you get that close to the edge up here," he said delicately. Raiden pulled back a maroon silk curtain that hung on one of the walls, revealing another cramped stairwell.

"After you," Raiden said, letting Kira and Jun go up first.

Kira was relieved to leave the sight of the drop behind, surprised at her own fear. She had never been afraid of heights, but, she supposed, she had never been in a building fortified with magic before.

At the top of the short flight of stairs, she emerged onto the final tier of the Spire. It was completely open on all four sides, with supports at the four corners for the roof.

Kira's stomach plummeted. She could see all of Heliodor, and the countryside beyond it, all bathed in the orange glow of the setting sun.

In the center of the floor stood an elaborate silver dragon sculpture, which supported a clear spherical crystal, mimicking the jade one several stories below. Beside the orb stood an older woman, a Shadow mage by her dark purple fitted robe and Spire pin. A silver streak of hair sprouted from her right temple, and though they were standing in the open perhaps fifty stories above the ground, her long, loose hair was perfectly still.

As both Jun and Raiden came up the stairwell behind her, Kira had to move closer to the nearest edge. She tried to keep her gaze on the countryside beyond; if she looked at anything closer the reality of the height became nauseating.

But there was no wind.

Curious, she slid an inch further toward the edge. Her heart racing, she lifted out a hand, but it encountered something solid.

"A protective barrier," Raiden told her as she reached out. "It is on all the levels actually," he admitted with a sly glance at Jun.

Her mouth open in awe, Kira ran her hand along the invisible barrier, her stomach still doing somersaults, refusing to believe that it was safe.

The walled city of Heliodor spread out in a rough circle in one direction, with the Spire at one edge of it. Mountains guarded the back of the temple, making that side of the city's wall nearly impenetrable.

"Wow," Jun said, coming up beside her.

Raiden cleared his throat and they both turned around. The woman had stepped forward, her long-fingered hands clasped in front of her.

Kira and Jun offered her a slight bow as Raiden said, "This is Lady Kesshō; she will be performing your Scrying."

Lady Kesshō nodded solemnly and beckoned Kira over with her long fingers. Her insides still squirming, Kira willed herself to step forward toward the dragon statue and orb, with no idea what was about to happen next.

Kesshō took Kira's hand in a business-like way as soon as she got close enough, and placed it palm-down on the crystal.

"The Scrying will reveal the magical capabilities of your soul," Kesshō said in a somewhat hoarse voice. "Keep your hand on the orb, and I will interpret the reading."

Kira's hands suddenly felt sweaty, and she briefly wondered if she was going to leave an unsightly handprint on the orb. Kesshō closed her eyes for a moment. When she opened them again, Kira felt a strange sensation run from her palm, up her arm, and all the way down her spine.

She almost yanked her hand back, but then she saw the colors. The orb began to glow with a delicate light, revealing the crystalline structure inside. And throughout the orb flowed a rainbow of colors, seemingly pulsing from the point where Kira's hand touched it. Perhaps half of the crystal glowed white, while the rest displayed shades of blue, purple, orange, and pink.

"Ah," Kesshō said, her gaze roving over the surface of the orb. "Very powerful indeed. These colors are vibrant. Though since you possess both Light and Shadow, I'm not surprised. See here, the light blue with yellow sparks? A proficiency in wind; very good. And the pool of darker blue melting into it; you might have a chance at weather magic as well."

Kira marveled at the array of colors; they seemed to move and morph with her breath.

"Now, there is a lot of bright white because of your Light magic, so I'd like you to pull on some Shadow magic so I can separate some of the fine colors in case you have any niche proficiencies—don't try to do anything with the magic, just access it—"

Without thinking, entranced by the magical capabilities of her soul, Kira reached out her consciousness and tried to pull Shadow magic from her surroundings.

The crystal drained of color and went black.

A sharp pain jolted through the back of Kira's neck, and she found herself looking up at the ceiling. Then, everything went black.

Chapter 7

Quarters

She awoke in an unfamiliar room, a strong scent of oranges in the air. She sat up quickly and realized she had been asleep on a futon-style mattress on the floor.

The room was quite empty, save for a brazier hanging from the ceiling in one corner, emitting whatever citrus incense she was inhaling, and the tatami mat floor. She ran her hands over the straw-like mat beside her, wondering how it was still in such good condition after so many years of neglect.

She shook her head to clear it—and immediately regretted doing so. Her skull ached, and she felt as if she had just rattled her brain around. She closed her eyes and cradled her head in her hands.

All she wanted to do was lay back down and go to sleep.

It was clear there was something very wrong with her.

She really *was* broken.

And now Raiden knew it too. She would never get to become a Gray Knight. Jun would go on without her, and she would never follow in her father's legacy.

She lay back down and found the small cylindrical pillow she had been resting on, and jammed it back under her head. It felt nice on her strangely aching neck. It was like she was overcoming a fever, but she wasn't hot or sick feeling. Just achy, tired, and depressed.

She closed her eyes and groaned. This wasn't at all how she had wanted her trip to the Spire to go. With a great effort she opened her eyes and forced herself to look around the room again.

I must be in the Gray Wing, in one of the private rooms, she thought. She brushed her fingers across the tatami mat again. *I wonder if it's preserved through Shadow magic. It must be.*

The thought of Shadow magic made her groan again.

A knock came at the door. "Kira? Are you up?" It was Jun.

She reluctantly sat up again and twisted around to study the room. The wall to her right was composed of sliding doors with paper paneling that she suspected led to a balcony like in the common room. In front of her, an array of cupboards behind wooden panels held storage space; she could see her trunk peeking out from behind one of the half-open doors.

If her trunk was here, how long had she been asleep? What time was it?

The answer came to her in the glittering light that began in her vision. The glow that signified that the sun had set, allowing her to see the Light magic in all her surroundings.

Surveying the room in the new glowing light, she noticed several paintings hung on the walls, much like the ones she had spotted throughout the common room and the kitchen. Just as she flung the covers off herself to go and study them, Jun called, "Kira? Are you all right? Can I open the door?"

"Sure," she grunted. She stood just as one of two doors opened, and she saw Jun standing there outlined in Light. He leaned against the doorframe but didn't enter.

"Good, you're up." His expression relaxed. "You've been out since last night. But Lord Raiden's healer said to let you sleep."

"Last night?" Kira glanced over at her trunk in the closet. "Oh, wow. I guess you're right. We were up at the top of the Spire at sunset, weren't we?"

Jun nodded. "The healer brought you down from the top after Raiden went down to go get her. I had to stay and do my Scrying alone, then walk all the way down."

"What, Raiden didn't walk?" Kira cocked her head.

He snorted. "Going down all those stairs after you passed out like that? No, he flew down on the wind after deactivating that invisible barrier. I didn't even get to watch. Then he came back with the healer, and she conjured a stretcher for you."

For a moment, Kira entertained the image of flying down the center of the tower. Then she cringed. "Did anyone see me?"

"How should I know? I was doing my Scrying."

"Oh, right... How did yours go?"

Jun's face lit up as if he'd been waiting for her to ask. "Well, my reading was just as bright as yours before—"

Kira raised her eyebrows at him.

"Before you passed out," he went on, "and Lady Kesshō found a ton of different proficiencies. They're going to put me in as many classes as the Spirekeeper can fit into my schedule." He beamed.

"What about my proficiencies? Do I have to do the Scrying again?"

"Um, I'm not sure."

"Any idea when I start lessons too?"

Jun shrugged. "I think Lord Raiden wants to meet with you tomorrow to talk about your skills," he said. "Hey, are you hungry? Zowan dropped by earlier to ask about you;

he and I had dinner. He made some fantastic fried noodles before he left for his new lodging down in the city."

Kira's stomach twisted at the thought. "No, but maybe some tea?"

"Okay. How about I bring it into your study, and we can sit in there? Yours is nicer than mine."

"Study?"

"Yeah, through here," Jun said, jerking his thumb over his shoulder and indicating the room he was standing in. He poked his head further into her room and pointed to the other door. "That's probably your washroom, and they brought in your trunk this afternoon. The wagon arrived from Gekkō-ji with Lady Anzu."

Kira drifted toward her trunk, glad to have her things, anyway.

Jun continued rambling on, "Oh, and the Spirekeeper won't let Lady Anzu stay in the Gray Wing with us; nor Zowan, I asked. Something about ancient traditions and blasphemy, I believe the woman said. It'd be nice to have them nearby though. I'm sure that's what Master Starwind would have wanted. But it's not like we need protecting anyway," he said with a smirk.

A chuckle escaped Kira. "All right, you go get us some tea while I change," she told him, straightening her keepsake box that someone had put on a shelf.

"Oh," she said before Jun closed the door, "what's up with the incense?"

"Something the healer left for you, she said something about promoting peace of mind while you slept," Jun shrugged, and left.

Kira shrugged too, taking a deep breath. "It's kind of nice," she said to herself.

The washroom held her very own bath tub, a large wooden basin beside a water pump much like the one in the kitchen. There weren't any towels or anything, so she conjured a few with Light magic, enjoying their softness as she washed her face. After she changed her clothes and summoned a comb for her hair, she padded out in her bare feet to the study.

With her Light magic, she could see every detail, though Jun had lit the three lanterns that hung from the ceiling, giving the room a nice cozy feel. He came in through another door that led out into the hallway, carrying a tray with a steaming white ceramic teapot, matching cups, and a plate of something that looked like biscuits. He set the tray down on the dark wooden desk in the corner, across from a small unlit fireplace. The study held a few more paintings, and the far wall was made up of sliding paper-paneled doors just like the sleeping quarters.

Kira plunked herself down in front of the desk in the only chair and rubbed the back of her neck. She was a little warm after waking up under the blankets in her heavily incensed room, so she leaned over to one of the sliding panels and let in some night air.

Jun conjured up another chair and set it beside the fireplace before pouring tea for the both of them. It was green tea, and the vegetal scent wafted heavily toward Kira as he handed over a cup. She grabbed one of the cookie-like biscuits, wondering if someone had made them, or they had come from the Spire's market.

They sat for a moment in silence. Kira sipped her tea and gazed unseeing at the dark fireplace, thinking.

"So did they say what happened to me?" she asked finally. "Maybe it's happened to other trainees before?"

Jun lowered his teacup. "They didn't really tell me anything, to be honest. Raiden just told Lady Kesshō to do my Scrying, then whisked away to get the healer. When I finally got back down to the wing, the healer was leaving here after settling you in your room."

Kira set her cup down with a clatter. Her hand was shaking slightly.

"Kira, are you..."

"So you start lessons tomorrow?"

Jun eyed her and apparently chose not to comment on her obvious change of subject. “Yes. First, it’s meditation at the pavilion down by the lake. All morning.” He grimaced and took another sip of tea. “And then into the Spire for levitation testing—I think like that kid we saw on our way up who was levitating that sphere, remember?”

Kira nodded, but couldn’t think of anything to say. They sat in silence for a little while, and Kira could hear crickets chirping just outside through the open door to the balcony.

Jun finished his tea. “Well, I’ll let you rest some more. I want to go clean up my quarters better. My father must have left them in a rush the last time he was here or something, they were in quite a state.”

Kira froze as she went to pick up another biscuit, and her heart leaped into her throat. “You’re staying in your father’s quarters? And whose are these—”

Jun grinned. “These were *your* father’s.”

CHAPTER 8

PERFECTLY POWERFUL

Jun was already gone the next morning when Kira emerged from her father's quarters into the common room. It had taken almost an hour to convince herself to get out of bed and get dressed. The back of her neck was still tingling strangely, and her entire body felt heavy and sluggish as if she were poorly recovering from an illness.

It had taken hours to fall asleep last night. She wasn't totally surprised, having been unconscious most of a day. She didn't know what time she finally drifted off after tossing and turning, wondering what the next day was going to bring. Every so often her thoughts would drift to her father, occupying this room more than twenty years ago.

Could she live up to his name? Would she be able to fix her Shadow magic and even get a chance to try?

She wasn't sure what to expect from her meeting with the Storm King, but she assumed a messenger would come for her when it was time like the other day.

She shut the door of her private quarters, and went to turn left toward the common room, but instead decided to finally explore the wing a little more. Turning right, she silently padded down the long hallway that housed the other private quarters. Her rooms were at the beginning of the hallway, closest to the common room. With a dozen doors leading off the hall, Kira figured out where Jun was staying when she reached the other end, where he had hung a small talisman wrapped in silky black fabric on his door. It had small flowers and a coin embroidered on it, which she had seen before on some of his clothing. She was pretty sure it was his family's crest.

Close to Jun's quarters, at the very end of the hallway were another set of double doors, and Kira pushed one side open to reveal a large empty room.

The wooden floors gleamed in the diffused morning light filtering in through the paper lattice doors at one end. *Jun must have cleaned it yesterday when I was unconscious*, she thought, wandering further in. A few dust motes hung in the air as if suspended there, and the quiet and stillness made it feel like she could have stepped in here at any point in time—as if her father might have just left this very room after a training session with his friends.

The room was otherwise completely barren. No decoration, no furniture. She supposed an indoor space to practice Light and Shadow magic didn't need any equipment, and any decorations were in danger of being destroyed by stray magic. Back at Gekkō-ji, they trained in the fighting rings in a wooded area, but they only practiced with traditional Light weapons. Here, the Gray trainees would be expected to practice with both Light and Shadow.

She bit the inside of her lip and turned to leave.

Back in the common room, Kira stood with her hands on her hips for a moment, suddenly wishing she had some company. But Jun was off to his lessons, and she had no idea where Anzu or Zowan were staying.

"I wonder where Thistle is?" she muttered to herself, but she wasn't surprised by his absence. Even back at Mount Gekkō, whenever she encountered the flying squirrel, he didn't stick around for very long. She wondered if he was conversing with the local spirits to find out about any suspicious activity that might reveal the Lord of Between. After all, that was why Gekkō had sent him.

She whiled away the rest of the morning in her father's study, breakfasting on the leftover biscuits from last night. She made the effort to make fresh tea, finding a tin in the kitchen that Zowan must have brought them. After heating the kettle on the stove with some fire she conjured with Light magic, she went back to her new quarters and curled up in the chair in the study with her hands wrapped around her tea cup.

As she breathed in the steam from her cup, she gazed around the study. A few more paintings were displayed here, and she now realized that it must be her father's artwork that hung all over the Gray Wing. There were a few rough sketches on paper laying on a shelf above the desk, a turquoise ceramic cup holding a few brushes, and even a wooden paint pallet with daubs of colors long since dried.

She had known her father had some artistic talent—Ichiro had shown her some of Rokuro's sketches—but she had no idea it was anything as good as what she had seen throughout the wing.

A snort of laughter escaped her when she thought of what her father might say about Kira's artistic talents—or, lack thereof. She could barely wield a calligraphy brush to write her own name, let alone create an entire painting.

The painting in the corner was a landscape she actually recognized now that she knew her father had painted it. It depicted the rolling hills just outside of the Starwind family estate, where Ichiro had taken her last summer on a brief trip shortly after they had found out she was his granddaughter.

They couldn't stay long, what with Kira's training, and Ichiro's duties running the temple, but she had gotten to see the large estate house where Rokuro had grown up. They had ridden right by those three hills featured in Rokuro's painting. Kira remembered stopping to stare at the strange rock formation in the foreground that somewhat resembled a bear. The blue and green features of the hills were deftly represented on the heavy paper; the scene fading into white around the edges as if it were a vision revealing itself from clouds.

A soft sound drew Kira's attention towards the door to the hallway. A piece of paper sat on the floor that hadn't been there a second ago.

"Hello?" she called. She untangled herself from the chair and went to the door to pick up the paper. "Who's there?" She opened the door, but the hallway was empty. A chill ran down her spine.

She turned the paper over in her hands and ran her finger under the black wax seal. For a second, it reminded her of the sealed scroll Ichiro had given her instructing her to pick a knight or mage to squire for. A wave of apprehension rolled over her. She had already forgotten about that. The longer it took her to decide, the longer it would take to advance to knight.

Brushing the thought aside, she forced herself to focus on the note.

Lady Gray,

I hear you are recovered. Meet me in the Jade Foyer at noon to discuss your training.

-R

Kira stared at the paper, dread creeping along her nerves despite how Raiden's nickname for her made her smirk a little. Was he going to make her climb all the way up to the top of the Spire again for another failed Scrying? Or worse, make her admit that she had lost her Shadow magic and send her packing?

She closed her door and tossed the note on the desk before glancing at the simple clock on the mantlepiece. She only had half an hour until noon.

Back in the bedroom, she folded up her sleeping mat and blankets, and put them away in the cupboard, with the reminder that the Spirekeeper said she was going to be making sure their quarters were clean. She selected some clothes from her trunk without really looking, and went to wash up.

A small wood-framed mirror hung just inside the washroom, a little satchel of long-dead herbs tied to the top.

Kira looked at her reflection and took a deep breath. For a moment, all she could see was the panic in her wide eyes. The fear that she would have to leave this place—her father's very own quarters—leave the Spire and never learn Shadow magic, all seeped into her like a sickly black oil over her skin.

She took another breath, trying to clear her head, and shrugged her shoulders a few times. "It's going to be fine," she told herself, then nodded. She just hadn't been feeling well is all. She must have come down with something; what else would explain all those weird chills and her passing out at her Scrying?

She couldn't just sink down into defeat and give up after one mere setback. She had to keep going. Figure out what was wrong with her magic, and go from there. She wouldn't give up the chance to learn Shadow magic in this place, the exact place her father had learned it all. She nodded at her reflection again with finality.

After closer inspection of her appearance, she ran a comb through her hair again and looked down at her carelessly chosen outfit. It was a little rumpled, and she was pretty sure she had worn the same trousers yesterday. She headed back over to her trunk and pawed through until she found her dark purple and black tunic and a clean pair of black wide-legged trousers.

Straightening her collar, she glanced at the clock in the study through the door. Time to go.

Kira strode toward the Jade Foyer, fiddling with her belt sash as she went.

Raiden wasn't there when she arrived, so she went to stand beside the fountain.

From the center of the foyer, she could see down each of the corridors leading off it. There was of course the massive stone staircase leading up to the inside of the Spire, the long Hall of Spirits with its many alcoves, the narrow corridor from which she had come, and several other hallways she hadn't yet explored. One led to a sunny corridor which was open on both sides, with wooden beams holding up the roof above it, leading out into the temple grounds.

The foyer was quite deserted until a moment later when the clean peel of a bell sounded throughout the temple. Kira couldn't tell where it was coming from, and she crossed her arms about herself as trainees began to appear through the sunny corridor, their dark mage's robes neat, their faces rather dour and serious.

It wasn't until Jun came up to her amid the crowd that she realized why everyone looked that way.

"Just finished with meditation," he told her, yawning as he joined her in leaning against the side of the fountain. "*Spirits*, my neck is stiff."

A short acolyte bobbed up to them and waved, "Hello again," she said, then she gave them a nervous bow. It was Yuki, the girl who had come to get them for their Scrying.

"Oh, hi," Kira said. "How was meditation?"

Yuki beamed. "The usual. I'm not that great at it yet though."

Jun snorted. "Me either."

One of the acolytes walking by threw a suspicious glance their way, and Kira couldn't tell if it was only intended for Jun and his impatience with meditation, or for both of them. She noticed no one else seemed to want to talk to the two newest trainees.

She was reminded of her days back in the Starless Realm, where she had moved schools so often that she never had time to make many friends.

But Kira couldn't tell if it was because she and Jun were new, or the fact that they were from the Light region that they were being ignored. *Well, at least no one is bothering us*, she thought in a bemused way. *Could be worse.*

"Oh, I better get going," Yuki said hurriedly. "I think I forgot to sweep our quarters. I don't want Kusari sending me to do weeding like last week."

Kira grimaced in sympathy and gave the girl a little wave as she ran off. "Well, she's nice," she said to Jun. "We better stay on top of cleaning the Gray Wing, I guess. Thanks for cleaning the training room, by the way."

"No problem," he said, shrugging. "I wanted to run a few drills yesterday and the dust on the floor was so thick I would have slipped just by walking in there. Wish I could have done some weapons training this morning instead of meditation though," he complained. "I mean, we were at it for *hours*."

"That bad, huh? Yeah, I wasn't really into it when Lord Raiden tried to make me do it back when he visited Gekkō-ji."

"Well, from the little speech the instructor gave me, it seems like it's the pillar of Shadow magic training," he said with a grimace. "Have you had your meeting with Lord Raiden to talk about your training yet?"

Kira shook her head. "I'm supposed to meet him here."

"Well, I'm heading back to the Gray Wing for some lunch, and then I've got to go up the Spire for levitation practice, and then I'm meeting up with an acolyte who has a really interesting Shadow skill—kind of like how you could hear things from far away, except he can project sound across a distance! Cool, right? I want to ask him more about how he does it. So I might not see you until later."

"Go on," Kira said, pushing him lightly. "You have fun in levitation. Try not to show off too much."

Jun grinned. "But how else am I supposed to impress the masters so they let me try the hard stuff? And besides, we've got Gray magic, it's expected that we're better than everyone else at magic, right?"

A jolt went through Kira's heart at his words and her shoulders slumped. Her world seemed to shrink around her.

"You're right, I should go," Jun said, oblivious to the impact of his words.

"Right," Kira managed. "See you later." She ran her fingers across the points of her crescent moon buckle as she watched him make his way through the steady flow of acolytes still passing through the foyer, all heading in different directions.

"Hey! Kira!"

She whirled around and saw Micah heading toward her. Her breath caught in her throat; she had completely forgotten just how striking his green eyes were along with his messy black hair that had an odd greenish-purple tinge to it, like the metallic sheen of gasoline. He seemed much taller than the last time she had seen him, too. She glanced down at her outfit, immensely glad she had changed. All thoughts of her broken Shadow magic dissipated from her mind.

He came to a halt in front of her and grinned. He wore a crisp half-apron over a thigh-length brown linen tunic and dark trousers, a small dagger visible at his waist.

"Wow, you're finally here," he said, "How have you been?" He scrunched up his face as he studied her. "Are you all right?"

"I'm fine," she said a little too abruptly.

His face fell a little.

She tried to recover with a smile. "Just tired. It's so good to see you. And how's Spectra?"

"She's well. Can't wait to see you. We've both been working all hours lately though; the Apothecarium is a little short-staffed at the moment. You should stop by if you get a break in your training."

She shuffled her feet. "I actually haven't started yet. So I'm not really sure what my schedule will be like. I'm supposed to be meeting Lord Raiden right now to discuss it."

And without warning, emotion burbled up in her chest. She flung her arms around Micah in a hug. "It's so good to see you," she said, breathing in his scent of frankincense and green things that she had forgotten until now.

His arms came around her and he whispered in her ear, "It's good to see you too, Starless girl. I missed you."

A shiver ran down her spine, and she pulled away smiling, feeling genuinely happy for the first time since she had left Gekkō-ji. They both reached out for each other's hands as they slid apart. Maybe everything would work out with her Shadow magic—and if it didn't, maybe it wasn't important.

Just then, Kira became aware of an incredibly tall figure cutting a path across the foyer. "Ah, Kira, there you are!" Lord Raiden called.

Her face grew warm as she peered around Micah and dropped his hand.

"Lord Raiden," they both murmured, bowing slightly.

"Kira. Micah," Raiden said, then he held out a gracious arm gesturing Kira to follow him. "Come. We have much to discuss. I've had tea prepared in my study."

Kira gave a hasty wave to Micah. "I'll try to come see you later!" she called, wishing she didn't have to say goodbye so soon. He returned her wave and smile before disappearing down one of the other corridors leading off the foyer.

Raiden led her through the crowded maze of corridors toward his study. He said nothing as they strode through the castle; his mere presence drawing the eyes of every acolyte, who lowered their heads or torsos in a bow as they passed. Kira couldn't help but notice a few suspicious glares aimed in her direction.

She wasn't surprised at the coldness of some of the acolytes; the two regions had been feuding for their entire lives. It was the same at Gekkō-ji with prejudice toward Shadow mages.

But when they brokered the peace, they all knew it wasn't going to be overcome so quickly. And apparently her having both Light and Shadow didn't make her immune to some of the mistrust and ire. Part of her was annoyed that they would be suspicious of her—everyone in Camellia knew she had grown up in the Starless Realm. How could these acolytes fault her for having Light magic?

Finally, they arrived at Raiden's study, and he held the door open for her. A boy was already there setting tea onto a large desk at the head of the room. There were leather settees and chairs in groupings around the large room, and everything was decorated in dark colors. Several open windows looked out onto the lake and grounds.

Sunlight twinkled off the edges of the lake, and Kira stared at it for a long while, a strange melancholy creeping up on her, but she couldn't really focus on why.

"Kira?" Raiden asked.

She jolted her head up, realizing it wasn't the first time he had called her name. "Sorry," she said.

Raiden gestured for her to sit at the desk across from him, where the boy had already placed a steaming cup of green tea, and a small plate with even tinier delicate treats. She inhaled the steam above the cup, wondering if it was the same blend of tea that they had back in their quarters.

"It's quite all right," Raiden said, resting both his elbows on the desk as he brought his hands together under his chin. "I can tell you are troubled."

Kira looked down at her cup of tea and bit her lip. Where to start?

Slowly losing her Shadow magic over the past year? Passing out at the top of the Spire at her Scrying? Staying in the same quarters as her father yet dreading being kicked out of them?

"I think there's something wrong with my Shadow magic," she blurted. Then she took a sip of tea, waiting for the ax to fall—or the storm clouds to roll in.

"Yes, it would seem so."

She whipped her head up to look at him.

"Lady Kesshō has done the Scrying for every acolyte who has passed through the Spire for the last fifty-six years. And she has never seen anything like what happened at your Scrying."

Kira drew a shaky breath as he confirmed her worst suspicions. "What's wrong with me?" she said in a near-whisper.

Raiden frowned and reached for his tea. "That is to be determined, I'm afraid." He took a sip. "I do, however, have a theory."

She stared at him. "Well?"

"Your encounter with the Lord of Between last year. I've been thinking. He did try to conduct whatever abominable experiment he was trying on the others on you as well, correct?"

"Yes, but we stopped him before he could—"

"I believe his goal was to remove your spirit—your soul."

"Right," she said slowly. "But he didn't succeed, otherwise I would have died like Mistress Tori and the other mage."

"Yes," he said gravely. "But my guess is that he might have done some damage before he was stopped."

"Damage? What kind of damage?" Kira's hand flew to the back of her neck, which was still oddly tender.

"That remains to be seen," Raiden said, taking another sip of tea. "I would hazard to guess it is impeding you from doing Shadow magic?"

Kira closed her eyes briefly. "Yes," she admitted. "I can't use it at all."

"I see."

"I know Lady Anzu arrived from Gekkō-ji," she said in a monotone. "Maybe she can escort me back while Zowan stays here with Jun."

"Back to Gekkō-ji?" Raiden cocked his head. "Whatever for?"

"I can't do Shadow magic anymore; I don't belong here; I don't even belong in the Gray Wing."

A deep chuckle rumbled through him. "Lady Gray, you have some of the most powerful Shadow magic I've seen at a Scrying in ages. Just because you can't access it at the moment doesn't mean you'll never be able to. Oh, no. You're not getting off that easily. We'll figure out exactly what the problem is, and proceed with your training."

"Really?" A glimmer of hope sparked in her chest. "But you said my soul was damaged. How can I possibly do anything about that?"

Raiden pierced her with his dark eyes. "Kira, you will find after living at the Spire for even a short time, that anything is possible if you work hard enough at it."

Kira found herself smiling.

"I know you are capable of greatness, Kira. But you must not let this setback weigh on you. Any kind of magic that affects souls is rather serious—it might have other effects on your mood or emotions. So be sure to check in on your own thoughts and actions."

"Is there... Can't the healers help me?"

He pursed his lips and shook his head. "No, this isn't a physical wound. Physical wounds can be healed with the right magic. Wounds to the soul take a lot more work, but it can be done. How is your Light magic?"

"Fine, I think."

"Well, regardless, I want you to keep up with your Light training and make sure it stays that way. Find time to practice with Kosumoso."

She nodded. The training room would see some use after all.

"As far as the rest of your training, I can't put you in any magic lessons until we address your problem. So you'll be attending morning meditation, followed by sessions with me. I'm going to reach out to a few mages who might be able to help you. I will inform the Spirekeeper of your schedule, so she shouldn't trouble you."

"Won't the other trainees think it's odd that I'm not in any of the lessons?"

Raiden twisted his teacup in a circle upon the desk. "It's unusual, but since you have Gray magic they might not be too concerned. I must tell you, our training at the Spire is much different than Gekkō-ji. The acolytes are sorted into different lessons by their proficiencies revealed at their Scrying—so they're not all in the same lessons anyway. But we can't very well have you go to the lowest level of classes and be unable to perform."

Kira felt her face grow warm. She didn't want that either.

"Report here to my study at midday from now on," he said. "We'll sort this out soon enough. I think soon we'll have a perfectly powerful Gray Knight on our hands."

Chapter 9

Imperfection

Kira's staff met Jun's with a loud *clack* and she pulled away in an instant. Jun danced back a few feet. The cavernous training room echoed with the sound of the strike for a brief moment. Lit by only a few of the lanterns that hung from the ceiling, they sparred in the exact center, even though there was plenty of room all around.

"Come on, don't you want to fight with real weapons?" Jun taunted as he darted to her right, jabbing out with his staff to try and sweep her legs.

With a huff she launched herself upwards to avoid the strike, bringing her staff around as she did so. Jun had to duck. The hair on his head rustled in the draft as her staff swept by. She landed in the next moment, feinted left, and swung right, nearly landing a blow.

Jun was too quick for her. She pulled back, eying him warily. "Not really," she finally responded, "the Storm King just wants me to keep up with my Light magic is all."

Jun grunted. "Well I want to stay on form too. I don't need to give Master Tenchi any reason not to advance me to knight when we get back to Gekkō-ji."

Kira shrugged. "Yeah, you're right, I guess we should practice for real. But not tonight." She twirled her staff, indicating she was ready to keep going.

"How come? Because you know I'll beat you?"

A snort escaped her as she lunged forward, and she let her momentum carry her past Jun's left side, where she clashed high with his staff as she pivoted. Shifting her weight, she brought the low end of her staff to the back of his knee and tapped it.

"I don't know about that," she joked with half a smile as they disengaged.

He chuckled and retreated a few paces, leaning on his staff for a break. He narrowed his eyes at her. "How are you feeling?"

"Fine," she replied quickly. From the way Jun was looking at her, she was beginning to regret telling him about her conversation with Raiden. "Really. Let's go again."

"All right," he conceded, "But we shouldn't stay up too late. It's amazing how hard it is to convince yourself to get up early just to meditate."

Kira chuckled. "I can't wait." She lifted her staff and took a wider stance.

"So did Raiden mention what you'd be doing during your meetings with him?" Jun positioned his staff across his body and widened his feet in a defensive stance.

"I'll find out tomorrow, I guess."

"Do you want me to write to my father about it?"

Kira lowered her staff. "What? No!" Her face flamed. "The fewer people that know about this the better."

Jun cocked his head. "Well, I'm sure Raiden can help you," he tried to reassure her.

"You know what? I think I'm done for the night. You're right; we should probably go to sleep early." She turned around and headed toward the door, blood pulsing in her ears. Suddenly she was too hot, and the world pressed around her, almost suffocating her.

"Kira, are you—"

"I'm fine!" she shouted, the ire surprising her. She whirled around when she heard Jun coming up behind her. "Really. Leave me alone. I can handle this."

Jun's forehead creased, and he huffed. "Yeah, I can really tell you're handling it well," he said with a note of sarcasm. "Look, I'm just trying to help—"

He reached out a hand toward her shoulder and she smacked it away.

Then she drew in a sharp breath. "I'm so sorry Jun," she said, hanging her head, her sweaty skin going cold. "I don't know what... I don't know what's wrong with me. In more ways than one."

He didn't reach out again but he tilted his head in her direction so she would meet his eyes. "I know you're not fine. But we can figure this out. Between Lord Raiden, his mages—Zowan if you want to tell him—hey, you could even ask Thistle to talk to the spirit of the mountain. If you want."

Kira slumped against the wall beside the door, sliding down and holding her staff across her knees. She stared at the hard wood of the staff she had forged with Light magic. "I just can't believe there's something wrong with my *soul*. I hate that the Lord of Between did this to me. I hate that we're no closer to catching them than when they first started creating portals."

Jun banished his staff and lowered himself to sit cross-legged in front of her.

Anger at the Lord of Between surged through her veins, the rage returning just as fast as it had fled moments ago. "They're the reason my mother was separated from my father, and the reason she died—and now they've damaged *my soul?* They need to be stopped." She pounded her fist on her knee.

"Hey, at least you're still alive—not like the others."

Kira bit off her next retort. "That's true." She bowed her head.

"Kira, we'll find whoever this is and make them pay. Trust me. With Lord Raiden and his mages, the Gray Knights, and all of Gekkō-ji's knights looking for them, the Lord of Between will surface eventually. They'll make a mistake at some point, and they'll get caught."

Kira didn't want to mention the last time the Lord of Between had been caught, they had escaped so easily through a portal, so she just nodded.

"You're right," she lied, voice cracking, her emotions spent. "We should really get to bed."

As she used her staff to get up from the floor, she noticed something that made her insides freeze.

A small crack ran down a few inches from the center. A crack that could only mean her Light magic hadn't been strong enough to keep it together. Hadn't had enough willpower to keep it solid.

She dispersed the imperfect staff back into their surroundings before Jun noticed.

Chapter 10

Projection of the Soul

For the tenth time, Kira tried to relax her face muscles.

No matter how serene the pavilion beside the lake was, how still she sat, or how peaceful her breathing was, she couldn't force herself to relax. She was sure her forehead and temples looked strained and would give her away again, earning another reproach from the mage leading the meditation session.

She had no idea how long she had been attempting to meditate alongside what must be nearly all of the acolytes—had it been hours? Or mere minutes?

A quiet chirp nearby made her ears twitch. Curious and dying of boredom, she cracked one eyelid open and spotted the source immediately. Thistle sat perched on a beam in the corner of the rafters nearby, grinning down at her.

She shook her head minutely. Now really wasn't the time. Any movement or whisper would disturb the dozens of acolytes closest to her. He would just have to wait.

After that it was entirely impossible to concentrate on clearing her mind, as she was supposed to be doing. She knew from her meditation sessions last year with Raiden that clearing her mind was imperative to get Shadow magic to work properly—it was finicky and would react to your emotions.

What does it matter? The thought kept floating through her brain. *It's not like I can even do Shadow magic. What do I need to clear my mind for?* She let out a deep sigh, her chest feeling hollow.

Finally, a little while later, the clear metallic peel of a bell echoed across the temple grounds. Carefully, Kira cracked open her eyelids, wondering if it was allowed yet.

The other acolytes still sat motionless, rows and rows of them side by side. But at the front of the pavilion, Mistress Korina, who sat facing them, had her eyes open now. With her petite frame and springy green robes, she was hard to see over the heads of the other acolytes, silhouetted against the wide green lawns of the temple. Korina clasped her hands in front of her chest and bowed to those assembled. Kira joined them all in bowing in return.

As everyone got to their feet, Kira sidled over to Jun who had been sitting in the row behind her. She nodded over toward where Thistle perched in the rafters, and Jun arched his eyebrows.

The two of them idled beside the large open pavilion as Mistress Korina and the acolytes made for the castle. Once they were all out of earshot, Kira went over to Thistle, and the flying squirrel soared down to land on her shoulder.

"Hey Thistle," she said, her hand going up to pet him. "What's going on?"

"Zowan wanted me to let you know he's leaving for a few days to report to the palace."

"Really?" she said, her hand stilling. "After we were ambushed on the road, I would have thought he'd want to stay put. We still don't know who those people were or what they wanted."

Thistle's eyes glinted. "I think he's rather glad for an excuse to leave Heliodor for a time."

Kira frowned. "Is it the way people in the temple are treating him? Is it that bad?"

"Oh, I don't think he cares an owl's pellet about what other people think of him. I would hazard a guess that the proximity of his uncle is the reason."

"Oh."

Jun nudged her in the side. "I have to get going if I want to eat before levitation, and I'm starving."

"Sorry Thistle, we've got to go. Do you want to come in with us?"

The fat little squirrel shook his head. "It's a fine day. I like it out here, thanks." And with that, he soared off Kira's shoulder. Not a second later, they saw him halfway across the sun-drenched lawn, landing on a stunted black pine tree, a trick of his magic it seemed.

They strode down the open corridor toward the castle. Above, dark wooden rafters contrasted against the white painted ceiling. Once they reached the Jade Foyer, they made straight for the Gray Wing.

"I never asked how your lessons went yesterday," Kira said as they arrived at the double doors leading into the wing.

Jun's face lit up. "Oh, they were great. I still have a few I haven't been to yet. I'm really looking forward to my exploratory study session. From what I've heard, it's for acolytes with high potential for unique proficiencies."

"That does sound cool," Kira admitted as they entered the wing.

"I'm sure you'll be in that one too. Oh, and levitation was a little trickier than I thought it would be."

"Really? Weren't able to impress everyone as—" Kira halted in her tracks at the edge of the common room. There was someone sitting on one of the floor cushions at their table.

"Anzu! You're here!"

The Light Knight grinned and stood, bowing her head slightly to them. Her round face was framed with a few locks of dark hair that had escaped her long ponytail, and she still wore her usual leather armor that started at her shoulders and went all the way down to her thighs. A deep maroon tunic stood out from under the brown leather, and at her waist, almost blinding in contrast to the dark tones, was her white sash signifying her status as a knight.

Kira grinned right back at her. Anzu had been her first friend here in Camellia; the woman had brought Kira to Gekkō-ji in the first place when she was lost and had only just discovered she had Light magic.

"I'm lucky Mistress Nari let me come, actually," Anzu said.

"What? Really?" Kira said.

The knight nodded slowly. "Yes, these new raiders are growing bolder—they've been spotted all across Camellia—there weren't too many knights to spare for Heliodor, but they finally agreed to send me."

"Is it that bad with the attacks?"

"They've been tricky to track, and they keep popping up in unexpected places. The other knights who were originally supposed to come here with me have been sent to various outposts across the realm so we have people on hand in each region."

"Wow," Jun muttered. "I wish we could help."

Anzu went on, "But we can't have you two alone in a city full of Shadow mages—even with the new peace between Light and Shadow, the palace advisors wouldn't approve. So Mistress Nari sent me."

"Well, I'm really glad you're here," Kira said, emotion suddenly burning her throat.

"Want some lunch?" Jun offered, heading for the kitchen.

"I'm fine," Anzu said with a smile. "Just thought I'd check in on my two Gray acolytes, or whatever it is they're calling you both these days. Oh, and I brought you something."

She pulled a small metal tin out from a pocket behind her armor and handed it to Kira with both hands.

"To celebrate this new stage in your training," Anzu said. "It's certainly a wonder, you two coming here to train in Shadow magic."

"Mmm," Kira said, gazing down at the plain metal tin. She pulled off the lid and wasn't surprised to see the dark green dried leaves of tea inside.

"It's from the village at Gekkō-ji," Anzu said. "Something to remind you of home."

A real smile drew up the corners of Kira's mouth at that. "Thank you."

Kira joined Anzu at the table and sank down onto a floor cushion. "So what happened on the day we left? Did you have to go take care of these raiders?"

Anzu fiddled with her right shoulder pauldron. "Yes. They had ransacked three farms near Andesine before we arrived."

"Did you see them? When we were attacked on the road, none of us even got a look at them."

Anzu shook her head, her jaw clenched. "They were long gone when we got there, and none of the farmers spotted them."

"Do you think they might be commoners, because I've been wondering if this could be—"

Jun bustled back in, chewing something. "Got to go!" he called, waving as he went by. The door to the wing boomed shut behind him. Kira gazed after him, an empty feeling in her chest.

"Am I keeping you?" Anzu asked. "Do you have to get to your lessons?"

Kira shook her head. "Oh, no. I've got time. I'm just meeting with Lord Raiden in half an hour; I haven't started lessons yet."

"I see. Well, I should let you eat and get ready for your meeting; I don't want to keep you. I just wanted to check in on the two of you and make sure they were treating you all right. You know, they refused to station me in the castle. So I had to find lodging in the city, but I'm close by. I'm sure Master Starwind and Mistress Nari wouldn't approve of you two being on your own like this, but they're a little overwhelmed at the moment, and that woman who runs the castle wouldn't hear of it. If you ever need me..." She frowned, thinking. "Can you send messages on the wind yet?" she asked with a sly smile.

Kira's throat constricted, so she shook her head. She couldn't tell Anzu what had happened. She couldn't tell her that she had lost her Shadow magic and was on her way to losing her Light magic too. She bunched up her fists below the table.

"Well, that's all right," Anzu said. "I heard from Zowan that you were accompanied by a certain mountain spirit's helper? Maybe you can send him if you need me. I'm staying at the Vitreous Lodge; it's as close to the Spire as you can get."

"Great idea. Maybe Thistle will drop in later; I'll ask him to locate the lodge in case I need you."

"I won't keep you," Anzu said, reaching over and giving Kira a squeeze around the shoulders. "Tell me if you need anything, all right?"

After Anzu left, Kira scarfed down some barley buns Jun had made the previous day, and headed out of the Gray Wing.

* * *

A little while later she found herself in Raiden's study, sitting in a plush leather chair across from a very peculiar mage.

Tall and lanky, he lounged in his chair with a cup of tea jauntily perched on his knee. His dark hair was spiked in a thoroughly *modern* way that surprised Kira—modern for the Realm of Camellia anyway. He wore the usual garb of the mages, the dark fitted robe that went down to his knees, with matching trousers, but he had intricate silver fastenings going up the length of the robe's opening.

"Ryn, this is Kira Savage," Raiden was saying as he brought a tray of tea over to the sitting area where Kira and the mage sat. "Kira, this is Ryn Kimura. He completed his training here at the Spire a few years ago, but I've called on him to help with your problem."

Kira managed a tentative smile. Ryn sipped his tea and lurched out of his position on the chair, leaning forward and putting his tea down so he could steeple his fingers in front of his face.

"Ryn specializes in auratic Shadow magic," Raiden said, sitting between them with his own cup of tea. "I think he might be able to see the damage to your soul and help us diagnose the issue."

The mage just sat there studying Kira with his eyes narrowed. She crossed her legs, then did the same with her arms. "Should I... do something?" she asked.

"No," Ryn finally said. "I'm trying to get a reading. Your aura is a little... hard to see."

Panic flitted across Kira's face.

"It's fine," Ryn said, apparently sensing her concern. "It's not because of the damage. I think it might be an inherent trait of yours—some people's souls resist access by other people. You're sort of walled-off."

"Should I—can I help you access it?"

He shook his head, still staring at her across his steepled fingers. "Just give me a minute."

Kira uncrossed her arms and instead placed her hands awkwardly in her lap, waiting. *This is even worse than med-*

itation, she thought. It was as if she were a horse on display, being inspected by a particular buyer.

Ryn abruptly leaned back in his chair and crossed one ankle over his knee, his long fingers still steepled together. "Your aura is very thin here," he said, pointing a wagging finger, "Near your head and neck. I've never seen one like that before."

Kira resisted the urge to bring her hand up to her now tingling neck.

"I'm seeing lots of blue and purple," he gestured vaguely at her with one hand, "but it looks like it's a new addition—it's covering up your normal gold and blue."

"And what does this all mean? How has her soul been affected?" Raiden asked, completely ignoring his tea on the table beside him.

Ryn pursed his lips. "The blue and purple I wouldn't worry about. Unless they turn black, anyway."

"But how would I know?" Kira said, perplexed.

A dark chuckle escaped Ryn. "Oh, you would know."

Kira furrowed her eyebrows.

Instead of explaining, he went on. "It's the thinning that's concerning." He locked eyes with Kira for a moment. "Your aura is a projection of your soul—or spirit some call it. The soul is your constant life energy, an energy that is supposed to remain untouched. Your aura can reflect the inner workings of your soul though. The thinness means that part of your soul is... Not as strong as it should be."

"Can she be healed?" Raiden said in a rumbling undertone.

Kira's face warmed. Now she was not only to be inspected, but spoken about as if she needed new horseshoes or something.

Ryn peered into Kira's face without meeting her eyes. "I can't say," he said slowly.

"Well if you're both done deciding whether my soul is broken or not," Kira suddenly burst out. "I don't want to waste anyone's time."

Blood rushed to her face and she was on her feet before she knew it. She couldn't take Ryn's shocked look, so she turned on her heels and stormed out of Raiden's study, her arms crossed tightly about her.

Chapter 11

The Apothecarium

So her soul was damaged. Her Shadow magic was gone, and her Light magic slipping.

That didn't mean she was going to submit to every mage Raiden wanted to bring in to gawk at her, and speculate over her like some prized horse.

She scoffed to herself and strode down the long empty corridors of the Spire, twice turning the wrong direction because she was so absorbed in her thoughts. On one of these wrong turns, she almost bumped into Yuki.

"Sorry," Kira muttered, warmth coming to her cheeks.

"It's fine," Yuki said with a slight smile, trying to look into Kira's face. "Are you all right?"

Kira shied away and mumbled something about needing to get back to her quarters. She turned back the way she had come and found her way down the halls until she made it to the Gray Wing. She burst through the double doors and found the common room thankfully empty.

With a scornful look out the balcony toward the Spire tower, she strode to her rooms, wanting more than ever to be alone.

What was she even doing here? She should just go back to Gekkō-ji and try to preserve what hold she still had on her Light magic.

Or maybe she should go to the Starwind estate, where her grandfather said she could live after her training was complete. Well, all her training might be over now that she was probably about to become common, magicless.

Inside her father's study, she flung open the sliding doors onto the balcony and stood at the railing, staring at the ever-looming Spire, trying to catch her breath.

And then panic began to set in as she realized what she had just done.

She had stormed out of Raiden's study like a petulant child, in front of a visiting mage, and who knows how many other people who saw her in the hallways and the foyer.

She closed her eyes, gripping the railing with clammy palms. She groaned, lowering her forehead to the railing.

"What is wrong with me?" she said in a strangled voice.

Whirling around, she went back inside the study and plunked herself in the chair at the desk, bringing her knees to her chest. Slowly her forehead came down to rest on her knees, and as she closed her eyes, she felt wetness trickle down her cheeks. "What is wrong with me?" she repeated, this time in a whisper.

The Storm King thought she was a prized mare who just needed a few adjustments—though what kind, no one knew.

Jun thought it wasn't a big deal at all, and was more focused on his own training, even doing extra research talking to mages about their specialties. She didn't fault him for it; he had grown up knowing that he had a high probability of becoming a Gray Knight. Magic had always been easy for him.

Kira hadn't even wanted to admit her problem to Anzu, but how could a Light Knight even help her? And Zowan wasn't even here, off running errands for Raiden to the palace.

She had no one else to confide in, no friends here at the Spire, and no family. Of course, she was pretty sure Raiden would have written to Ichiro about her soul damage by now, but Kira wasn't exactly on the most comfortable terms with her grandfather just yet. Though she hated to admit it, Ichiro might consider her problem just as Raiden was doing—cold and speculatively. And she cringed to think of how Mistress Nari would treat her. She would probably kick her straight out of Gekkō-ji when she found out Kira's Light magic was slipping.

And then she remembered Micah. Hope surged in her chest at the memory of their meeting in the Jade Foyer. And there was his sister Spectra too. Neither of them had any magic, so they couldn't exactly help with her problem, but it would be nice to talk to people who weren't speculating over her broken magic, and just wanted to speak with her.

She was up and walking halfway across the Jade Foyer before she realized she had no idea where the Apothecarium was. She paused beside the enormous spherical jade fountain, the gently trickling water the only sound she could hear in the spacious foyer. The acolytes were all in the middle of lessons. With a pang of jealousy, she looked up at the inside of the dizzying Spire, wondering just what she might have been learning right now if she hadn't gone and ruined her powers chasing after the Lord of Between.

"Lady Starwind? Can I help you with something?" It was the Spirekeeper, Kusari Kashjian.

"Oh, um, Mistress Kusari—" Kira stammered, taking a step back at the sudden appearance of the exceedingly tall woman. Her short pixie-style hair was as out of place as it had been when they first met. And one glance down at the woman's soft leather shoes explained how she had come into the foyer so quietly.

"No '*Mistress*', please," she said crisply. "Just Kusari is fine."

Kira bowed her head a little. "Kusari. I was thinking about visiting my friend Spectra in the Apothecarium, but I just realized I don't know where it is..." she trailed off, not wanting to sound disrespectful, but still a little irked that no one had bothered to show her and Jun around the temple yet.

Kusari hummed. "Ah, yes, Lord Raiden did tell me about your—er—irregular schedule. You will find the Apothecarium just down that corridor," she pointed to a brightly lit interior corridor just beside the staircase that led up the Spire.

"And let me see," Kusari continued, then bent to put a hand on the side of the stone fountain. "Miss Spectra is indeed at her work. Be sure not to bother her too long."

"Oh, I won't," Kira said. "But, h-how do you—"

A smug smile crept across Kusari's face. She twiddled her fingers. "That? It's my proficiency. It's why I'm adept at arranging schedules and the workings of the temple. With a touch, I can identify the whereabouts of individuals within any structure. I can see who is where," she clarified further, no doubt in response to Kira's blank look.

"Oh, wow," Kira said, her brow furrowing as she thought about it. It sounded a little creepy.

"It's nothing intrusive," Kusari explained, seeming to interpret Kira's concern. "It's a little like seeing a blurry speck on a map of the castle inside my head. And it only works if I know the building well, and the people inside it."

"Oh."

"Yes, well, you might want to get going, Lady Starwind. A group of mages is returning from scouting near the border to the Stone Mountains, and they'll all be clamoring through the foyer in a moment."

With a swift glance down the Hall of Spirits, Kira darted toward the hallway Kusari had pointed out. Just as she turned the corner, she heard raised voices entering the Jade Foyer.

Still marveling at Kusari's proficiency, Kira followed the narrow corridor for a minute, the smell of herbs and tinctures growing stronger by the second. It was reminiscent of the apothecary back at Gekkō-ji where Kira and Jun had learned of non-magical ways to heal people.

At the end of the corridor, she came out into a wide circular room, the afternoon light streaming in from the multitude of windows in a glass dome above. The walls were composed entirely of wooden compartments, each filled with tins or bottles. Kira stepped inside and gazed around at the herbs in dark glass jars, the small metal tins, the clear bottles of all different sizes, filled with liquids ranging from one end of the color spectrum to the next. It was almost like a library but for healing ingredients. There were even wooden ladders on rails to access the higher-up ingredients.

The healing staff all wore crisp white aprons over their clothes as they bustled about the rows of supplies in the center of the room. The smells were overwhelming; Kira could pick out peppermint, clove, and sage, among a number of foreign scents assailing her nose.

She found her footing on the top of the handful of steps leading down into the enormous Apothecarium. She didn't see either Spectra or Micah anywhere, but Kusari had said Spectra was here.

It was quiet, save for the sound of water sloshing in an alcove to Kira's left, where someone was cleaning bottles. She saw the familiar black glossy hair with a green sheen and started forward.

"Spectra?" Kira said in a hushed voice.

The girl turned and gave Kira a startled smile. "Kira! Oh, wow, you actually came! Um, I'm kind of busy at the moment though," she mumbled, turning her head down to the longneck glass bottle in her hand.

"I'm sorry, I should have let you know I was coming beforehand."

"Kira? Is that you?" another voice called from behind her.

She turned to see Micah coming over with a tray of dirty glass bottles. His sleeves were rolled up over his forearms, and his apron strings were wrapped twice around his waist, accentuating his narrow torso.

Before they could talk, a group of three people entered the Apothecarium, breaking the heavily perfumed silence.

"I'm fine," a man was saying loudly. "It's not a big deal." His two companions carried him in; he sat on their linked arms. They turned toward where Kira stood, and she recognized them at once.

"Starless girl!" called the man being held. "What are you doing here?"

She snorted and came toward them. "Tai! Are you all right?" She glanced between the two people holding him; stoic Sagano was looking around for a healer, and the woman on the other side was Ayana, her longbow hanging across her back.

"Oh I'm fine," Tai drawled.

Then Kira noticed his leg and gasped. A huge rip in his pants revealed a jagged wound that seemed partially healed. The pant leg was covered in blood, but the skin had been washed clean.

"That doesn't look fine," Kira said, coming closer.

"Oh, the healer'll have me cleaned up in no time," Tai said. "We had to do a quick and dirty patch-up heal; there was no time on the road. So Sagano here wanted to make sure it gets healed up correctly."

Spectra finally looked up from her bottles and gave Tai's leg a cursory check over. Then she bustled off to another room, leaving Kira standing awkwardly beside Micah.

"How come you didn't have time?" Kira asked. "Were you the Guard that was scouting near the Stone Mountains border?"

Kira wasn't too familiar with the area, but had had an unnerving encounter with a mage from the Stone Mountains last year. When Lady Madora had found out Kira's parentage, she had wanted Kira to join her as an ally in the Stone Mountains. When Kira refused, Lady Madora had tried to keep her by force, until Kira's friends had shown up, anyway.

"Aye," Sagano said. "We were. Until we were attacked by raiders. Precisely the reason we were scouting that far south. There have been some interesting reports in the past few weeks. Well, I'm afraid—" he glanced around and checked no one was eavesdropping. "I'm afraid these raiders are *coming from* the Stone Mountains region."

"Really?" Micah said in a hushed voice, inching forward.

"Really," Sagano said, "But don't you breathe a word of that to anyone until I brief Lord Raiden on it."

"You know me," Micah said, putting a finger to his lips.

Sagano grunted as he saw Spectra return with a matronly sort of woman, her long black and gray hair tightly plaited in two braids that ran down her back, with delicate wrinkles framing her eyes. "Bring him through here," she directed, motioning to the arched doorway from which she had come.

"Be seeing you, Kira," Tai said, tipping his fingers toward her from his forehead in a salute of some kind.

Sagano and Ayana left them with silent nods as they carted Tai away.

"Do you need something too?" the matron asked Kira, giving her a look up and down.

"No, Mistress," Kira replied, bowing.

"Very well." The woman turned and beckoned to Spectra to follow her. Kira gave Spectra a little wave, though she tried to hide her disappointment in not being able to talk to her.

"I'd better get going," Kira told Micah, glancing at the doorway the matron had disappeared through.

He frowned. "Yeah, maybe that's a good idea. Mistress Tetsu is in a terrible mood today; one of the acolytes nearly burned down the mixing lab." He jerked his head in the direction of one of the other doors.

"Oh?" Kira said in concern.

Micah shrugged. "It happens. Some of these mages in training think they can do everything with magic."

Kira snorted. "That's why at Gekkō-ji they make us do a lot of chores and stuff by hand. So we don't abuse our magic."

"It sounds like a good idea," he said, absently brushing the sides of his apron. "I should probably get back to helping clean up the lab. But we should try to meet up sometime, maybe outside of the temple? We could go into Heliodor."

"That would be great," Kira said earnestly, her face lighting up as the thought drove out all of the worry over her magic. She looked deep into his eyes, and her heart soared from the depths it had sunk to. "Thank you."

"For what?" He cocked his head, his messy black hair falling across his forehead a little.

Instead of answering, she leaned forward and pressed a kiss to his cheek.

Chapter 12

Soul Reading

That evening, Jun left the Gray Wing before they had a chance to spar, claiming he was meeting with another acolyte he had met that afternoon.

"He's got a really unique proficiency," he told her, one foot already out the door of the wing. "He says it's not much, but he can tell time without looking at a clock. I want to hear how he does it. Maybe I can too."

And with that, he left, leaving Kira alone in the common room with her thoughts. She frowned, part of her wishing she could go with Jun and learn about interesting Shadow proficiencies, and another part wishing she could hole up in her quarters for a month. The latter was looking more and more attractive the longer she thought about it.

She grabbed a bowl of rice and bean sprouts she and Jun had made earlier, then fled into her study. After downing the food, she really wished she had made some of the tea

Anzu had left her, but she didn't feel like getting back up and going to the kitchen again.

So she sat at the desk, summoning throwing knives with Light magic over and over again. She was supposed to be practicing her Light magic, anyway.

The knives winked into existence as pure white in her hand and dispersed like mist when she released them. She could feel the Light magic in the world all around her, she could see it now that the sun was down, and she could draw it in with her senses, mold it into whatever she wanted. But her will needed to be strong enough. She banished a knife with a puff of breath, letting the magic sink back into the earth before pulling on it again, forming another identical blade.

Maybe the crack in her staff had been her imagination last night.

Or maybe she was losing her Light magic too.

She summoned another knife into her palm, trying to focus on making it as strong as steel, as sharp as possible. She let out a huff.

Would she stop being able to see Light in the world around her if her magic really was slipping? Would the pearlescent glow fade from her sight, so short-lived after a life in the dark?

She drew the knife back up by her shoulder and sent it flying toward the wall beside the door.

It sunk into the wood paneling with a thud.

At that same moment, a knock came at her study door. Stifling a groan, she called, “What?”

“May I come in, Lady Starwind?” a somewhat familiar male voice called.

“Um, sure?”

Jun and Micah never called her that; who else did she know here?

She untangled her legs from where she had perched on the chair and stood up just as the door slid open.

The lanky form of the mage called Ryn took up the entire doorway, a skinny arm perched on his hip. “I’m sorry. I knocked at the entrance to the wing, and called out for you before busting in, but... Nice holdings you have here,” he said, peering inside but not stepping over the threshold. He gave her a respectful bow. “You don’t even want to know how small the regular acolyte quarters are,” he said in an undertone.

“Oh?” Kira didn’t know what to say after her outburst in Raiden’s office earlier.

He spotted the knife sticking out of the wall, at the same height as his face. “Nice.”

With a thought, Kira reached out and dispersed the magic in the knife, leaving only a wedge of a hole in the wall as the only evidence it had been there.

"Even nicer," he commented at the knife's disappearance.

Kira went back to her chair. "What are you doing here?" she blurted.

Leaning against the doorframe, his short hair brushed the lintel. "I thought you might want to talk more about your aura. Maybe not in front of Lord Raiden."

Kira leaned an elbow on the desk and stared down at the wood.

"Well?" Ryn said, crossing his arms.

"All right," she said. "But not here. Let's go out into the common room." She didn't trust herself to summon a chair from Light magic. She couldn't bear the idea of it breaking when Ryn went to sit in it.

She led Ryn out into the common room. "Wait here," she said, leaving him to sit on one of the floor cushions beside the low table in the center of the room. The hanging lamps all around the room glowed with flickering flames. Of course, since the sun was down, she could see a subtle highlight of Light magic in everything around her, but the lanterns pooled their warm light over the common room just the same. She often had to remind herself that Shadow mages couldn't see in the dark as she could.

She headed into the kitchen and picked up the tin of tea Anzu had given her. In minutes, she had a tray loaded with tea things to bring out into the common room.

"I want to apologize for earlier," Kira said as she came back into the room with the tray.

Ryn eyed the tray with curiosity. As soon as she put it down, she poured them both tea. The green leaves had been infused with a wonderful fruity floral scent that seemed to lift Kira's shoulders from the simple act of inhalation. She took a sip, wondering if the taste would do the same. She closed her eyes briefly as the warm liquid soothed her throat and soul.

"I understand," Ryn said lightly. "I can't imagine what you're going through—what you're feeling, and how it's affected your magic. You've got a right to be angry about it."

"But I don't want to be angry," she admitted. "I want to fix it."

He set down his cup and stared down at it. "That is *fantastic*. What kind of tea is that?"

"I have no idea; my friend Anzu bought it as a gift near Gekkō-ji."

He bobbed his head. "Anyway, I'm here to try and help you fix your problem. I'd like to do a more in-depth reading on your aura. But Lady Starwind, if I ever make you uncomfortable, we can always stop. I've been told sometimes I can be a little... insensitive."

Kira shrugged. "I can do it. And you can call me Kira. You're just going to look at my aura again, right?"

Ryn took a long draught of his tea. "Actually, I was thinking we could try something else."

She bit her lip. "Like what?"

"Like a soul reading."

"You can do that? How is that different than what you did before?"

Ryn recrossed his long legs and leaned forward. "Lord Raiden told me about your Scrying with the Dragon Crystal. That's kind of what gave me the idea."

She narrowed her eyes at him. "You don't need me to try to access Shadow magic, do you? Raiden told you I passed out, right?"

A chuckle came over him. "No, I wouldn't suggest that either. No, what I'd be doing is trying to do a reading like what the Scrying produces—to tell us the colors of the magic of your soul."

"Oh. Well, that sounds okay. What do we have to do?"

Ryn drained his teacup and set it back down. "Just take my hands, and I'll do all the work. I've never done this before, so I have no idea if it even *will* work. There's a reason the Dragon Crystal is what they use to help sort out acolytes' capabilities."

"What *is* that crystal, anyway? I've never heard of any other magical objects like that here in Camellia."

"They're really rare, I know that much. It reacts to the magic that gets channeled through it. Something in the crystalline structure reveals mage's skills, but I've heard there were other crystals once upon a time. So, what I'd be doing is trying to pull the same Shadow magic through you, to get your soul to show me the answers, instead of channeling it through a crystal. I *think* it's similar to how I read an aura."

Kira squirmed a little on her floor cushion. "If you think it will work."

"It can't hurt," Ryn said brightly, reaching out for both of her hands.

"I mean... it could," Kira said pointedly.

He *tsked*. "You'll be fine," he assured her. "You won't be attempting to access any magic yourself. I'll be doing all the magic. We're just looking."

With a sigh, she reached her hands out and said, "All right. I'm curious anyway. Let's try it."

Ryn's long fingers encircled hers, and he closed his eyes as he scooted closer to her. Not sure what she should be doing, she closed her eyes too, feeling a little silly. At least she wasn't on display being stared at by anybody.

A slight tingle began at her fingertips, but it didn't bother her. She was beginning to suspect that the weird feverish sensation at the back of her neck had something to do with the soul damage, but all was calm there at the moment. She took a shaky breath, wondering how long this might take.

"Your aura is blocking me again," Ryn complained.

"Sorry?" she muttered. "I'm not really sure how to stop that."

Ryn gave an exaggerated sigh. "I'll get around it."

"Why would my aura do that anyway?"

"Hush, I'm trying to concentrate."

Kira bit back a giggle and waited, sort of enjoying the tingle in her hands. It was like warmth returning to them after they had been out in the cold too long.

"I think I'm getting something," Ryn said so quietly she almost didn't hear him.

She held her breath and waited.

"Ohh, this is interesting."

But he didn't elaborate. "What?" she finally snapped after several minutes.

"Oh, sorry. I think I'm actually getting through to the color signature of your soul's makeup, just like the way the Dragon Crystal projects them. Your aura is acting as the crystalline structure. I've never seen anything like this before. I honestly never thought to try it."

Kira opened her eyes, but she couldn't see anything different about herself. Ryn was staring at her hands, eyes wide.

"Well, can you think of a way to fix the damage?" she asked quietly.

"I'm not sure yet. I can see a hole—no, no, it's more like a wound across part of your soul—so your soul is still intact, but this wound is preventing you from accessing the abilities."

"Oh," she managed.

He hummed a little, still studying the air around her tingling fingers. She wondered if what he was seeing was as beautiful an array of colors as she had briefly seen in the Dragon Crystal.

"I think what we need is someone or something that can heal your soul. All I can do is view what the damage looks like; I can't do anything about it."

"Do you know of anyone with that kind of magic? Are there healers in the Spire that could do it?" But she knew the answer to her question before it slipped from her mouth—if there were, Raiden would know; he would have gotten them to heal her by now.

"It wouldn't fall under normal healing," Ryn hedged. "Soul magic isn't something that's even studied here. Souls don't normally get wounded like yours did."

Kira studied the grain of the table in front of her, thinking. "Well, does the Spire have a library? Can we check there?"

Ryn chuckled. *"Does the Spire have a library?"* he repeated incredulously. "Girl, has no one shown you around this place yet?"

"Nope," she said. "I don't think the Spirekeeper or the other trainees are too excited about having people with Light magic here, to be completely honest."

Ryn rolled his eyes, but Kira could see some hesitation in his expression. "That's ridiculous. I'll show you around tomorrow," he said, finally dropping her hands.

"Really? How long are you staying at the Spire?"

With a shrug he said, "Who knows? There isn't much demand for auratic readings these days, so I might stick around a while."

Kira found herself smiling for once.

"Ah! Yes—" he said, pointing to her head and hands. "That was the other thing I wanted to tell you. Your aura brightened just now when you smiled. You should try focusing on positive things more, if you can. They'll feed your soul and help stave off the wound."

"Do you think... Could it be getting worse?" The thought made her heart hammer painfully in her chest.

"I think it's possible," he admitted with a frown. "So try and do things that make you happy; make sure you take care of yourself. I imagine the wound is already messing with your happiness, which kind of makes it hard to be happy in the first place. But sometimes even simple things make people happy, like smiling or going for a walk. Writing, drawing, whatever you like to do."

She snorted. "Well I'm terrible at drawing, but I'll try and be more aware of it, I guess."

"Well, we're all good at *something*," he said with a wink. "No one's good at everything."

"Oh I don't know," said a voice from the hallway. Kira turned to see Jun appearing from the entrance to the wing. "I'm pretty good at a lot of things."

Kira scowled at him. "Yeah, but that's just 'pretty good', so that doesn't count."

Chuckling, Jun came over to join them.

"How long have you been standing there?" Kira asked.

"Who's your friend?" he countered.

Ryn unfolded his long legs and stood; he gave Jun a slight bow of his head. "Ryn Kimura. Lord Raiden invited me back to the Spire to help Lady Starwind with a problem."

Kira rose up off the floor to join them. "Please, it's just Kira. And we can talk about it... Jun knows about my problem."

"Jun Kosumoso," he said, returning the bow. "Were you reading her aura?"

"Sort of," Ryn said. "It was my proficiency when I trained here."

"Really? Can you show me how to do it?"

With a soft laugh, Ryn said, "It took me seven years to perfect, but... maybe I could tell you the basics sometime."

"Deal. And you'll have to tell us all about your training here. What do you do now that you've finished?"

"Oh, this and that," Ryn said vaguely.

A clock chimed from the open door to Kira's study just down the hall.

"It's probably late," Ryn said. "I'll leave you two be. Don't need old Kusari coming in here and yelling at you for having a visitor so late."

With a jolt, Kira recalled Kusari's unique Shadow proficiency. She almost chuckled, wondering at the fact that Ryn had been in the Gray Wing with her and she hadn't even worried about the fact she was alone with a boy she barely knew. He seemed genuinely harmless and concerned for her welfare.

But things in Camellia were a little different than the Starless Realm, with surprisingly more freedoms for women, she had noticed. No one had blinked an eye putting Kira and Jun together in the wing, though they did have completely separate quarters at different ends of the hallway. But she supposed for a realm that trained women and men to be equal warriors alongside each other, it wasn't suspect like it would have been back in the Starless Realm.

"Did you want to try a reading again tomorrow then?" she said.

Ryn nodded. "I'll talk to Lord Raiden in the morning," he said delicately. "I think we should do frequent readings just to be safe. And I don't think having him there will be that productive. Let's meet in the Jade Foyer at midday. You have meditation in the morning, correct?"

"Yes," Kira said without enthusiasm.

The mage's face brightened. "I think that would be a great time to focus on the positivity we talked about."

Kira stifled a groan.

"Kira," Ryn chastised. "You know I can see what your aura is doing, right?"

She let out a strangled chuckle at his jibe. "All right, fine, I'll give it a try."

CHAPTER 13

THE STONE MOUNTAINS

Breathe in the good, breathe out the bad.

Kira tried to focus on the mantra that Ryn had suggested she try before departing the Gray Wing last night. Sure, she could match up her breathing with the well-meaning mantra, but was it really doing anything?

She hadn't slept well again. It was hard to relax when she kept picturing a dark splotch on her soul. And to sit in perfect stillness with her eyes closed wasn't as restful as it should be after a night of tossing and turning.

She took another deep breath and tried to envision the wound inside her, a mangled portion of her soul she pictured as a black spot at the back of her neck. She tried to imagine the blackness leaving in small pieces as she breathed out. Breathing in, she pictured white light entering to displace it. Over and over, with each breath she tried to focus her mind. In and out. Black and white.

This is stupid, drifted across her brain.

No, no, don't think like that, she told herself. *Breathe in the good—*

The clear peel of the bell echoed into the pavilion, interrupting her warring thoughts. She huffed out a frustrated breath. How in the world did Ryn think she was going to become more positive with these long hours of meditation? Maybe she would just have to try something else later. She just hoped he wouldn't be able to tell she hadn't done well when he read her aura this afternoon.

Or, even worse, what if she was making the wound worse with all these negative thoughts?

She resolved to find *something* to raise her spirits today.

After the acolytes all bowed to Mistress Korina, Kira stood and met up with Jun, who had picked a sunny spot to meditate in near one of the open sides of the pavilion.

"Meeting Ryn now?" he asked.

Kira nodded, and they both made their way inside the castle through the covered walkway. Before they reached the Jade Foyer, however, they were approached by the Spirekeeper.

"You two, come with me," she said, towering more than a head above each of them. She turned and began to walk away, expecting them to follow.

Kira and Jun exchanged frantic looks. Did she know about Ryn visiting the Gray Wing last night? How often did Kusari look in on each part of the castle? Would they really get in trouble for that? Or had they not cleaned the wing to the Spirekeeper's liking?

Kira recognized the path Kusari was leading them on, and they soon found themselves standing outside of Raiden's study. Surely this wasn't something the Storm King would need to punish them for, right?

Kusari knocked.

"Enter."

Raiden wasn't alone inside his study. To Kira's surprise, Jovan Kosumoso stood in front of Raiden's desk. Jun's father, and the leader of the Gray Knights, he kept his graying hair cropped short. He was suited up in full armor, diamond-patterned chainmail across his chest under leather pauldrons that curved up at the ends of his shoulders.

Kira and Jun both sunk into deep bows, and Sir Jovan returned them with grace.

"Thank you, Kusari," Raiden said, and the Spirekeeper backed out through the door and closed it.

"Greetings to both of you," Jovan said, clasping his hands behind his back. "I must apologize for not coming sooner. I had hoped to join you on the way to the Spire, but Lady Sasha, Sir Dorado, and I were deep in the Seven Days Forest dealing with a deranged headman of the Ga'Mir." He shook his head. "And now Camellia is beset by another brand of raider. I suspect they think we are weak now that we have achieved peace between Light and Shadow. Well, there will be time enough later for your formal Gray training and assisting in the defense of the realm. It is enough that you are here, and you are learning."

Kira twisted her mouth and looked down at her shoes.

"Now, to business," Jovan said. "I've been told you were ambushed on the road to Heliodor with Lord Zowan, is that correct?"

Scrambling her thoughts as she remembered that day, Kira blurted, "Yes." The attack felt like ages ago, after everything that had happened at the Spire so far, but it had only been a few days.

"Zowan briefed me on the attack when you arrived," Raiden explained, "but I'd like the two of you to go over the details for Sir Jovan."

"This happened near Andesine?" Jovan asked.

"Yes, sir," Jun chimed in.

"What else can you tell us about the attack?" Raiden asked. "Zowan isn't due to return from the palace until tomorrow, and I want to verify some new theories."

Jovan nodded in agreement and added in an undertone, "If it is as we suspect, I'd like to send word to Gekkō-ji and the palace straight away."

Raiden looked like he wanted to roll his eyes at the mention of the palace, but he waved Kira on to speak.

"Oh, well first they shot Briar in the leg with an arrow," Kira began, and together she and Jun unraveled the story of the brief skirmish.

Jovan rubbed his chin thoughtfully as they finished speaking. "And there was no magic of any kind, is that correct?"

"Not that any of us saw," Kira said.

"Very well, thank you," Raiden said.

Kira glanced at Jun, wondering if they were being dismissed just like that. But they were the next Gray Knights. Weren't they supposed to be involved in the realm's affairs? "Do you think—could it be raiders from the Stone Mountains?" she wondered.

Raiden clenched his fist, and Kira could have sworn she saw tiny crackles of lightning dancing there. "What makes you say that?" he snapped. Jovan shifted slightly on his feet.

"Oh, I don't know," she hedged, "I mean, they're too far southwest to be from Ga'Mir, aren't they? The Stone Mountains are the only other region nearby..." she trailed off, hoping she sounded natural. She didn't want to get Sagano in trouble for saying anything.

Kira was surprised to see Raiden and Jovan share a mutual uneasy glance, and then Raiden sighed. "Why don't you both come sit down? As Gray Knights in training, I suppose you're entitled to be included in the conversation. Jun, I'll explain away your absence from lessons."

They perched in two chairs in front of Raiden's large bare desk, and Kira retained an upright posture, feeling a little awkward sitting here discussing the problems of the realm with Raiden and Jovan, as if she were important. As if she had as much say as they did. As if she were her father's daughter. She smiled sadly to herself, trying not to think of her malfunctioning magic.

Jovan seemed to relax a little as he turned toward them. "As Gray Knights, you will be charged with the protection of the realm—not just individual regions and factions, but the realm as a whole—and for the good of all people," he explained. "These raiders are becoming a blight worse than the haphazard Ga'Mir. These new raiders are clever. I sent Dorado to scour the area—the attack on the three of you has not been the only one in the past week. And the rumors of where they are coming from..." Jovan trailed off, glancing at Raiden.

Raiden frowned. "Well, let's just say I hope they're not coming from the Stone Mountains," Raiden admitted.

"Lady Madora isn't pleased with either you or me as you may recall," he said to Kira.

Kira's insides twisted. The memory of the old woman in the caravan, a cloth covering her blind eyes, yet she had the power to look into the past at will with her Shadow magic...

"But she has magic," she said. "So why did you want to know if the raiders have it or not? Do people there not have magic?"

Raiden rubbed his thumb over his clenched fist. "Magic is rarer there in their people. And whenever anyone from there does exhibit magic, they usually leave the Stone Mountains and come to train at the Spire or Gekkō-ji, never to return. We've had a smattering of Shadow mages from there over the years; Kusari is one, and I trained with another called Kage when I was an acolyte... It has developed some spite in the people there when they don't return.

"Lady Madora, of course, chose to return to her holdings there after honing her magic, thus making her one of the most powerful people in the region. And her guards are highly skilled in combat, giving her another edge."

"Oh," Kira said. "So when she wanted me to come to the Stone Mountains with her and I said no... You don't think this has anything to do with that, do you?" she said in a quiet voice, not wanting to admit such a thing in front of Sir Jovan, but wanting to voice it nonetheless.

Raiden brought one hand down the front seam of his robes, smoothing the crisp fabric. He flicked his eyes to Jovan and away. "That is yet to be determined."

"How do we know this isn't…" Kira began awkwardly, "the commoners from before? The Lord of Between could be rallying them again. It doesn't necessarily mean they're coming from the Stone Mountains. The Lord of Between could be trying to deceive us somehow."

Jun grunted beside her. "And they've tried to attack Zowan before too."

"Oh, I remember," Raiden said darkly.

Kira would never forget the sight of Zowan slumped against the wall of a basement, beaten and bloody at the hands of the Lord of Between's rogue commoners. Her fists clenched at the memory, her fingernails digging into her palms.

Raiden began rummaging in the top drawer of his desk to retrieve paper and a brush pen to write with.

"The Third Shadow Guard witnessed a group of these raiders coming from the Arashi Pass," he said as he slipped a piece of parchment onto the desktop. "That leads straight to the heart of the Stone Mountains. And from their clothing and weapons, they didn't look like they were from this region. They wore sandy-colored cloaks that are indicative of the Stone Mountains. I had merely hoped you two could remember something that would mean they were more common raiders."

Kira furrowed her eyebrows at him.

"It makes things far more complicated if they're from the Stone Mountains. But alas, it seems our suspicions are not to be unfounded."

"Oh."

"Well, let's alert the palace," Jovan said grimly, nodding at the paper Raiden had taken out.

Kira didn't see what he wrote, but after a few minutes Raiden finished his letter with a flourish and pulled out a stick of navy blue wax from a drawer. With admirable precision, he summoned flame with his index finger and thumb to melt the wax just enough to drip on the letter. But he didn't press a seal to it. Instead, he appeared to summon Shadow magic into the palm of his hand, which he lowered toward the cooling wax. When he drew his hand away, the wax had formed a unique design—the magic had swirled the wax into a spiral pattern, with the letter "R" intact in wax in the center. It had taken only a second.

Kira and Jun glanced at each other out of the corner of their eyes.

"Very well," Raiden said. "Perhaps my nephew can bring a reply if he is still there."

Jovan nodded, and said, "I'll send word to Gekkō-ji myself before I mount back up."

"You're leaving?" Jun asked his father.

"Yes, but I'll be patrolling south of the Kaidō road, so I'll still be in the region. We've split the Gray Knights across the realm since these raiders keep appearing all over. I'll try and return as soon as I can. Even though they seem to be coming from the Stone Mountains, we've had to spread thin to watch for them."

"Yes, well I can spare more mages in the north if you'd let me," Raiden growled.

Jovan shook his head. "You know as well as I do how the people would react to seeing your Shadow Guards patrolling. No, it's best they remain in the Shadow region; there have been plenty of attacks here, too. And Mistress Nari has dispatched as many knights as she can afford elsewhere. The Gray Knights will just have to remain vigilant in leading counterattacks. I'll try to visit the Spire again when I pass by next," he added to Jun, clapping him on the shoulder.

Jun bowed his head at that, accepting it. Kira was sure he was used to his father's absence.

Raiden put his brush pen away into the drawer. "Jun, you should return to your training. Kira—"

"I'd like a word," Jovan said to her.

Kira's insides squirmed as Jun stood to go and she remained pinned to the chair.

But before Jun left, Raiden cleared his throat and said, "The information about the raiders doesn't leave this study." Kira and Jun nodded. "I truly hope our assumptions aren't true, but I don't want a rumor spreading. Oh, and I don't want either of you leaving the walls of the city until I say so. No quests outside of Heliodor until we address these rogues. Your squireships might need to be put on hold for a while."

Kira saw Jun's face fall before he acquiesced with a nod and left the study. She looked down and studied her fingernails, her stomach clenched in a knot, waiting for Sir Jovan to speak. Sure, Raiden had thought she was worthy to stay in the Gray Wing—to stay at the Spire— because he thought she could be healed, but what about Jovan?

She felt a weight on her shoulder and looked up to see Jovan's hand there. He had a kindly look on his face, his eyebrows pinched in worry in a way that reminded her distinctly of Jun.

"Kira, I'm sure this hasn't been easy on you," he said. "Lord Raiden has spoken of the soul damage you suffered at the hands of the Lord of Between. If there is anything I can do..."

Her mouth dropped open a little. "I—um—no, there's nothing."

"You shouldn't have had to suffer this," he said with sudden ire. "We *will* find the rogue and hold him accountable for his actions. I must only apologize that I was not there to prevent this fate, that you had to face him alone to rescue Lord Starwind."

She gave him a weak smile.

"Well, she wasn't alone," Raiden growled. "I was there too, though your knights and the palace still see me as untrustworthy."

"I'm aware of the situation, Raiden. And Empress Mei acknowledges you and your Guard's assistance in the matter, but prejudice doesn't just disappear after a kind act or two. Healing Camellia could take decades."

Kira sat up straighter in her chair. "Oh, Sir Jovan?" she began, noticing Raiden didn't have a reply to that, "That reminds me. If Lord Raiden told you about my—er—soul damage, well do you know of any type of magic for healing a soul? Ryn says there is a wound on it, that's preventing me from accessing my magic..." Her words lowered in volume as she made the admission.

He rubbed his stubbled chin, gazing into space. "None that I'm aware of. Traditional Shadow healing will do nothing for a soul, I'm sure you know," he said to Raiden. "But you say you had someone look at the damage?"

"Ryn Kimura," Raiden supplied. "He specializes in auratic Shadow magic."

"Ah, yes. I remember him," Jovan said. "Are you sure it's wise—"

Raiden held up a hand. "Ryn is perfectly capable. He has my fullest confidence."

Her brows pinched; Kira opened her mouth to ask about Ryn but Jovan went on.

"Then I'm afraid we'll just need to keep looking, Kira. But I'm sure we'll come up with something. You've got your father's strength, and your mother's perseverance, I know that much. I know you can beat this."

Speechless, Kira blinked away the tears threatening her eyes as she bowed herself out of the study.

Chapter 14

Poems of Peace

She found Jun waiting for her in the hallway. They started walking back toward the center of the Spire together.

"Well? What did he say? Did he know how to help your soul?"

"How do you know what he wanted to talk to me about?"

He scoffed. "Come on, he's my father. I know he's concerned about you; we all are—"

"No, he didn't know of anything," she said before he could go on, blood rushing to warm her cheeks. "But he didn't really seem too worried. I mean, he's got bigger things to worry about with those raiders..."

They discussed the idea of the raiders coming from the Stone Mountains until Jun reached the room in which his levitation lesson took place, and she bid him goodbye.

Surprisingly no longer jealous of his lessons, Kira was beginning to find her lack of training strangely freeing. She made her way through the empty halls, alone and silent but for the sound of the floorboards chirping under her feet.

For almost two years now her life had been busy with training at Gekkō-ji; the daily combat drills, the strength of will it took to learn more and more intricate Light magic, and the never-ending chores. She rarely had any free time with her friends, except for a few seasonal festivals here and there. And she was normally so busy, she didn't even have time to mourn her lack of leisure time.

She was quite looking forward to Ryn showing her around the temple. He was a little quirky, but he didn't seem to be afraid or resentful of her and her magic like the acolytes who had been politely ignoring her.

Ryn was waiting in the deserted Jade Foyer when she arrived, sitting cross-legged on the side of the fountain.

"Sorry I'm late!" she gushed when she spotted him. "Lord Raiden wanted to talk to me and Jun about something."

"It's fine," Ryn said, standing to join her. "Let's head outside first, shall we? That ought to perk up your aura some. Sunlight is an underrated miracle."

Kira made a pleased sound and followed him through the open walkway she normally took to the meditation pavilion. Instead of continuing toward the pavilion, Ryn led her off to the right toward the lake.

The early afternoon sun glittered on the small lake, and Kira felt the same rays warming her skin. It was nice to be out in the sun for once; she had spent almost all of her time indoors ever since arriving. She wondered if her aura was brightening, or if it was just her imagination now that she was aware of it.

They entered a beautifully manicured garden, with narrow little paths of loose stone winding around perfectly groomed shrubs and trees. Here and there, patches of bright summer flowers bloomed, their petals reaching for the sun.

"The gardens are maintained by the acolytes with plant proficiencies," Ryn told her as they crossed a small bridge over a stream that flowed into the lake. "They practice during their training sessions, and none of the other acolytes have to do any weeding," he chuckled.

Admiring a pink flowering tree, Kira let out an amused breath. "I wish it was like that at Gekkō-ji. Although, once I get my Shadow magic back, I should have some proficiency with plants. I was able to control vines last year."

"What else can you do?"

They reached the water's edge, where an enormous tree leaned out over the water, its long trunk practically growing horizontal to the water's surface. A spray of evergreen boughs at its end was mere inches from the water. Kira had never seen anything like it.

"Oh, well not much really," she told him. "I was able to move water around, and use wind a little. Oh, and once I was able to hear someone speaking from pretty far away."

"Really? That's an interesting one. The amazing thing about Shadow magic is it can manifest in so many different ways. It's not all just wind and levitation."

"I'm beginning to see that," Kira said, still staring at the horizontal tree. "I just wish I could use mine, and figure out what I'm capable of. Do you... Do you think I can really get it back?" she asked, not looking at him.

"I've heard a lot about you, Starless girl, and if anyone can get back their magic, you can."

Heat rose to her cheeks, but she was pleased nonetheless. "Can we go to the stables?" she asked suddenly. "I'm not actually sure how to get there, and I haven't even seen my horse Naga since we arrived." Guilt rushed over her at the thought. She desperately hoped someone had been taking care of her.

"Of course," Ryn said, casually nudging her shoulder in the direction of the castle. "It's the next stop on our tour."

They crossed a large stone courtyard between the castle and the lake, and Kira had difficulty suppressing the memories of the battle that had once taken place here. They had battled the lake spirit on this very spot—well, the Gray Knights, Raiden, and some mages did.

"The Spire is held up by magic, right?" she asked him, glancing up as they walked across the stones.

"Oh yes," Ryn said. "I don't really know how it works, but there are mages with building proficiencies. The ones that built it put some serious willpower into magicking the structure. It's the highest in all of Camellia."

Having lived in New York City briefly during her life back in the Starless Realm, Kira had seen taller buildings, but none held up by magic, of course. In a land like Camellia, the Spire was an incredible feat.

They found the stables on the south side of the castle and began looking for Naga. But before they could find her, a small weight dropped onto Kira's shoulder. She jumped, then realized what it was.

"Thistle! You scared me!"

He chortled his musical laugh. Ryn's eyebrows rose high on his forehead, but he said nothing. His eyes wide, Kira suspected he was trying to read the intelligent squirrel's aura.

"It's about time you came to visit Naga," Thistle chided. "She misses you."

Kira frowned and tilted her head. "Really? Is she all right? Where's her stall? I feel terrible."

Thistle leapt off Kira's shoulder and swooped ahead, leading them down another hallway. It wasn't much different than Gekkō-ji's stables, that is, until Kira spotted a small group of mages standing around a horse's stall, patting the animal and talking to it in low voices.

After they passed, Kira whispered to Ryn, "What in the world was that about?"

"Animal proficiencies," Ryn said with a shrug.

They found Naga halfway down the second corridor, munching on a pat of hay in the corner. Her ears perked up at Kira's voice, and she turned and whickered in their direction before continuing to eat.

"Oh, she's pretty," Ryn said, admiring Naga's smooth dapple-gray coat as he leaned against the stall door.

"She was a gift from Zowan," Kira told him, unlatching the door and going in to pat her. Her coat had recently been brushed, and when Kira lifted Naga's front hoof, she saw that they had been picked as well. Perhaps the animal proficient mages had been taking care of her.

Again, guilt assailed her. She had been moping about the Gray Wing for two days without even a thought for poor Naga. At least someone had been feeding her. Kira went over and patted Naga's cheek, then buried her head in the mare's mane. "I'm sorry," she whispered. "I'll be back to see you every day from now on."

She drew away and rejoined Ryn and Thistle in the corridor, bolting Naga's door. "Where to next?"

But Ryn's posture stiffened as he gazed down the corridor.

Kira looked at where he was staring, and spotted Anzu walking toward them. She had on her usual knight gear, full-body leather armor, and the usual white sash at her waist.

"Ah, Kira, I was just coming to check on Naga," Anzu said.

"Were you the one taking care of her?" Kira asked. "Thank you; I really should have been doing that."

Anzu looked in on Naga through the bars on the door. "It was nothing, I had to come in to take care of Panji anyway." She nodded at her horse in the stall across the way. "Although, a knight taking care of a squire's mount—usually it's the other way around." She chuckled.

Kira smiled, but her insides began to squirm. Surely Anzu knew that Kira had to pick someone to squire under for her last year of training. But Kira hadn't even had a chance to consider who she might ask. Did Anzu want

Kira for a squire? Or should Kira choose a mage, like Zowan?

Her unease deepened when she remembered her present troubles. *First things first, I need to actually get my Shadow magic back. I can decide then.*

Ryn still hadn't said anything, so Kira said, "Well, Ryn is showing me around the temple, and then we have to do something for my training, so we'd best be off. And... I'll take care of Naga from now on," she added. "She's my responsibility, I can't pawn that off on you."

Anzu gave her a graceful smile and a nod. "Don't forget to send word if you ever need me. I'm here in Heliodor to protect you and Jun, but short of lurking around all day when you're trying to train, I don't have much else I could do."

Kira's smile widened. "Thanks Anzu."

Thistle leapt back onto Kira's shoulder, joining them as they left the stables. Ryn was surprisingly quiet, his shoulders stiff.

"Anzu's all right, really," Kira assured Ryn as they emerged into the sunlight, coming out a different door than the one they had entered, into yet another garden. Still, he said nothing, which seemed quite out of character for him, even though Kira barely knew him.

"Light Knights aren't really all that intimidating," she went on, feeling as though she were defending *herself*. "It's those Shadow mages you have to worry about," she joked weakly.

Ryn arched his shoulders up. "Well, I must admit it's not an easy sight to have sprung upon you," he said, his voice thoroughly lacking in his normal aloofness. "Seeing a Light Knight stalking toward you—inside the Spire grounds for that matter—after all those years of fighting, it's a little disconcerting is all." He shivered. His face had a closed look about it.

"But you're not intimidated by me?" she said, intending it as a statement, but delivering it more as a question.

He finally loosened his shoulders and gave a little chuckle, shaking off the sudden melancholy. "Well, you're the Starless girl. The honored visitor from that realm—although, I know, I know, you should have been born in Camellia. And besides, you're just so *cute*."

"Cute? I'm not cute! Why would you say that?" She wrinkled her nose.

"Have you seen yourself? And then there's the fact that you're not all decked out in leather looking like you'll skewer me on a magic sword if I step any closer to you."

"Hey, I could summon a very sharp blade at any moment, Ryn, just as well as a knight, I'd say."

He gave her a mock-appraising look. "Show me."

Without thinking, she pulled on some Light magic from the garden around her. But then she shrank inside herself. What if she couldn't do it? What if there was a flaw?

Ryn's forehead wrinkled. "What's going on? What are you thinking about?"

She huffed. It was almost like he could read her mind, with her every emotion being broadcast across her aura for him to read. "I'm... kind of afraid my Light magic is slipping too," she admitted in a whisper, all joking forgotten.

He frowned, then pointed to a stone bench nearby. "Sit. Let's do the reading."

Though lacking in flowers, this garden was covered in greenery and stone. Walkways, benches, and statues were coated in delicate green moss, and ivy vines curled up trees and over trellises.

Kira obeyed, and they sat cross-legged facing each other. Thistle hopped down first onto Kira's lap, and then onto the bush nearby. Though he stared at them with his wide black eyes, Kira wasn't bothered by his curiosity. In fact...

"Thistle," she began as Ryn took her hands, "Do you know anything about souls and auras? Apparently there's a wound on my soul, keeping me from doing Shadow magic. We think we might need some kind of magic to heal it..." she trailed off, her hopes hanging on the words.

Thistle cocked his head, thinking. "It's not something Gekkō is capable of," he admitted easily. "But I can ask around with the other spirits, and send a message along to Gekkō to look for others."

Shrugging, Kira said, "It's a start; thanks Thistle."

He chittered in reply, then sat back on his haunches, gazing curiously at their hands.

Ryn didn't close his eyes this time, so Kira didn't either. The familiar tingling sensation began at the tips of her fingers, and she wondered—not for the first time—just what her aura looked like to him.

After a few minutes of silence, Ryn said, "Well, I think this sunshine is doing you good. I don't know if I'm mistaken or not, but I think the wound is a little bit smaller than before."

"Well, it definitely wasn't the meditation," Kira muttered.

He snorted and pulled away, breaking off the tingling sensation.

Without a word, Thistle disappeared into the bushes, no doubt having seen what he wanted to see of their aura reading.

"We better head back inside the castle," Ryn said, unfolding his long legs and coming to a stand. "There's a lot more to show you inside."

"Oh, and I want to see the library," Kira said, following him down the path. "I want to see if I can find anything on soul healing magic if I can. Just in case there's something obscure Lord Raiden or his healers wouldn't know of—I mean, I know this hasn't happened to anyone before, but there could be *something*."

"Good idea."

They entered in through the Hall of Spirits, and Kira smirked at the statue of Gekkō and Thistle again, reminding herself to tell Thistle about it next time.

From the Jade Foyer, they ascended a few levels of the Spire so Ryn could show her some of the rooms where lessons took place. At this point, melancholy began to creep up on Kira again as she wondered whether she would ever join them.

When they returned to the ground level, Ryn took her to the kitchens where they kept bushels of things grown in the vegetable gardens, and huge sacks of grains, tea, and other staples brought in from around the region. They skipped over the Apothecarium since Kira had already found it, but not far from it was the entrance to the Spire's library.

Even though Kira had grown to love Gekkō-ji's almost mystical underground library, with its long rows of books and glittering stone ceiling, she had to admit that the Spire's library was impressive.

It spanned two levels, with the second being an open gallery that ran along the long rectangular space. Kira marveled at the long stacks of books on the first floor, while gazing up at the second floor, where wooden cubbyholes—much like in the Apothecarium—covered the walls, except instead of ingredients, these held a vast number of scrolls.

But what really drew her eye was the ceiling.

She craned her head back to take in the incredible mural painted there. Portrayed entirely in black and white paint, two massive koi fish encircled each other amid the ripples of a pond. But as Kira stepped further into the library, she noticed the detailed scales of each fish glittering in silver. At first, she thought wildly that it was Light magic that she was seeing, but no, it wasn't yet past sunset. Kira halted in her tracks for a second, studying the sparkling details.

Ryn followed her gaze upwards. "Ah, yes. Creative proficiencies," he said in explanation.

"I doubt I'd have one of those," Kira said to cover up a pang in her heart at the idea that she might never find out her proficiency. Then she cursed herself for sinking back into despair so soon after the bright positivity she had experienced outside.

Ryn said to try to be positive. I'll get my magic back. I'll figure out my proficiencies and join those lessons just like everyone else.

Somehow.

Ryn chuckled at Kira's self-deprecation, drawing the attention of a mage standing nearby, a thick white streak running down her hair from one temple. She surveyed the two of them, and though her face seemed set in a permanent scowl, surprise lit up her eyes. Her robes were made of dark green silky fabric, by far some of the nicest Kira had seen.

"Why, if it isn't Ryn Kimura," she said in a monotone, raising a thin eyebrow. "And Lady Starwind; it is a pleasure to make your acquaintance. I am Ji Sato, I head the Spire's library."

"Please, call me Kira," she said, offering a slight bow.

The woman returned the gesture, then studied Kira's face for a long moment. "Ah, yes, I can see Rokuro in your face."

Kira's heart surged. "You knew my father?"

"Of course. His favorite book was *The Poems of Peace*. He would re-read it every time he came to visit the Spire, even after he completed his training."

"Wow," Kira said. "How do you remember his favorite book?"

Ji smirked, her long eyelashes fluttering for a second. "I remember all the books in this library; it's my specialty, an incredibly focused memory. I could tell you where any book in the library was, and even who read it last."

Kira was speechless for a moment and her eyes wandered over the rows and rows of shelves. Then she remembered something. "Do you know if there are any books on magic for soul healing?"

The librarian bit her lip, her eyes flicking to the books behind where Kira and Ryn stood. She paused for a few moments, thinking. "I'm afraid I don't know of any."

Kira's heart sank at the short-lived hope.

"But that's only because soul healing isn't in any of our book's *titles*," Ji went on. "I've only memorized titles, I haven't had the chance to read every book in the library—yet."

"Oh," Kira said, her hope rekindling. "Well, do you know what section I could start looking in? I'm not taking the usual training classes at the moment, so I do have some free time to search."

Ji held up her hand. "Not to worry. We do catalogue all our books and their subjects. It will take some time for me to search through it though." She walked over to a podium just behind Kira and Ryn, where an enormous book stood open, a long white ribbon trailing down the center. "The books are catalogued in a sort of code of ours, so you wouldn't be able to do it yourself."

"Thank you so much," Kira said, bowing again. "There's one more thing; can I borrow that book you said my father used to read? What was it called?"

"*The Poems of Peace*," Ji said, turning to her left down a row of books. "I'll go retrieve it for you."

A few minutes later, clutching the book across her chest, Kira left the library with Ryn. After the sunshine, the promise of Thistle and Ji helping to look for the healing magic, and the book that her father had loved, Kira couldn't help but think that her aura must be glowing with happiness now.

Chapter 15

The Commonality

Still aglow from the first pleasant afternoon she'd had here, Kira agreed to spar with Jun that evening. She was really starting to worry that if she didn't use her Light magic, it would fade too. After a light dinner of rice and steamed peas with some oil that tasted like sesame, they headed into the training room. Unlike Jun, she didn't mind the vegetarian offerings of the Spire's food stores. When living with her mother all those years in the Starless Realm, they weren't that well off, and they'd had to subsist on rice and whatever vegetables or beans were on sale a few nights a week. Kira made more of the tea Anzu had given her, and she was still in unusually high spirits for the first time in a while.

She was starting to realize the effect the wound on her soul was having on her emotions. Sometimes she felt fine, like now, but other times she sunk quickly into melancholy at the slightest thing, which was not like her at all.

She made a mental note to keep an eye out for weird mood swings like Raiden had originally told her.

Jun lit the lanterns in the training room with a few flicks of his hand, sending small balls of flame zooming toward each corner, and across the ceiling. Kira sunk into a leg stretch while he lit the room, then proceeded with a few more poses to loosen up her muscles. Jun was right, if they didn't keep practicing, they would be well out of shape when they returned to Gekkō-ji. She couldn't afford to slack off and hide in her quarters feeling sorry for herself. And the exercise would do her good.

In the center of the room, Jun was reaching both hands up high, and bending from side to side. Kira rolled her shoulders and came to join him, the old polished wooden boards beneath her feet creaking slightly as she crossed the room.

She took a centering breath, pulling Light magic in as she did so, taking extra care to focus on the sensations.

At the same moment, the soft, twinkling radiance in her vision told her that the sun had set, setting aglow the Light magic in everything around them. She grinned at Jun, and summoned a tall polearm, a long staff with a sharp blade at the end. Jun's hands were suddenly filled with an elegantly curved Katana blade, complete with an intricately wrapped hilt. She knew he had been honing the artform for quite a while to craft such a detailed weapon.

Kira lowered her eyes for a moment, discretely assessing her own weapon. She couldn't see any cracks in the wood-like shaft, and the blade at the end looked sharp, though they kept their blades dull during these practice sessions. She took another deliberate breath and tried to focus. She locked eyes with Jun, and they began.

With her long weapon pointing directly at him, it was difficult for him to get an easy opening. Light on his feet, he darted back and forth, bringing his blade in close a few times, feinting, testing. Kira waited patiently, her guard drawn.

Then suddenly on one of those light-footed advances, Jun ducked under her polearm, keeping his back to her weapon as he emerged on the other side, and brought his sword down and around toward her right hip. She leapt back, bringing the polearm up and across her body to deflect the strike.

Lowering the polearm again, she kept him at bay, her blade following his slight movements back and forth as he tried to break through. He smacked the right side of her polearm with his katana and she wrenched her weapon toward him, then tried to jab him with the end. But he danced out of the way.

Growing tired with her defensive stance, Kira struck out again, thrusting at him several times in quick succession to distract him from what she was going to do next. With a burst of Light, she dissolved the polearm and immediately pulled the magic back within her to form it into her own katana, the handle nearly as beautifully wrapped as Jun's, the blade just as sure. She had been practicing, too.

With the combination of the flash and change of weapon, she took advantage of Jun's momentary distraction and charged, sweeping her sword down and across. Met with Jun's blade, she shifted her momentum and whirled around behind him, bringing her blade down toward his back. He ducked out from under the attack, slicing upward as he did so. Their swords met with a clang, sliding down their lengths until Kira disengaged.

They continued on with the katanas for quite some time, equally matched as always.

Eventually, Jun held up a hand. "I want to try something."

"Okay," Kira said, lifting her blade in a question.

"Yeah, keep your sword. That should make it interesting. Just give me a minute." He backed away to the far end of the room. Kira stood in the middle, wondering what in the world he was planning.

She sunk into a fighting position, hips low, sword raised across her body, and waited.

Jun stood there focusing on something for a moment, then he began running at her. Bracing herself, she sunk lower into her stance. Then Jun was running on air, gaining height, with his sword drawn back and ready to strike. Kira's heart raced as he came speeding toward her, each footstep landing on air.

But he sailed over her—right over the top of her head—nowhere near striking her. She yelped and spun around, lowering her sword. Jun had landed a few yards away, and sunk to his knees. He banished his sword and began laughing. The sound echoed around the training room.

Kira chuckled, still shocked. "They can't have taught you that in lessons yet. Are you *trying* to hurt yourself? At least warn me next time and I'll dull my blade more; I don't want to skewer you."

Jun shrugged, getting to his feet and brushing his hands on his wide-legged trousers. "You wouldn't have skewered me," he said confidently. "But maybe I'll keep working on it with a block or something before we try that again."

"Good idea," she scoffed. "Where'd you get the idea to try that, anyway? I thought you were just levitating spheres in those lessons."

"I've been reading a book I found in my father's study," Jun said. "It's an old book on Shadow fighting techniques."

"Nice," she said. "I got a book from the library today too—have you been there yet? The librarian has the coolest proficiency. But the book was apparently my father's favorite. I haven't opened it yet though."

"I looked in on the library quickly, yeah. Why, what's the librarian's proficiency?"

Kira told him all about Ji's memory skills. "And she's going to look for some books in their catalogue for soul healing magic," she told him.

"You and Ryn think that'll help?"

She nodded. "He says the magic of my soul is still there, just covered by this wound. If we can heal it, I'll be fine again."

* * *

Zowan was due to return from Meridian the next day, so Kira went to meditation with a little more enthusiasm than usual despite the early hour. The chill of the early summer morning brought a straightness to her spine as she settled in on the soft woven grass mat she had chosen.

When the bell tolled across the temple grounds hours later, Kira opened her eyes and a jolt ran through her. Standing just outside the pavilion was the Storm King and a woman she didn't recognize. Raiden, exceedingly tall next to anyone, completely towered over the short woman. Her stature might have been lacking, but between her surly round face framed with long drawn-back hair, and the full-body leather armor she wore, she cut an imposing figure herself. And two curved katanas at her sides spoke volumes.

Kira had no doubt who they were here to see.

After the acolytes bowed to Mistress Korina and were dismissed, Kira glanced at Jun to see if he had noticed Lord Raiden. Jun was eyeing the diminutive woman just as Raiden called, "Kira, Jun—a word, if you please."

Brushing non-existent dust off her trousers, Kira paced over to the two of them. The rest of the acolytes were busy heading for the castle and bowed their heads at Lord Raiden as they passed.

When it was just the four of them, Raiden began, "Kira, Jun, this is Commander Aita, she would like to meet with the two of you." His jaw ground together as he said these words, and Kira bit the inside of her lip as she stepped closer. She had never heard of a commander of anything before. Was she a Shadow mage?

Commander Aita bowed slightly, a few strands of her dark hair swinging out of their braid. "It is an honor to meet you," she said, though her words were curt.

Kira and Jun returned her bow and muttered greetings.

"Her Imperial Majesty, Empress Mei, has sent me here to protect the realm's newest Gray mages. We received word that there has been violence in the area by some raiders, and the Empress wanted to do everything she could to ensure your safety."

Speechless, Kira glanced at Lord Raiden to see his reaction, but his face was drawn, and only the subtle crackle of electricity around his wrists gave away his emotions.

The commander went on, oblivious to Raiden's subdued rage, or in spite of it, "I command Her Majesty's newly formed group of soldiers," Aita informed them passively, her right hand resting on the sword at her hip. "We are called the Commonality, and our purpose is to protect the realm from violence and war, outside of magical politics. And with the recent commoner violence, Her Majesty thought now was the time to form a force by commoners, for commoners."

Kira licked her dry lips. Not a mage then.

"I am here to ensure your safety from these raiders and to recruit more common folk to the Commonality." Aita gazed up at Kira and Jun now, making eye contact with both of them. "Personally, I would rather you return to Gekkō-ji, or come to Meridian where you would be better protected, but Her Majesty didn't see the need for that just yet."

Jun burst out, "What? We just got here. The raiders aren't any threat to us inside the city."

"Indeed," Aita said. "Which is why while you are in Heliodor, myself and the rest of my force will help keep you safe. You two are highly valued by Her Majesty, and she didn't want any trouble to befall you. The Commonality was formed just for this purpose—protecting the realm's people from violence of other common folk. After last year's uprising against the peace between the two temples," she nodded deferentially in Raiden's direction, "Her Majesty saw the need."

"It is most wise of her," Raiden said. "However, as Kira and Jun and anyone else will tell you, they are quite safe inside the Spire."

"I'm sure that's true," Aita said, "but Her Majesty commands that our two Gray Knights in training are protected at all costs—under my direct supervision, especially since the fully-trained Gray Knights are otherwise occupied across the realm." She turned to Raiden. "We will require lodging inside the Spire, as close as possible to Starwind and Kosumoso."

"Absolutely not," Raiden said swiftly. "The Spire has a strict tradition—"

"These are the terms Her Majesty instructed me on. Otherwise I am to escort Starwind and Kosumoso back to Gekkō-ji."

Kira stood frozen. Would the Empress really make them abandon their Shadow training just because there were a few raiders in the region? They were training to become Gray Knights! They would be the sole protectors of the realm once they completed their training. Did the Empress think they couldn't even protect themselves?

Raiden's jaw dropped. He quickly closed it, and Kira saw his hands bunch into fists, a wink of lightning dancing on each. He flung his hands behind his back to clasp them when he saw Kira notice. "Very well, you can stay in the Spire. But you absolutely *will not* stay in the Gray Wing. I will have the Spirekeeper find you lodging on the ground floor nearest them."

"That is acceptable," Aita said. "I will also require knowledge of your schedules as well," she said to Jun and Kira.

"The Spirekeeper can supply that to you," Raiden said, to Kira's relief. "Come, I'll bring you to her. Where is the rest of your... group?"

"My soldiers are surveying the temple grounds; I sent them to assure the Spire's safety once Lord Zowan led us inside."

"I see," said Raiden through clenched teeth.

Kira snuck a glance at Jun. He was staring blank-eyed at Aita, hands clasped behind his back.

"Kira, Jun, you best be about your day," Raiden said finally, dismissing them.

Feeling rushed back into Kira's frozen body and she gave Raiden and Aita a quick bow and hurried off with Jun, eager to be rid of the Commander.

They sped along the covered walkway and into the castle. Kira looked back once they had reached the Jade Foyer, and she could still see the silhouettes of Raiden and Aita standing in front of the pavilion, Raiden's back stiff, and Aita still clutching one sword hilt.

"Well, this isn't good," Kira whispered to Jun as they reached the double doors to the Gray Wing.

"Who do they think they are?" Jun raged as soon as the doors closed behind them. "They can't bring us back to Gekkō-ji just because of some stupid raiders!"

Kira crossed her arms and stared out onto the balcony. "On the Empress' orders."

"You know what?" Jun said, pacing behind her. "I'm going to try to send my father a message. Maybe now Zowan's back he can send a letter on the wind for me. My father'll get the Gray Knights to come to the Spire—there's plenty of knights and mages protecting the realm. We don't need these soldiers breathing down our necks just because the Empress thinks we can't protect ourselves."

Kira gasped and spun around to face him. "The Empress. The palace. How do we know Aita isn't some part of the Lord of Between's scheme? We know he—or she—has a connection to the palace. And," her stomach plummeted, "they're a shapeshifter. How can we even trust this Commander Aita at all?"

The clock on the mantel chimed and Jun jumped. "I'm going to be late for levitation. Look, maybe you can find Zowan and see what he thinks, if they came here with him from Meridian. I'm sure Ryn won't mind."

She nodded. But how would they even be able to tell if they could trust Commander Aita?

Ryn knocked on the doors to the Gray Wing just as Jun was rushing out of them. They exchanged greetings and Ryn stepped inside.

"How are you feeling today?" he asked.

"Fine," she said, her arms still clutched about herself. "No. Not fine. The Empress sent some soldiers to watch over Jun and me. To protect us."

Ryn arched his eyebrows. "But didn't they send a Light Knight here to protect you two? How many do you need?"

"Well, yes, exactly, Anzu is here to watch over us. I'm just worried..." she trailed off, not wanting to reveal her suspicions about anyone associated with the palace. "I just want to make sure I can trust these people. They say they're called the Commonality—common soldiers to protect the realm from other common folk."

"Oh," Ryn said, scratching his chin. "Well that's something new."

"Hey—" Kira said suddenly. "Do you know if there's a way to tell if someone has magic?"

Ryn smiled slyly. "You're talking to him."

A wide grin spread across Kira's face.

Chapter 16

Hard to Grasp

The next couple of days fell into an uneasy rhythm for Kira. Each morning was spent trying to meditate in the lakeside pavilion, even though she woke up groggy and bleary-eyed from the continued lack of sleep. Then she would meet with Ryn in the afternoon to do an aura reading. In his brutally honest way, he reported no new changes, which didn't do much to encourage her. Sometimes after going outside, her aura would brighten, as he would call it, but she knew it didn't last. And she didn't have much else here at the Spire to make her happy besides practicing and caring for Naga, both of which were more duties than actual fun activities.

In the evenings she would spar with Jun, whose Shadow training Kira was trying hard not to resent, despite knowing that she needed to keep an eye on her negative emotions. But knowing he was learning all kinds of new Shadow magic without her left her with a gaping hole in her thoughts. Outside of lessons, he also met with mages and trainees to talk to them about their proficiencies—it was like he was collecting ideas for powers to try.

Whenever Kira walked through the halls of the Spire, she felt eyes on her and saw whispers traded behind hands. The other acolytes never seemed to want to talk to her, a feeling she knew well from her first days at Gekkō-ji, when everyone thought she was from the then-hated Shadow region.

"People are starting to think you're really advanced since you're not in any of the regular lessons," Jun admitted one evening after Kira broached the subject. She had wondered if they were treating him with the same cold looks. "The y... think you're training with special masters in secret or something."

That almost hurt more than the truth of her reality.

Commander Aita and her Commonality soldiers constantly followed Kira and Jun as they went about their days. Kira kept her meetings with Ryn inside the Gray Wing, where she could have some privacy as he read her aura. But they followed her and Jun to meditation each morning, and there were two soldiers posted outside the double doors to the wing at all times. It was lucky no one else was allowed to live in the Gray Wing, or surely

Commander Aita and her Commonality soldiers would have moved right in with them.

Kira had already gotten Ryn to assess whether Commander Aita and her soldiers were common or not. She wanted to rule out any of them being the Lord of Between in disguise, or one of their magic-using recruits.

Ryn read all of their auras and assured her that they didn't possess any magic. Kira was fascinated by the process, so had Ryn explain what auras looked like with and without magic.

"Well, all auras are an amalgamation of color, a projection of the soul, and also one's emotions and personality," he had explained one afternoon over tea after he had read Aita's aura. "A mage's aura is surrounded by a layer of what looks like sparkling jewels. And Light practitioners, well their auras have this pearly glow all over them. Commander Aita's aura is purple and yellow, but nothing sparkling or glowing to worry about."

That still didn't rule out a connection to the Lord of Between. Not having magic didn't make her innocent.

"We know they've convinced commoners to join them before," Kira told Jun, Anzu, and Zowan that evening as they had dinner in the Gray Wing's common room.

The two came by to visit each night before Kira and Jun sparred. Sometimes Zowan would bring some food to help make dinner, and sometimes Anzu would stick around and spar with them. It was almost like their own little family.

"We'll just have to continue to tread cautiously," Zowan said. "Knowing none of them have magic is useful though. And perhaps they'll be of some use with these raiders. But don't become complacent," he told them. "It's possible any of them could be working for the Lord of Between. Don't trust any of them if you can help it."

* * *

On one particularly rough morning after she had gotten almost no sleep, Kira slogged through meditation and went to meet Ryn for lunch in the Gray Wing. She wasn't looking forward to today's reading. It was never good when she felt this tired.

Eyeing her from across the table where they sat in the common room, he finally said, "Honey, we need to take you to the healer's and get you something for sleep; you look terrible."

"Thanks," she said wryly, wrapping her hands around her tea cup.

"I'm serious."

He eyed her in a way that made her think he was reading her aura, so she blurted, "Fine, let's go." It would be a distraction from him trying to look at her soul damage, at least.

When she entered the Apothecarium with Ryn trailing behind her, she first looked around for Micah. She hadn't seen him at all since her last trip here, not wanting to get him into trouble with his work. And after all of the meditation, soul-reading exercises, and sparring, she was always too exhausted for much socialization. She was glad Zowan and Anzu's evening visits were so casual that she barely had to speak. And next to Anzu's tight-lipped quietness, Kira's tired silences went unnoticed.

As she emerged into the bright Apothecarium, she tucked her loose hair behind her ears and blinked heavily a few times, trying to will herself into looking less tired. She didn't see Micah anywhere in the large round room, but the matron was bustling toward them, so Kira straightened up.

"Yes?" the woman asked, the wrinkles around her eyes deepening.

Ryn pushed her forward a little. "Lady Starwind needs something to help her sleep. A tincture or potion—uh, Lord Raiden doesn't want any healing done on her right now, it'll interfere with her training."

A wave of apprehension washed over Kira at Ryn's words. She hadn't even thought of that. There was no way she wanted anyone using Shadow magic on her—what if she passed out again like at the top of the Spire?

Of course, anyone else could probably have their insomnia cured with Shadow magic, but she didn't want to let anyone else know about her soul damage, either.

The matron surveyed Kira for a few minutes, then nodded and turned around, heading toward a door to their right.

Kira watched her go, her hands stuffed into her deep pockets.

"You know, there's nothing wrong with asking for help," Ryn said.

She shrugged, too tired to talk about it.

A few moments later, it wasn't the matron who returned from the other room, but Micah. His eyes lit up when he spotted Kira. She suddenly became aware of her rapid heartbeat.

A small glass jar of clear liquid held in his hands, he skirted around the circumference of the room toward them.

"Hey Kira," he said. He handed her the bottle, and she saw there was a tiny slip of parchment hanging from a string wrapped around its neck. Micah pointed to it and said in a voice that was very different from his usual tone,

"Instructions are on the bottle; start off small and don't exceed the dosage."

She nodded, cringing internally, waiting for him to make a comment about her need for sleep help, or her obviously disheveled appearance, but he only stood there smiling at her, his hands on his hips where his apron strings went around his torso. But he didn't say anything.

"Thanks," she said finally, mustering up a real smile.

"Hey, Kira," Ryn suddenly announced, "I'll be right back, I want to ask the matron about something."

"Okay," Kira said, and she and Micah watched him lope across the wide room.

"So," Micah said, "I have tonight free from work—do you want to go out into Heliodor with me and Spectra? There's a summer market down by the east wall I thought you might like."

"Oh, um, sure. That would be nice."

He tilted his head to the side. "Are you busy? I don't want to interfere with your training—"

"No, no, it's fine," she assured him, "I just normally practice combat in the evenings with Jun, but skipping one night shouldn't hurt."

"You sound just as busy as I've been," he said.

"Eh," she shrugged.

He chuckled, his green-tinged eyes glinting. "So can I stop by the Gray Wing later to come get you?"

"Sure. I'll tell those Commonality soldiers to let you in. And maybe I can convince them that Lady Anzu will be enough of an escort into the city," she added bitterly.

But Micah didn't seem bothered about it. "We probably won't even notice them. The summer market always has a lot to see, and in the first few days they always have the best vendors from all over the region."

"I can't wait," she said, meaning it, but a hollow ache in her chest made her second-guess even wanting to go out with Micah. She didn't know if she had the energy for such an excursion. Sure, it would be fun to go into Heliodor, but she hadn't spent any time alone with Micah. What would they talk about? Would she even enjoy it as sleep-deprived as she was? She looked away from his green eyes, and down at her sleeping concoction. Her mouth twisted.

His hands covered hers.

"Are you all right?" he asked.

When she looked up at him, the concern in his eyes was so genuine that she couldn't stop the emotion from welling up in her face.

"No," she said thickly. "I'm not." She bit the inside of her lip. She knew if she kept talking that she would cry.

And on top of everything else going on since she arrived at the Spire, she really didn't want Micah to witness that.

He squeezed her hands within his own. They were incredibly warm.

They stood there in silence. Distant sounds in the other rooms of the Apothecarium filtered into the large room, of tinkling glass bottles, of herbs being ground, and the soft sound of string music coming from somewhere.

Finally, after focusing on her breathing for a few moments, she relaxed. She looked back up into his eyes.

"Thank you," she said, taking a shaky breath. "I just—it's been a rough time since I got here. And," she gestured with the bottle in her hands, "I've been sleeping terribly, and..." she sighed, unable to go on.

"I totally understand. And we don't have to go out into Heliodor, I shouldn't have said—"

"No, no, I want to go, I really do. It will be nice to get out of the castle. It'll be good for me." It would probably brighten her aura some, too.

"Are you sure?"

"Yes. Can I just—" she hesitated, sighed, then reached out and put her arms around his middle.

His arms encircled her, and his head rested against her shoulder. She closed her eyes and breathed, feeling his light touch across her shoulders and back. For a moment, her eyes felt restful. For a moment, she actually felt happy, felt the tension leave her neck and shoulders.

She heard footsteps coming from another room and pulled away. Micah trailed his hand down her arm and grasped her fingers briefly before letting them drop.

It was Ryn. He was slipping a small sachet into an inside pocket of his robe as he returned.

Kira crossed her arms over her middle, already missing the feel of Micah's arms around her. She darted a look at him; he had his hands on his hips and was smiling genially at Ryn as he approached.

"Well, we better get out of your hair," Kira said to Micah, eyeing the room where the matron had gone. "I don't want to get you in trouble for not working."

He shrugged. "All right. How about I stop by the Gray Wing right after Spectra and I finish? I'm not exactly sure when it'll be though," he added apologetically.

"That's fine," Kira said, aware that Ryn was smirking at the two of them. "Come by whenever."

They bid him goodbye and left the Apothecarium. As they entered the Jade Foyer, Ryn said, "You two are so cute together."

"Stop it," Kira said, her face flaming; she punched him lightly on the shoulder. "Well, do you want to do a soul reading?" she started heading toward the corridor for the Gray Wing.

"Actually," Ryn said, "I was speaking with Lord Raiden this morning, and he said he wants you to try accessing your Shadow magic."

Kira halted in her tracks. "What? Why?" she asked in a hush. "I passed out last time." Her eyes flicked up toward the top of the Spire, where she knew the Dragon Crystal stood.

"Well, Lord Raiden said you didn't actually *use* your Shadow magic—it was being pulled through you. Come on, let's go to your training room." His voice lowered to a mumble as they approached the two Commonality soldiers standing guard at the double doors into the Gray Wing.

The soldiers wore dark green robe-like jackets over leather armor. One of them carried a spear, the other a curved katana.

Kira and Ryn went past them into the wing without another word.

"Those two must get bored," Ryn said as he followed Kira into the common room.

"Mmm," she agreed. "I wish they would go away. It's ridiculous, like Jun and I are children who can't even protect ourselves. I mean, we're in a walled temple inside a walled city. How are the raiders a danger to us?"

"Well, let's see some of your magic then," Ryn said. "Where's that training room anyway?"

Kira glanced down the hallway. "Do you want to have tea first? I still have some of that one you liked."

"Stop stalling." He took her by the arm and turned her in the direction of the hall. "Come on. I think it'll be fine. Raiden says you should try."

"Fine," she groaned, then led him toward the training room. She dropped off her sleeping draught in her room on the way there, not sure if she was going to try it tonight or not. At least it had gotten Ryn off her case about looking tired.

She opened the heavy training room door with a loud creak.

"This wing is huge," Ryn remarked as they went inside. "Do you ever get spooked living in here with just the two of you?"

Kira shook her head. "I mean, the entire Spire is huge. And I haven't had such a big bedroom to myself since the Starless Realm."

Ryn eyed her speculatively. "Well," he said, "Now you have to tell me all of your Starless Realm stories, now that you brought it up."

She burst out laughing. "I don't think we have that much time. I mean, I lived there until I was thirteen. Who's wasting time now? Didn't you want me to try some Shadow magic? And I'm meeting with Micah and Spectra later. I might need time to recover."

He gave her a knowing look. "Yes, of course. You'll have to tell me all about your exploits in the Starless Realm another time. How do you want to start?"

The training room was lit by the sunlight filtering in through the paper panels on the doors at the opposite end, which led out onto a balcony. It was a warm, buttery glow, giving them just enough of the afternoon sunlight to see by. Kira went to sit in the center of the training room, and Ryn followed. They sat cross-legged across from one another.

"I can try wind?" Kira suggested. "I should probably try to focus first though."

She closed her eyes and got into a comfortable position, her palms resting casually on her knees. She tried to calm her pounding heart with steady breaths. What if it didn't work?

What if it did?

She took one long deep breath in and opened her eyes as she let it out. Ryn had tucked one knee under his chin as he sat and waited. Kira reached out into her surroundings to feel for Shadow magic. As always, she could feel the presence of Light magic there, ready to be drawn upon and shaped into whatever she willed it to. Its presence was tangible and familiar.

Shadow magic, on the other hand, was slippery, intangible, and hard to grasp. She had to search for it with her mind, seeking it out as if searching for, well, a shadow.

She tried to reach out to the particles in the air around them to encourage them to move. In her mind's eye, she could picture them like dust motes floating in a sunbeam. She reached out with a tendril of thought and tried to touch them.

And then she felt the strangest sensation. It was as if her tendril of thought, like a phantom finger, slipped through oil instead of air. She shook herself, a shiver running down her spine.

Ryn cocked an eyebrow. "What happened?"

"I don't know," she said, shaking her head. "I tried to reach out to the air, but it felt... *oily.*"

"Hmm," his eyes narrowed at her in a way that she knew he was looking at her aura. "I could see a brief amount of magic moving about your aura, but it's gone now. Why don't you try it again? Even if it's oily," he said in response to her grimace.

"Fine."

"Maybe it doesn't recognize you? I don't know. But if you got this far..."

She took another long, deep breath, and focused on the air particles, dividing them until she could feel what she thought was the Shadow magic buzzing inside them. She reached out.

The oily feeling coated her thoughts, but she pushed through it. She knew it was just Shadow magic. Maybe her soul damage was just making it feel strange. Maybe underneath it was the same, just like Kira's soul.

"All right," Ryn said, "I can see a little again. Why don't you try engaging with it?"

Kira tried to push the oily magic, willing the air particles to float in a breeze instead of the pile of sludge they resembled.

She could tell it didn't work.

And even worse, the back of her neck was tingling unpleasantly. It had been a few days since this had happened, but it was as odd as ever. The chill, the fever-like ache.

She backed off, her wide eyes meeting Ryn's.

He assessed her, resting his chin on his upraised knee and hugging it. "What was *that*?" he asked.

"I can feel something here," she said in frustration, rubbing the back of her neck. "And it seems like I'm able to touch the Shadow magic, but I can't influence it without getting this weird ache."

Twisting his mouth as he searched her aura around her neck, he said, "I'm still wondering if it doesn't recognize you because the wound alters your aura signature somehow. Have you found out anything about soul healing magic by any chance?"

"No," she said. "Nothing from the librarian yet, and nothing from Thistle or Sir Jovan. How about you?"

He shook his head. "I've sent messages to some mages I know but I haven't heard anything. And I think you and I both know that if Lord Raiden had figured anything out, he'd be the first to tell us."

She grinned. "Yeah."

"Well, that's enough for today. I don't want you straining your grip on your Shadow magic any more than it already is. Besides, you have your romantic excursion with Micah to get ready for anyway."

Kira felt herself turn crimson as she got up off the floor.

"It's not a date," she said as they headed for the door. "I mean, Spectra's going to be there, too. And probably Anzu if I can convince her to watch over me instead of one of those Commonality soldiers."

"Uh huh," Ryn said. "Well, I'll see you tomorrow. I think we should keep trying to practice Shadow magic.

Maybe you should try a different proficiency other than air. That might help."

Kira shrugged. "Yeah, sure."

Secretly, she was incredibly relieved. She had been able to touch Shadow magic for the first time in a while, and nothing bad had happened.

It was a start.

Chapter 17

Protection

She bid farewell to Ryn at the doors of the wing and went straight back to her quarters and into her washroom.

She glanced at the sleeping draught on the sink basin. She didn't normally like taking things like medications if she could help it. And if the sleep deprivation was from her soul damage, it might not even work anyway.

She stared at her reflection in the mirror. There were dark shadows under her eyes, and her hair was in need of a wash. "Perhaps I *should* take the sleeping draught later," she muttered to herself, inspecting the dark circles beneath her tired eyes.

She went over to the bath and began pumping water into it. After a few good pumps, the water flowed continuously into the large wooden tub, already hot from some mixture of magic or mechanical engineering. It was almost like plumbing back in the Starless Realm, which she did miss from time to time.

While the bath was filling, she headed to her trunk in her room, at the bottom of one of her closet doors. She rifled through for something to wear, for the first time wishing she didn't only own the garb of a Gekkō-ji trainee. *Perhaps I can buy something at the market*, she thought to herself and smiled, glad for something else to look forward to.

Finally, she settled on navy-colored calf-length pants, which were wide legged like all of her training gear—to help hide her leg movements while fighting—and a cap-sleeved navy and black wrap shirt. Though she wished she had lighter colors to wear for the increasingly beautiful summer weather, at least the style would be suitable for the temperature.

She sunk into the bath and warmth cascaded over her skin. Leaning her head against the back of the tub, she felt the tension release from her neck and shoulders as she breathed in the steam.

After a few minutes she had to force herself to get moving and bathe; she still had to get dressed and ready.

Toweling off her hair with a plush towel she had summoned with Light magic, she looked at herself in the mirror again. The dark blue outfit fit a little looser than normal, and she still had to put her belt sash on with her steel dagger. With her magic so patchy, there was no way she would go anywhere unarmed.

After staring at herself in the mirror for too long, tying—then re-tying—her belt sash, she went out into the common room to wait. She paced around awkwardly for a few minutes, unsure of what to do while she waited for Micah and Spectra to show up.

A rustle came from the balcony, and she had a throwing knife summoned into her hand in an instant.

Then she saw a small puffball of gray fur sitting on the railing. Letting out a shaky breath, she dispersed the magic and went through the open doors and onto the balcony, the Spire looming over her.

"Hey Thistle," she said, leaning her arms on the railing.

"Jumpy today, are you?" he chittered.

Her face warmed.

"It's a good thing," he said. "A little fear keeps you on your toes. Better to live in fear than die in stupidity."

She snorted. "Fair point."

"But actually, I was out there for longer than before you heard me," he went on. "You should really pay more attention to your surroundings. Even though the castle seems well protected."

"You're right," she said, gazing up at the dark tiers of the Spire. "The Lord of Between or his people could be anywhere. Though I know the Commonality soldiers don't have magic, at least. Oh, hey that reminds me, can you go ask Anzu if she'll accompany me into the city so the soldiers don't have to follow me?"

"Sure," he said, wrinkling his nose. "But you know, Lord Gekkō sent me here to be more than just a messenger," he grumbled.

"Sorry, but it's not as if I can use magic to send her a message. I don't even know how to do the Light magic one like Mistress Nari does when she sends those glowing fox messengers all around Camellia."

"Well maybe you should work on that," he said, but it was more of an encouragement than a complaint. And with that, he soared off the balcony and leaped from tree to tree until he was out of sight.

She paced around the common room some more after he had gone. She went into the small kitchen to see if anything needed to be tidied up, but Jun must have cleaned it before he left for his afternoon lessons.

Not sure how long Micah was going to be, Kira finally went into her study and grabbed the book, *Poems of Peace*, and brought it back out to the common room so she could hear when Micah arrived. She moved a few floor cushions together and curled up to read.

She could see why her father loved this book. The poems were simple and thoughtful, though mostly she just liked to picture Rokuro reading this book, his hands turning the same pages that her hands turned, his eyes reading the same words. Perhaps he had lounged on these very cushions, holding the book above him.

There was one poem she got stuck on and kept reading over and over:

A heart cannot live
Without the soul's radiance.
A soul cannot shine
Without the body's strength.
A body cannot explore
Without the mind's inquisitiveness.
A mind cannot learn
Without the heart's acceptance.
A heart cannot love
Without the soul's peace.

A knock came and she slammed the book shut and rolled off the cushions.

Breathing fast, she went to the door but paused before opening it to slow down her heart rate. Then she realized she still had the book in her hands. She rushed over to put it on the table. Back at the door, she pulled the handle, and there stood Micah, his black hair tousled after a long day working, the scent of mysterious herbs wafting about him.

The smile that rose up from his lips sent a shiver down her spine.

"Hi," she said.

"Hi Kira," Spectra said brightly from behind Micah, then leaned around her brother. "We better get going before we miss the drummers."

"Drummers?" Kira echoed, a little crestfallen. She had imagined how their meeting would go and had pictured inviting Micah inside the Gray Wing to show him around.

"Yes, drummers," Spectra said, reaching out and pulling on Kira's arm.

Kira relinquished her hold on the door and allowed Spectra to pull her along.

Micah shot Kira an amused look. "Spectra is quite fond of the music festival that takes place at the market."

"Oh, I can't wait," Kira said as they entered the Jade Foyer. It wasn't often she got to do anything fun, even when she wasn't cooped up in the Spire trying to regain her lost magic.

She glanced over her shoulder to see one of the Commonality soldiers who had been posted at the door following her.

"I'm meeting Lady Anzu," Kira informed the soldier, pausing to stop. "I don't need you to escort me, but th anks..."

The guard rested her hand on her sheathed katana. "But my lady, Commander Aita wants you to be protected—"

"I'll be fine," Kira insisted. "Lady Anzu is a knight, I'll be perfectly protected."

The soldier hesitated and Kira began walking to where Micah and Spectra waited at the entrance to the Hall of Spirits.

"I'll be back later!" Kira assured her.

A thrill running through her at losing her Commonality tail, she followed the others into the long statue-filled hall.

She grinned at Micah. "I didn't know if that would work or not."

"They're really serious about protecting you, huh?" Micah said.

"Yeah, it's a little ridiculous. That's what Anzu came all the way from Gekkō-ji for. And I'm not in any danger inside the Spire." *Well, maybe a danger to myself on occasion*, she thought.

Down the Hall of Spirits, across the wide lawn they went, where the dying rays of sun fought to make their light seen. Anzu was crossing the bridge toward them when they got there, Thistle on her shoulder.

“I received your message,” Anzu said with a rare smirk.

Kira chuckled and Thistle swooped over to her shoulder. “Do you want to come with us?” Kira asked the flying squirrel.

“Yes, I think I might,” he said, surprising her. “Though I detest the idea of crowds and these buildings, I think it best if I accompany you too.”

Kira frowned. This was supposed to be a fun outing. Why did everyone think she needed protection?

Micah led the way down the city streets, Kira beside him with Thistle on her shoulder. Spectra walked with Anzu, though the Light Knight wasn’t much of a conversationalist for Spectra’s commentary about the market and the various houses and streets they passed. They walked together through narrow cobble-paved roads with wooden houses on either side, many with all manner of potted plants lined up at their foundations. Dusk in Heliodor brought out a magic of its own, with lanterns being lit on every dwelling and shop, some with intricate metalwork, some square lanterns with paper on all four sides, and some freestanding stone lanterns, the posts almost as tall as Kira. She marveled at all of the illuminations.

“It’s funny,” she said, turning her head back to Anzu, “I just realized there really aren’t many lights at Gekkō-ji.”

Tight-lipped as always, Anzu merely smiled. From Kira's shoulder, Thistle chortled.

As if on cue, the reason why Gekkō-ji didn't have many lights sparkled all around them as the sun set and Light magic became visible to Kira and Anzu. Kira could see every cobblestone outlined in a faint light, every lantern glowing with extra luminescence.

And then a warm hand slipped into hers. She looked up at Micah, his startling green-tinged eyes studying her. Swelling in her chest seemed to crowd out any embarrassment that almost made an appearance, and so she squeezed his hand.

They heard drumming before they arrived at the market. Coming to a halt as they reached a wide street filled with people. Kira stared at all of the different people laughing, buying special sweets, and admiring brightly colored floral fabrics and clothing at the different vendors. There were a few weapons merchants visible from where they stood, and Kira thought she might ask Micah if he wanted to look at the knives with her, when they heard someone shout her name.

"Lady Starwind!" a woman called.

Kira turned to see Commander Aita marching toward her, her face disapproving even as her stature was dwarfed by the soldier who had let Kira leave the Spire.

"Uh oh," Thistle sang quietly by her ear. Kira slipped her hand out of Micah's with regret.

"Lady Starwind," Aita said again when she stood in front of Kira. Surprisingly, she still afforded Kira a slight bow. Her voice grew shrill the more she spoke, "You are not to leave the Spire without protection—there are many dangers—"

Anzu cleared her throat.

"Empress Mei ordered me to see to your protection," Aita started again, more calmly. "I will not let you go out into Heliodor unaccompanied. I will remain with you until you return to the Spire."

Heat rushed to Kira's head. "I'm not unaccompanied," she said quite loudly, flinging her arm to point at Anzu. "Lady Anzu is an accomplished Light Knight, and she is more than enough protection for me. And what do I even need to be protected from?" she demanded, not caring that some of the festival-goers were starting to look around at the shouting.

"There are many dangers in Camellia," Aita said, unable to hide the hint of annoyance in her voice. "I understand since you grew up in the Starless Realm you might not—"

"I know how dangerous Camellia can be," Kira said, lowering her voice. "And Lady Anzu is more than capable of protecting me from the worst."

Aita stole a glance at Anzu, whose face remained impassive, clearly not wanting to anger the commander.

"I'm sorry, Lady Starwind," Aita continued, "but if you attempt to leave the Spire again without proper protection, then I will be forced to—"

"That's it!" Kira shouted, her ire sending Thistle to leap onto the edge of a nearby lantern statue. "Fine! I'm a helpless little girl from the Starless Realm who can't protect herself, so I'll just go hide in the Spire. Is that what you want?"

Without waiting for an answer, she stormed away without looking back to see who might be following her. She could see the Spire from anywhere in the city, so she knew she could easily find her way back herself.

Thoughts clouded her head in a tangle of rage as she strode down the cobblestoned streets. Why did the Empress saddle her with these soldiers now? She could take care of herself. She had proven it last year, hadn't she? Confronting the Lord of Between to rescue Ichiro had been no easy task.

Yet a nagging voice in the back of her thoughts reminded her, *But you let him damage your soul. Maybe you* can't *protect yourself.*

Yes, I can.

She shook her head violently. *Yes. I can.*

But when she summoned a polearm to carry with her for comfort as much as to show off to the Commonality soldiers who were no doubt trailing behind her, she refused to look at it for fear that it might be flawed.

Chapter 18

A Starry Night

Kira barely noticed where she was going. In that moment, she didn't know or care what Micah or any of the others thought. All she wanted to do was hide in the quarters that had once been her father's, and cry.

She threw her polearm from her as soon as she entered the Hall of Spirits, then quickly dispersed the magic before it made contact with the floor. Her face was like a mask of fury as she stormed into the Gray Wing, brushing past the one guard left at the doors.

She slammed her study door shut and flung herself into the chair at the desk, bringing her forehead to the surface of the desk, her arms around her head. But no tears came. It almost hurt to breathe, and she felt like she had a knife between her ribs near her heart.

What is wrong with me? she wondered, lightly thudding her head on the desk.

Why can't they all just leave me alone? I was having a hard enough time trying to work on my Shadow magic before those soldiers showed up. I just wanted to have some fun with Micah and Spectra.

Micah. She banged her head again, suddenly flooded with remorse at the scene she had caused. What would he think of her outburst? She was being childish, she knew.

In the back of her mind, she knew—she *knew*—her emotions were all over the place because of her soul damage. Lord Raiden had told her. And Ryn had told her to avoid negativity. But she couldn't help it. Knowing there was something wrong with her emotions didn't mean she had any control over the situation. In fact, it just made it worse.

She got up from the desk and groaned. She paced across the study, muttering to herself a little as she relived the dreadful scene in her head. "Ridiculous... Can't believe they'd threaten to send me back..."

Her roving gaze landed on the painting of the three hills, and she halted. She went over and studied it, noticing something she hadn't seen before, now that the sun was down and she had her enhanced sight. There was a faint square outline in the center of the painting.

Abandoning her anxious thoughts for the moment, she went closer to examine it.

But when she touched the heavy paper, the square didn't shift with it. The square outline was coming from behind it. She moved the painting carefully to the side, and saw a small indentation in the wooden wall. Automatically, she poked at it.

A click sounded beneath her feet, and she leaped back. A rectangular section of the floor about three feet wide sunk an inch downward.

Forgetting all about her troubles for the moment, she fell to her knees and examined the strange recess. She put her palm to it, and the boards shifted to the right a little, so she pushed the panel aside some more.

She gasped as a small cache appeared in the dusty hiding place beneath. It was mostly filled with books, though she spotted a few pieces of jewelry and a trinket or two. She gazed at the collection, drinking in the sight of it, what must be her father's most prized possessions that he had chosen to leave here at the Spire. A whisper of Rokuro seemed to waft from the hiding place.

Gently, she moved aside a few scrolls of dusty parchment to remove the books one by one. They didn't have any titles. She opened one of the thick black leather-bound volumes and realized it was a journal. Her father's handwriting was scrawled across each page she leafed through.

Pages and pages of entries. All words her father had pressed to paper.

Suddenly deflated, she sank back on her heels as her eyes stung and the first few tears slid down her cheeks. Her chest ached at the sight of those words.

But curiosity made her brush away the tears and pull the rest of the books out of the hole to bring them over to Rokuro's desk, stacking them in a neat pile. Excitement zinged through her fingertips as she ran her hands over them. What would she find?

She curled up in the chair with the black journal and opened it to the first page.

Tonight I climbed to the top of the Spire at midnight while no one was around in order to look at the stars. In all their magnificent Light, it reminds me of the evenings at home when I would lay out in the grass and fall asleep outside gazing at the sea of stars. Or even back at Gekkō-ji when I would hike up to the top of Mount Gekkō, until my father caught me that one night and gave me early morning bath house cleaning duties for a month.

Kira snorted, picturing a younger Ichiro disciplining her father.

There is peace here, even if I have to be away from the Starwind lands and the sight of the beautiful Risandra. I swear, when I finish with my training, I will finally ask her to attend the spring festival with me.

Blushing, Kira closed the journal, a pleasant calm settling over her nerves. She hugged the journal to her chest and got up to open the sliding wooden doors onto her balcony.

The stars were magnificent.

A sea of stars, her father had said, and it was true.

Though the world she had grown up in—she no longer referred to it in her head as the *real world*—had stars, it was *starless* compared to Camellia. And with her Light magic, the heavens were a luminescent masterpiece, much like that Van Gogh painting she had once seen at the museum in New York with her mother.

"It's a beautiful night," a voice said.

She turned to see Zowan step from the shadow beside the balcony entrance to the common room.

"Zowan! You're back."

"Anzu told me what happened," he said simply.

She didn't reply. She didn't know what to say. For a few precious minutes, she had forgotten all about her outburst, about her soul damage, about everything bothering her.

"It's going to be all right Kira, I know this must be scary for you—"

"How do you know?" she blurted. "How do you know it's going to be all right? How do you know I won't lose all my magic? I'll be just like I was before I came to Camellia, except I'll know all of the things I've lost."

A sigh escaped her. She hadn't intended on airing her complaints, but the words had just poured out of her.

Zowan came over and leaned on the railing next to her. "I don't know. I'm sorry. I guess I can't know exactly what you're going through right now. But I know you have a lot of people who will be there for you no matter what happens, and—and I'm one of them."

Something inside her chest broke and she found herself falling into Zowan. His arms went around her, and her eyes stung with tears once again. After reading her father's journal, it was almost like having a father of her own embracing her.

"Why do I feel like this?" she asked miserably. "What's wrong with me?"

Zowan pulled away but put his hands on her shoulders, looking into her eyes. "There's nothing wrong with you. Sometimes bad things happen and we have no control over them. And all we can do is cope the best we can.

"You had a major thing happen to your soul. I'm not surprised you don't feel like yourself. But I want you to try and take care of yourself, all right? Now go get some sleep, you look like you could use it."

Kira nodded and wiped her eyes on the back of her hand.

As she was on her way back into her study, she turned to ask, "What would you do, if you were me?"

"Me?" he rubbed his chin, "I'd keep fighting until I got what I wanted, and if I never got it, well, then I'd find something else to fight for."

CHAPTER 19

BLACK MIRE

As Kira readied to go to meditation early the next morning, Jun knocked on her study door. She went through her room and into the study to open it. He held up a small piece of paper with the words "Lady Gray" written on the outside.

"This just floated into the common room."

Kira rolled her eyes at Raiden's pet nickname for her and snatched the note from Jun. She had slept a little better last night, having taken the smallest amount of the sleeping draught. After Zowan's advice about taking care of herself, she figured she should probably accept the help of the healer's potion.

"Thanks. Oh, he wants me to come meet with him and Commander Aita."

"I wonder what about," Jun said.

"Well, I get to find out sooner rather than later. It says I should skip morning meditation and come straight away."

"No way," Jun said, his forehead wrinkling. "Sounds important. Maybe I should come with you just in case."

The slight smile that played at Kira's lips faded almost as quickly as it had come. "It's probably about yesterday."

"Why? What happened yesterday?"

Kira bit the inside of her cheek. "I... *might* have gone out into the city with just Anzu and then stormed off on Commander Aita when she followed me."

Jun's mouth popped into an 'O' of surprise, then he said, "Well, serves her right. Does she think we're little kids or something?"

She shook her head in resigned disbelief. "I don't know, I think she's just bound to whatever the Empress ordered her to do. But I guess I better go meet them and get this over with."

A few minutes later she finished getting ready. "Have fun meditating," she called into the kitchen where she could hear Jun clanging about with the pots and the water pump.

"Ha, ha," he replied darkly.

A sinking dread began to fill her as she trudged toward Raiden's study. What if Commander Aita demanded that Kira be sent back to Gekkō-ji?

No, she wouldn't let that happen. What had Zowan said to her last night? To keep fighting. And fight she would.

Starting with my magic.

At least yesterday with Ryn I was able to feel Shadow magic again, even if it felt weird. I need to try to heal this wound, and keep practicing both magics as much as I can.

She knocked on Raiden's study door when she arrived, but it was slightly ajar already. "Come in," he ordered.

The scent of tea and freshly baked bread overwhelmed her and even made her forget about the remaining fears about being sent back to Gekkō-ji. A black and gold cast iron teapot with matching cups had been laid out on a small table beside Raiden's desk, with a large tray full of fresh buns, fruit, and small pastries.

Kira's mouth watered, but she figured she should first sit down in the chair beside Commander Aita that Raiden was pointing to.

He sat behind his desk, hands clasped under his chin. "Well? Commander?"

Kira cringed, then stuck out her chin.

"Lady Starwind," Aita began, leaning toward her slightly, "It has come to my attention that you might have some involvement with the conflict arising out of the Stone Mountains, and I wanted to discuss it with you."

"What? Oh. Um, okay," Kira said, her eyes flicking to Raiden and away. She couldn't read his closed expression and had no idea what she should tell Aita.

"You met with Lady Madora of the Stone Mountains last year, is that correct?" Aita demanded.

"Yes, she came to Gekkō-ji to meet me."

"Why would she do that?"

"Um, Lord Raiden invited her. She has Shadow magic that can read people's histories."

"What do you mean?" Aita asked impatiently.

"Well, that's how I found out that I'm a Starwind. That I'm Rokuro's daughter. Lady Madora read my history and was able to see when my mother fell through to the Starless Realm—and that her husband was Rokuro."

"Ah, I see," Aita said, waving her on. "But you had some sort of altercation with Lady Madora...?"

Kira glanced at Raiden again, and this time he nodded slightly. "Yes, when she found out who I was, she wanted me to go back to the Stone Mountains with her. And I told her no."

"That's it?"

"That's it. That was right when my grandfather had just been kidnapped by the Lord of Between, so my friends rode in to get me. We didn't fight the Lady's guards or anything, I swear. We just rode off."

Aita stared at Kira and cracked her knuckles seemingly without realizing it. "Very well. As Commander of the Commonality, I believe we should send an envoy to the

Stone Mountains—to Lady Madora. It's likely that these are members of her guard that she's sending into this region to harass us and draw the attention of the Shadow mages—for one reason or another," she added delicately.

"What will that accomplish?" Raiden scoffed. "Lady Madora is clearly trying to provoke a reaction out of us."

Kira could tell Aita had refrained from rolling her eyes.

"It will accomplish *answers,* Lord Raiden. How else are we to find out what she really wants and how to stop this senseless violence? These raiders have sacked countless villages; Dorogon nearly burned to the ground only a few days ago. Luckily, a small contingent of the Commonality had been patrolling nearby. Even the Gray Knights are no match for these raiders—they are skilled at evasion and destruction. I shudder to think what they *want* from us."

"We know what she wants," Raiden growled. "She can't have it."

It took Kira a second to realize what he meant. "But why would she send these raiders now?" she asked. "It's been a year since that happened."

Aita seemed ready to speculate. "Perhaps because you recently moved to the region? Or perhaps these raiders are just a distraction while another force attempts to kidnap you?"

Kira didn't know what to say to that. Instead, she glanced at the tea and food, then back at Raiden.

"Commander, why don't you send your envoy and let me know how I may be of service," he said, clearly dismissing her.

"As I said, I will," Aita agreed. "And I'll alert the palace. I don't suppose you would be willing to send a message for me? I must admit your methods of communicating are extraordinarily effective."

Raiden grunted. "I must train with Kira today, but you may bother my nephew if you need to send a letter. He is my palace liaison after all."

And with that, Aita left. Raiden lifted the black and gold teapot and poured two cups of steaming tea. Kira took hers, the cast iron cup warm in her hands but not too hot. She took a sip and found the earthy green tea just the right temperature.

"Training?" Kira said, cringing a little.

Raiden nodded gravely. "Ryn tells me that you attempted to access your Shadow magic yesterday to some end."

Kira scowled. She had sort of hoped Ryn wasn't reporting her every move to Raiden, but she supposed Raiden had summoned the young mage here to help her. She couldn't really fault him for it. She made a mental note to rib Ryn about it later.

"Yes," Kira finally admitted. "But it was... weird."

"I can imagine, with that wound on your soul," Raiden said, sipping his tea. "And Ryn said you only tried to move air?"

She shrugged. "Yep."

He set down his teacup and steepled his fingers together in front of him. "I seem to remember you utilizing a unique Shadow power last year when we raided that estate to rescue your grandfather. You were able to hear sound over a long distance, isn't that right?"

Kira nodded. "But I haven't tried it since then."

"Well, what better time than now? We already know you have an affinity for it. All right, let's try it."

"What, now?"

"Yes, now. You're already missing meditation, and your aura readings with Ryn in the afternoons are helpful to check on your soul, but they're not getting you anywhere. Your session to test your magic yesterday is the best progress you've made so far. And since you were able to touch Shadow magic without losing consciousness, I take that as a good sign."

He lowered his voice. "All right. Commander Aita was given quarters just down the hall from here, and the first door is her study. Why don't you try focusing on searching for her voice to listen to?"

Kira jerked her head back. "Listen for Commander Aita? What for?"

Raiden lowered his chin and looked at her seriously. "You think I enjoy having a group of Imperial soldiers occupying part of my castle? I don't believe the Commonality is here just to protect you. I think it would be an opportunity for the palace to finally place someone near enough to spy on me. I'm sure the advisors have wanted to do that for as long as we have had this peace."

"I mean, I guess they could be doing that," Kira said. "Commander Aita just seems really obsessed with her orders from the Empress to protect me. It's annoying, but I don't know if they'd be up to anything suspicious. Unless you think they're in league with the Lord of Between," she added quietly.

"We can't rule that out."

"But we know none of them have magic at least, thanks to Ryn."

"There is that," he conceded. "But that doesn't prove they are harmless. So, let's get to work. Try to listen down the hallway to the left; the second door on the right is her study."

Kira took a deep breath in and out. The last time she had done this, she had been in a panic to find her grandfather before the Lord of Between performed an experiment on him—she had been under a lot of pressure to find him before the time ran out. If she could do it then, she could do it now while sitting calmly in Raiden's study.

She put her hands in her lap and closed her eyes. She could only hear her own breathing. Raiden's study was silent, and the castle and grounds the same; every acolyte was down in the lakeside pavilion meditating. But Commander Aita was just down the hall.

She tried to picture herself gliding down the hall, her ears searching for any sound.

A little guilt crept up on her at the thought of possibly eavesdropping on the woman. After all, she claimed she was just trying to do her duty. But then Commander Aita's smug face from yesterday at the market bubbled up out of Kira's memory, and she let the guilt go. If Aita wanted to interfere with Kira's life, Kira would interfere with hers.

If she could pull it off, anyway.

All she could hear was silence. Again she pictured herself floating toward where she needed to go, ears straining to hear anything, a word, a sound.

And then she felt something. It was like her thoughts were coated in oil this time.

She pulled back. "Ugh." She opened her eyes and shook her head in disgust.

"What happened?" Raiden asked.

She wrinkled her nose. "It's like I'm trying to reach out to Shadow magic, but I can't grasp it; it's like, greasy."

Raiden pursed his lips. "Interesting. Perhaps there's some sort of veil you need to get through to access it since your soul is injured. It could be your own soul preventing you from accessing magic while it is damaged, protecting itself. As long as you feel comfortable, I want you to try again."

She nodded. She could do this. She was ready to fight for her magic.

Closing her eyes, she tried to repeat what she did before. But when she reached out with her thoughts and felt the unpleasant oiliness, she pushed on.

She could feel her face muscles straining, so she tried to relax as she trudged on, pushing her thoughts into the greasy mental mire.

The Shadow magic was almost in her grasp. Trying to keep her own thoughts calm and focused, she pushed a little harder, and the sickly oily feeling surrounded her brain.

"...summon the Defector, will you? I'm not sending one of ours..."

The words hadn't been spoken inside this room.

Kira's eyelids snapped open.

Raiden was leaning halfway across his desk. “Yes? Did it work?”

She nodded but didn’t speak. She wanted to try again. It had been so long.

Ignoring the slight ache at the back of her neck, she shut her eyes and sent her thoughts where they needed to be. She knew how to do it now; how to seek out and send the magic to listen. She just needed to push through the murky barrier—

It happened in an instant. The oily feeling drowned her senses, and a feverish ache radiated from the back of her neck with a sharp twinge.

Her eyes fluttered open, but the edges of her vision were black.

She caught sight of Raiden hurtling toward her before everything went black.

CHAPTER 20

INTO THE DARK

"You're up early," a voice remarked from outside Naga's box stall.

Kira looked up from Naga's beautiful dapple-gray coat which she had been rhythmically brushing.

Zowan was standing there, leaning over the side of the stall and looking in.

"Well, I—er—fell asleep early last night."

"Oh really? I'm glad you're getting some sleep."

Kira felt her face flush and she turned back to Naga, not about to divulge that she had passed out again. She had awoken at an ungodly hour in her own room, and after she realized what happened decided to pay Naga a visit before morning meditation.

"You're up early too," she said, changing the subject. "Are you going to the palace again or something?"

Zowan grunted, his eyes shifting to the side. "I'm going to the Stone Mountains."

"What?" Kira demanded, turning all the way to face him. "Why?"

He glanced around the nearly empty barn before speaking. "Commander Aita came to see me yesterday. She wants to send an envoy into their region to look into the situation with the raiders. I don't mind going—they're terrorizing the Shadow region; we need to get to the bottom of this."

"But why you? You should be here." She bit her lip, not wanting to bring up what happened to him last year when he had been kidnapped. She was sure he didn't need to be reminded. "You're supposed to be here to protect me and Jun when you're not doing palace liaison stuff, right?"

He snorted. "I think you two have enough people protecting you. And Commander Aita..." He grit his teeth. "Unfortunately, when the Empress created the Commonality, she afforded Commander Aita a rather high rank in the realm. I can't exactly say no."

"Then I want to go with you."

"Absolutely not," he said immediately. "And do you think Aita would even let you?"

Kira looked down at the brush in her hands. "Fine. You're right. She wouldn't even let me go to the market. Probably wouldn't let me go to the bathroom alone if it wasn't in my own quarters. Well, promise you'll be careful?"

He put a hand across his heart. "I always am."

"Who else is going with you?"

"Two Commonality soldiers and two other mages. We'll be fine, Kira," he assured her.

"I wish Anzu could go with you or something."

"Well, *she* is definitely supposed to be here to protect you. Though I know she's upset that they won't let her lodge inside the Spire—especially since the Commonality were given quarters."

"Yeah, but Lord Raiden was really against it. I'd let you and Anzu stay in the Gray Wing if I had any say."

"Thanks, Starless girl," he smiled. "But you forget, I was raised and trained in the Spire too. I'd love to be closer, but even I know the Gray Wing is only for Gray Knights and trainees."

She chuckled. "All right, I understand. Well, come see us when you get back, we can all have dinner together again."

"Of course," he said, bowing with a grin. "You take care of yourself and get some sleep while I'm gone, agreed?"

"Agreed."

He left to go get Briar ready, and Kira finished grooming Naga, alone with her thoughts, now worried about Zowan's trip into the Stone Mountains.

She had an idea what Lady Madora wanted, but she also knew that no one in either the Spire, Gekkō-ji, or the palace would allow them to take Kira. And she certainly didn't want to go to a place she had never even seen to be used as a pawn.

She shook her head. *It's not about you*, she told herself. *You're being so full of yourself. They wouldn't be raiding the entire countryside and drawing the ire of all the knights and mages in the realm just to get me.*

After she settled Naga with some fresh hay for breakfast, she headed to the lakeside pavilion for meditation.

For once, when she got to the pavilion, she was looking forward to the practice. She squared her shoulders and sat down, focusing on breathing.

Far from discouraging her, her session with Lord Raiden yesterday had lit a fire in her.

She could still do Shadow magic. It wasn't lost.

So she sat stiff-backed all morning while she and all the acolytes focused on simply breathing. She felt the warmth of the rising sun on her skin as the rays undoubtedly reached the pavilion. She could hear a few birds playing down by the water and the far distant echo of the inhabitants of Heliodor beginning their day.

But each feeling and sound washed over her, and her only thought was on her breath, in and out.

After a while, she became aware of a warmth radiating from the center of her chest. Curious, she tried to bring her awareness to it.

A sick feeling rolled over her, and the dreaded achiness in the back of her neck returned.

Wow, okay, don't do that again, she thought, desperately returning her attention to her breath.

But it was hard to concentrate after that. *Did I draw in Shadow magic without realizing it? Maybe this meditation is good for something after all.*

When the bell rang out over the temple grounds, Kira felt like she hadn't wasted her entire morning. The purpose of the meditation was to assist with focus for using Shadow magic, after all.

After Mistress Korina dismissed them, Kira sauntered over to Jun.

"Feeling better?" he asked.

"A lot better," she said, following him down the covered walkway back into the castle. "Hey listen, I want to do some Shadow training tonight. I know we missed Light practice last night—"

"First of all, *you* missed it, I still practiced," he said. "And second of all, are you crazy? I know the Spirekeeper and Yuki brought you into your quarters yesterday. You passed out again?"

"That's who brought me?"

He gave her a look.

"Fine. Yes, I did. But I was able to access my Shadow magic when I was practicing with the Storm King. It's not completely gone."

"That's great to hear," he said, "really, but I'm not picking you up and carrying you to your room when you pass out in the training room."

She scoffed at him as they entered the Jade Foyer and walked around the fountain.

"Besides," he went on, "I doubt Lord Raiden wants you using Shadow magic again so soon after that. Especially unsupervised."

"How do you know? He was the one who said I should try—" she stopped talking as she spotted the two Commonality soldiers posted outside the Gray Wing. She kept her mouth shut until they were in the empty common room. "He told me to try to listen down the hallway on Commander Aita."

Jun's eyes grew wide. "Really? What, does he really think she's involved with the Lord of Between or something?"

Kira frowned, shaking her head. "I don't think so. I think he just doesn't like her because she could be spying on him for the palace. And Zowan doesn't like her either—she's sending him and some other mages into the Stone Mountains."

"What?" Jun paused on his way to the kitchen.

Kira told him all she knew while they both went in and found some rice balls Anzu had apparently made last night while Kira was passed out.

"I wish we could go with him," she said when she was finished.

Jun rolled his eyes, mouth full of rice. "Like that's going to happen. I don't know how we're supposed to even fulfill our squire duties when we can't go on quests with our chosen superior if this keeps up."

A jolt ran through Kira's core. "Have you figured out who you're going to ask yet?"

He shook his head. "I wanted to consult with my father, but he clearly doesn't have the time right now." He sighed.

"Do you think he's okay?" she couldn't help but ask.

"I'm sure he's fine. Just another duty of a Gray Knight."

Kira nodded. "I was hoping to meet some more of them. Especially since..." She glanced at the back wall of the kitchen, in the direction of her quarters.

Brushing stray grains of rice from his hands, Jun began cleaning up his meal. He handed Kira the last rice ball in the oiled cloth they had been wrapped in. She took it, looking down on it carefully.

"I did kind of want to ask the Gray Knights about my father," she admitted. "After staying here where he lived while he was training and everything." Her thoughts drifted to the journals she had found under the floor. She hadn't told anyone about them yet and had replaced them that night.

"Well, I'm sure they'll finish with this raider business eventually. I mean, they're the only ones in the realm who can help us learn how to become Gray Knights."

Kira forced a smile. "Yeah, we'll need to learn how to combine Light and Shadow."

"Right. But we really *should* pick who we're going to squire under, even if we're not allowed on quests right now. Any idea who you're going to ask?"

"I don't know. I kind of always thought I'd ask Anzu... but I've been wondering about asking Zowan, too."

"Maybe write to Master Starwind and ask what he thinks?"

Kira tilted her head to the side. "I guess I could. I hadn't thought of that."

"I better get going," he said. "I'm supposed to move up today in Levitation."

"What, like lift larger spheres?" she sniggered.

"Ha ha. No, I think this will be moving them around instead of just keeping them levitating in one place. Should be fun."

She tried to keep the bitterness out of her voice as she bid him goodbye.

She was getting used to being alone in the Gray Wing. It was quiet and homey, unlike the girl's dorm house back at Gekkō-ji, which was comfortable but filled with other girls.

Back out in the common room, she opened one of the sliding doors that led onto the balcony.

"Thistle? Are you out here?"

A rustle in the trees beside the balcony revealed his plump gray form, and a moment later, he soared onto the balcony railing.

"I'm glad you were around," she said.

He chittered. "Well, Gekkō told me to keep an eye on you. What else am I supposed to do?"

Kira shrugged. "Hey, so, Zowan is going to the Stone Mountains. Would you go with him? I can't go and I would feel a lot better if you went, in case they run into any trouble."

His little black nose twitched. "Do you want me to go with him, or follow him without saying anything?" he said with a mischievous glint in his eye.

Kira felt herself smiling for once. "Either is fine with me. I don't think he'll mind if you go. But maybe stay hidden just in case, I don't know what Aita would think—or the people in the Stone Mountains."

He chortled and pranced about on the railing before swooping away into a branch. "Be careful while I'm gone then," he said, then disappeared into the upper branches and away.

"Nothing here I need protecting from," she muttered to herself as she wandered back into the common room. "Besides myself maybe."

A note sat on the floor just inside the common room, and Kira had a feeling she knew how it got there. She picked it up and read,

Lady Gray,

No more Shadow magic until we figure this out. I'm sending Ryn this afternoon to do a reading.

-R

Kira huffed and paced back to her rooms. "That's it? No more magic?" she said to herself, crumpling up the note and throwing it into the empty fireplace in her study. "It's not like yesterday was my idea."

But she had done it. Her Shadow magic wasn't completely broken. How could Raiden make her stop now?

Well, it wasn't as if he would know if she tried on her own. She glanced over her shoulder into the empty hallway, but she was alone in the wing, not even Thistle was watching over her.

She settled herself into the chair at the desk and closed her eyes. But as soon as she did, she heard a distant knock. She groaned.

Vowing to try later, lest she lose what little grasp on the magic she had, she got up and went to answer it. But it wasn't Ryn.

She was face to face with Micah for the first time since she had stormed off out of the market, and she was struck by his piercing green eyes. The way his black hair fell casually into his eyes made her momentarily forget who she was.

She smiled, staring at him.

And then she remembered the marketplace. "Oh Micah, I'm so sorry about the other day," she said, feeling her face grow warm. "Commander Aita just showed up and—" She glanced at the two soldiers at their posts a few paces away.

"It's all right." He leaned against the door frame and she admired the professional way he looked in his white apron. Then she blinked and looked up into his face.

"Look," he started, "I know you're busy with training and everything, and I've been stuck working all these extra hours at the Apothecarium, but I thought maybe we could have tea or something?"

"Now?" Her heart raced at the idea of inviting him inside the wing and making tea together in the cozy kitchen. What would she even talk about? Would she get in trouble with the Spirekeeper for having a guest that wasn't Ryn?

"Whenever you're available," he said. "But I did bring some tea from the Apothecarium for you."

He held out a small tin covered in beautiful white and gray rice paper. Her eyes lit up.

"I'd love to." And then her heart sank. The lanky form of Ryn was loping towards the doors to the Gray Wing. "But I have some extra training I usually do in the afternoons."

Micah turned to see Ryn approaching and shrugged. "Another time, then. How about I check back tomorrow?"

Kira smiled sadly at him, and said quietly, "Sure. I'm sorry. Thanks for putting up with my schedule."

"Hey, it's really no problem. That's what you're here for right? Training to be a Gray Knight? I'm the one trying to steal you away," he said with half a grin.

Ryn arrived and appeared to size up Micah, a mischievous gleam in his eye. "I don't believe we've officially met."

Kira said, "Ryn, this is Micah. Micah, this is Ryn, he's teaching me—er—"

"Aura reading," Ryn said loftily. "Nice to meet you, Micah. Kira, we should go to the library, Mistress Ji said she found a book title."

Kira gasped. "Really?" She turned to Micah, who stepped back, ushering her forward with a gesture.

"I'll see you tomorrow, then," he said.

"Thanks, Micah."

Micah turned and headed off.

"So what did Ji say?"

Kira shut the door to the Wing, regretfully watching Micah go.

"She found a title, that's all I know."

Excitement zinged through her as they set off for the library. But about halfway across the Jade Foyer, Ryn stopped walking and narrowed his eyes at her. "Wait a moment."

She squirmed, knowing he was reading her aura. Was something wrong with it?

"Did you do something?" he asked slowly. "Raiden said I should read your aura, but he didn't say why."

Kira glanced at the jade fountain and away from Ryn. "Why? What's wrong with it?"

He studied her. "Well, overall it's actually better, but there is a haze of black hovering about here." He gestured to himself at the area below his neck. "I'll need to do a soul reading to look at it further."

"Was that not there before?"

"What did you do?"

"I, uh, tried using Shadow magic again," she said. "Lord Raiden wanted me to try." She stuck out her chin.

He *tsked*, shaking his head. "I know we tried together, but you should really take it easy on this. You could make the damage worse. You did take it easy, right?"

"I was with Lord Raiden. It was fine. I was able to actually use it! Ryn, I don't want it to go away again."

"I just want you to be careful. Your soul is still wounded. It's vulnerable."

"I know," she said, gazing unseeing at the floor. *Why is he being like this? I got my magic to work!*

"Kira, this is your soul we're talking about," he said, lowering his head so he could look her in her shifting eyes. "I know this might sound harsh, but your soul is more important than getting your magic working again. If you lose your magic, you only lose your magic. If you lose your soul..."

"It's fine Ryn," she snapped. "Lord Raiden was there, and I really do need to practice. Meditation can only do so much. I need to *do something*. I need to fight for it. I can't just sit around waiting for a cure."

He shook his head. "I still think—"

"Let's just go to the library," she said, pushing off from the fountain.

"Kira." He grabbed her arm. "You're going to do some real damage if you keep going at this pace. You need to find something to heal the damage first."

She whirled around him to get out of his grasp. "I'm fine," she said again, a little too loudly this time. "Seriously."

"But—"

"Ryn! Leave it alone. I have to do this."

"You're not still going to try?"

"Wouldn't you?"

They stood facing each other in the foyer, their shouts echoing up the open Spire long after they were spoken.

Ryn took a long blink. "Fine," he said quietly. "Do what you're going to do. But I won't watch you spiral into the dark and lose it all."

And he stalked off.

Dumbfounded, Kira stood there staring after him for a long time, wondering why in the world she had fought with Ryn, the only person who was really trying to help her.

Chapter 21

The Spirit

She stalked through the halls until she reached the library, playing her fight with Ryn over and over in her mind. Guilt riddled her at the thought of what she had said to him. He had only been trying to help.

But he didn't know what it was like to be failing, losing your magic.

Sure, she had spent most of her life not knowing that magic existed outside of books and movies and Santa. But to have it all, Light and Shadow, and then have it stolen from her...

It hurt like another wound on her soul.

Another loss in a life of losses. But this was something she could actually get back. She just had to fight hard enough.

The wide doors to the library were already thrown open, so Kira wandered in, still on edge from her fight with Ryn. But she knew her emotions were too high to speak with him right now. She would probably just end up yelling at him some more.

She would just have to wait until later and apologize. Though since she still wanted to try her Shadow magic, she wasn't sure if he would accept.

Mistress Ji looked up at the sound of Kira's soft footsteps and came over.

"I suppose Ryn told you?" Ji said, and Kira winced. "I found a book in the catalog that contains information about a type of magic you were looking for. One of the subjects in *An Introduction to Alternative Healing* is soul healing magic."

"Really?" Finally, something was going her way.

"Yes," Ji said, looking down her long nose at Kira, "but the book is not where it should be. Someone must have borrowed it and not returned it." Ji frowned, wrinkling her nose at the very idea.

Kira closed her eyes for a brief moment, and everything troubling her rushed back in a dizzying wave.

She found herself mumbling a barely coherent "thanks" to the librarian, turning around, and stumbling from the library.

She began wandering the castle, allowing her feet to take her—somewhere, anywhere. Her mind was busy cataloging all of her hurts, as if naming them would somehow help.

There was a book, but it was nowhere to be found. She would never fix the damage to her soul now, and she would lose her Shadow magic forever, or risk passing out if she even tried. And her Light magic was probably on its way to disappearing too.

She had alienated herself from Ryn, the one person trying to help her. Zowan was off to the Stone Mountains where he'd probably learn the raiders were attacking all because of her.

And as always, she was no closer to even finding the Lord of Between.

Then she realized she was already back in the Jade Foyer. But with one glance at the short hall that led to the Gray Wing, she decided to take the large stone staircase up instead. She didn't want to have to walk by those Commonality soldiers, and she certainly didn't want to run into Jun or Ryn right now—if the latter still even wanted to speak to her.

The stairs up seemed like a good penance for her problems. She looked up at the inside of the Spire and decided to climb to the very top. It wasn't like she had anything better to do.

Her legs soon grew tired, but she pushed through it as she climbed level after level. Voices filtered out of the rooms she passed, instructing acolytes in things Kira might never learn. Levitation, weather magic, plant proficiencies—her fingertips ached at the very thought of the magic. She flexed her fingers, empty of Shadow magic. She walked faster, to get away from the sounds of the acolytes learning, even though her thighs were becoming fatigued.

Soon the tiers grew smaller, the stairs steeper, the levels deserted. Her frenzied thoughts subsided, and there was only the sound of her light footsteps on the stairs and her tired breaths.

As if the height of the Spire had lifted her heart, she felt clear-headed by the time she reached the top and went through the hanging curtain that led to the very peak.

Now it was only curiosity pushing her forward. She crept up the last staircase and emerged into the open platform.

Heliodor was awash in the yellow glow of the afternoon sun, under a pristine blue sky.

The Dragon Crystal stood on its silver podium, and Kira noticed that the silver dragon's eyes were embedded with shiny black stones. Carefully she inched toward the sphere, the last of her wild thoughts chased from her head by the height and beauty around her. She could smell the fresh air but felt no wind, and she wondered without jealousy what kind of Shadow magic could make a barrier like the one protecting the top of the Spire.

She took several deep lungfuls of the lofty air, feeling as if she had left her troubles fifty stories below. Not wanting to return to reality at ground level anytime soon, she sat cross-legged on the floor close to the crystal's statue, as far away from the edges as she could get.

She stayed there until the sun went down.

The riot of reds and gold strewn across the sky soon faded into a light blue that was sprinkled with the silver of Light as the magic became visible to her.

Finally, she stood, thinking she should begin the long walk back down the stairs before Jun started to worry about where she was. A wave of apprehension pulled through her at the thought of going back down. She had no idea why she had even come up here—but it had been worth it. It had cleared her head, and she no longer felt like her world was crashing in around her.

Her eye was drawn again to the Dragon Crystal, and she inched closer to it, still not wanting to touch it. What if it made her pass out, and no one came up here to look for her?

She twisted her mouth, her hands awkwardly limp in front of her as she examined the sphere. The crystalline structure was beautiful and infinite in the blue dusk, each hairline highlighted by the Light magic she could see.

A recklessness seized her, and she reached out her hand to touch it.

Nothing happened. A giggle escaped her. Of course not; Raiden had said Lady Kesshō used Shadow magic to make it work. She let out a relieved sigh.

"That's an interesting stone," an ethereal voice said behind her.

Kira spun around, her heart trying to throw itself out of her chest. "Oh my—!" She flung a hand to her thumping heart as she spotted the woman. "You scared me!"

She was dressed differently than anyone Kira had seen at the temple. She wore a cream-colored dress with long flowing sleeves, with a loose red shawl draped about her arms that seemed to float in the wind—until Kira remembered there was no wind up here.

Kira's breath caught in her chest. She had a feeling this wasn't one of the mages or anyone else from the temple. She would bet her entire savings of coin that this was one of the spirits of Camellia. Kira sunk into a bow from the waist up, running her suddenly clammy hands down her thighs as she went.

The woman smiled, her beautiful face lighting up as she did so. "What has happened to your soul, child?"

Eyes wide, Kira drew in a sharp breath as she straightened. "I—don't really know. It was damaged when someone tried to... remove it."

For a few moments, the beautiful woman studied Kira. "Hmmm, yes," she said finally. "*That* dark soul will perhaps never be redeemed. They've gone too far. Much too far."

"Do you—do you mean the Lord of Between?"

The woman raised an elegant eyebrow. "I know not this soul's name, merely the black stain they've left upon Camellia, wreaking terror across the realm's very fabric, endangering the spirits. I can see they've left a mark on you too. It's... curious."

"Can you fix it?" Kira couldn't help but ask, her chest swelling.

The woman pursed her lips. "I do not fix. I merely... assist. But your soul called to me up here, alone, high above the conglomeration of souls gathered in this city." She stared out toward the horizon as if lost in thought.

Kira wasn't sure what to say next, so she waited for the spirit to speak again.

"You are going about it wrong," the spirit went on. "When your soul was nearly taken, it had begun to detach itself from your body. When the theft was stopped, your soul wasn't able to fully reconnect with your body. The brief time outside of your body changed part of your soul so that it no longer resonates the way it should, leaving it disconnected."

Subconsciously, Kira reached up to touch the back of her neck. She wasn't sure if she was imagining the tingling sensation there or not.

The woman walked toward the railing opposite Kira, nearly gliding there with her dress whispering over the wooden floor. She turned her back to Kira, looking out at the horizon. "You don't need to heal the damage; it is not damaged. In order to return it back to normal, you will need to reveal the true nature of your soul."

"Reveal?" Kira asked. "But how do I do that?"

The woman turned around swiftly, her dress swishing around her feet. And without warning, the woman blinked away in a swish of fabric.

Open-mouthed, Kira looked all around, but she knew the spirit had gone.

"You couldn't give me more of a clue?" she muttered under her breath, hoping the spirit wasn't somehow still listening.

She drank in one last look at the evening cityscape outlined in Light before resigning herself to the stairs. She lingered for a moment, waiting to see if the spirit would return, but Kira was all alone again.

Feeling clear-headed for the first time in days, she wasn't looking forward to the prospect of returning to the ground level, where all her problems seemed to reside. But she squared her shoulders and began her descent nonetheless.

There was nothing she could do besides face her problems. Suddenly, the words of a poem in her father's favorite book popped into her head:

What's gone is lost.

And when all's lost,

Even the fiercest soul can find peace.

Even the fiercest must overcome.

CHAPTER 22

DUTY

Descending from the top of the Spire took a lot longer than she expected. Perhaps it was because her legs were tired, or her reluctance to rejoin the temple on the ground slowed her steps. In either case, it was rather late when she arrived in the Gray Wing, so she crept quietly across the common room and into her quarters. She didn't want any questions from Jun right now after she had missed dinner and Light practice.

She decided not to attempt any more Shadow magic right now. Fantasies of laying on her pallet bed and attempting Shadow magic in a safe place would have to remain fantasies. After her talk with the unnamed spirit, Kira didn't want to risk disconnecting her soul any further.

And tomorrow afternoon she would apologize to Ryn for telling her the same thing when he had just been trying to stop her for her own good.

Trying not to feel bad for being a terrible friend, Kira got ready for bed and took a small swig of her sleeping draught. She really needed to take better care of herself.

But before she could climb under her covers, the small hidden compartment she could see in the corner of her study caught her eye. She pursed her lips, thinking. She wondered if there was anything about souls in one of Rokuro's journals. She still hadn't read all of them yet.

Pushing off sleep, she padded bare-footed toward the painting of the three hills and pressed her finger to the notch behind it, opening the secret panel in the floor.

Bringing all the books over to the desk, she leafed through them, trying to figure out where to start. They were all dated, and from what she knew of Camellian dates, they were all before the Fall of Azurite. *Of course*, she thought, *after the feud started, he wouldn't have come back here at all. Not as an ally.*

She began to flip through them, despite her heavy eyelids and jaw-cracking yawns. She was beginning to regret taking any of that sleeping draught.

Every so often she would skim a page here and there, not knowing what she was looking for, but reveling in her father's handwriting and his inner thoughts.

In one of the older journals, clearly from Rokuro's time training here, she caught the word soul a few times, so she went back and read the whole entry.

31st day of the 10th month, year 604

Sometimes I wish I wasn't going to be a Gray Knight.

Matsuya made me and Jovan come to his study today when he let young Kage know he was being sent home. Kage wasn't happy, to say the least.

I haven't really interacted with the boy much, but Matsuya came down on him quite hard for experimenting with some banned magic. I think he wanted Jovan and me there in case anything happened. Watching Kage break down wasn't how I wanted to spend my afternoon. After he stormed out of Matsuya's study, we then had to accompany him while he packed. That was where I found the book. Kage said he had brought it from the Stone Mountains, said he bought it second-hand—but to be perfectly honest, I think he stole it. It's horrible. No wonder they kicked him out. Magic should be limited to Light and Shadow, and that's it. Only spirits should use soul magic—they're pure magic souls, right?

When I questioned Kage about it further, he became defensive and said he had only practiced on himself, but from his shifting expression and the fact that he was being forced from the temple, clearly he was lying about that too.

Why would Kage try to alter his own soul? Souls are sacred. It's an affront on the spirit Kamellia.

So I took the book. I'm going to give it to Matsuya next time I see him. But maybe I should just burn it. Jovan was more concerned about where Kage was going after he left the Spire—Kage clearly didn't want to return home to the Stone Mountains a failed mage. I'm sure he'll settle down in Heliodor or something and try to make his way among the common folk, now that he won't be a mage.

Well, tomorrow I can get back to training. I just hope not all of my Gray Knight duties are this unpleasant.

Then Kira noticed a book in the stack that wasn't a journal. It was likely the book in question that Rokuro confiscated from this acolyte who had been removed from the temple. *Alternative Magicks* was embossed in faded gold lettering on the black cover. Curious, Kira began to flip through it, at first not seeing anything off about it. There was even a section about crystals such as the one at the top of the Spire. But then she came across a chapter on soul magic. At first, she grew excited, wondering if there would be something here that would tell her how to reveal her true soul as the spirit said, but the only soul magic in here seemed geared towards utilizing your soul's energy to produce magic, much like how Kira pulled Light and Shadow essence from the world, then used them to create or alter things. She shuddered, her face drawn in disgust as she put the book down. Even not having grown up in Camellia, the idea of using magic like that didn't sit well with Kira, especially if you used it on another person.

But as Kira crawled into her bed that night, she had another unpleasant thought.

Perhaps the Lord of Between had studied at the Spire. And perhaps he had been kicked out.

But knowing the true name of the Lord of Between wasn't much help. Obviously, he was going by another name—and another face, with his shapeshifting magic.

She would ask Raiden about him the next time she saw him. Maybe he had trained at the Spire at the same time. And Sir Jovan was still posted in the countryside helping fend off the raiders, so she couldn't ask him just yet.

Now more than ever, she wished the Gray Knights were here—not just for training, but for answers.

* * *

Early the next day, Kira took the long way out of the Spire to get to the stables to care for Naga, and went out through the Hall of Spirits.

The statues of Camellia's spirits always fascinated her, because she knew they were real, though she had only met a few. Unlike in the Starless Realm where mythology and ancient gods were little more than fairytales, these spirits were present and meddled in human affairs, though some of them were for luck or health.

She studied each one carefully as she passed, searching. She didn't find the beautiful woman until the very end, near the doorway leading outside.

Carved from stone—though, likely by magic—the woman was identifiable by her sash and eye makeup. Kira crept forward to read the plaque beside her.

Kamellia, spirit of souls.

Kira blinked a few times, staring at the words. Then she whispered, "Wow."

She had heard of Kamellia before, because she was one of the major spirits of the realm, who shepherded lost souls on after a person died. But she had never expected to meet her. She just wished she had known at the time. She would have asked her plenty more questions. But the spirit probably wouldn't have answered her.

Still surprised that the spirit had chosen to visit her, Kira headed for the stables to take care of Naga. When she got there, Anzu was already there.

Kira smiled. "You really don't have to take care of Naga for me."

But the knight had already brushed Naga's beautiful dapple-gray coat and was combing out her mane. "I was up early," she said, shrugging. "I thought I'd make myself useful."

"But it's my responsibility," Kira said, joining her in the stall. "If anything, I should be taking care of your horse!"

That drew a small smile from the knight. "Have you decided who you'd like to squire for then?"

Kira's mouth popped open and she felt her face grow warm. "I—um—"

Anzu turned back to Naga's mane. "Oh, I understand," she said quickly.

"No, it's—Anzu I'm sorry. I just haven't had time to decide. And..." She sighed. "When I get my magic back," she said, balling her hands into fists, "I'm not sure if I should squire for a knight or a mage. I... I'd love to ask you, but I don't know if I should ask Zowan too."

"Hmm," Anzu said softly, turning back to face Kira. "Well if it's between me and Zowan, I'm all right with that."

"Really? I thought you'd be disappointed. So I didn't want to talk about it..."

Anzu chuckled. "I know I can't help you with Shadow magic like he can. As long as you weren't going to ask another Light Knight."

"Oh, please! Who else would I ask? You're the best Light Knight in Camellia."

Throwing her shoulders back, Anzu laughed again. "Well, that's very kind of you, but you don't have to win my favor. I would be honored to have you for a squire. But if you end up choosing Zowan, I'll understand. He would be good for you too."

"You're the best, Anzu," Kira said, gathering up all the brushes, combs, and the hoof pick as she cleaned up. "Do you want any help with Panji?"

Kira helped Anzu groom her own horse before setting off for meditation. Though she was glad Anzu was amicable about the squire position, she still didn't know what to do. *I need to get my magic back before I decide*, she thought, bunching up her fists again.

She got to meditation just as everyone was settling onto their mats, an atmosphere of quiet already rolling over the pavilion much like the incense Mistress Korina had lit. She beelined for the place beside Jun, but she would have to wait to talk to him until after, lest she draw dirty looks from the other acolytes and Mistress Korina. So she settled for a hasty smile at him before they both sat down and closed their eyes.

It was even more difficult than usual to concentrate, after her revelations and theories about the Lord of Between, and her impending talk with Ryn. What would she say to him? Where would she even find him? She doubted he was going to come to the Gray Wing after what she said to him.

Amid her bouts of somewhat rhythmic breathing, her thoughts drifted back to the book that she had discovered with her father's journals. *Perhaps I should look at it some more, maybe there's something in there I can use; the book wasn't* all *bad.*

Her eyes shot open the second the peel of the bell rang out over the peaceful grounds. A light breeze came in from the lake, dispersing the incense hanging around the pavilion like heavily scented clouds. Kira breathed in the fresh air and turned to talk to Jun, but he started first. "Where were you last night? I had to practice Light combat with a dummy."

"Oh, um it's a long story," she said, glancing at the passing acolytes. "I'll tell you everything when we get back to the Gray Wing."

He levered himself up off the ground in a graceful motion. "Can it wait 'til later? I'm meeting with someone from the Shadow Guard."

From the bright look in his eyes, Kira could tell he wanted her to ask, "What is it this time?"

A grin spread wide on his face. "I think I'll tell you when I figure out how to do it myself. It's a good one."

"Okay," she chuckled.

They parted ways before they even entered the castle, as Jun went to meet his latest mage to study. Kira found herself dashing to the Gray Wing, the *Alternative Magicks* book on her mind.

Pausing only to grab a pear from the small kitchen, she went straight to her study to get the book out from the hidden hole in the floor. She had figured if her father had left the journals and book hidden away, she should too, just in case.

Avoiding the section on using soul channeling magic, she perused the rest of the book, looking for anything that might be useful in revealing her soul as Kamellia had told her. Her heart leaped every time she read the word *soul*, but it wasn't until she read the section that mentioned the Dragon Crystal that she found something of note.

Of Certain Crystals Possessing Magick

There exist only a few crystals capable of channeling magic, the most powerful being the Dragon Crystal that Shadow mages have long used to identify the soul's capability for magic. The Dragon Crystal possesses a unique structure, projecting the soul's magic in a rainbow of colors, allowing interpretation.

Another crystal of note is the Tiger's Eye Crystal, though not as widely used, it is far more powerful. This crystal possesses the ability to project the colors of the soul outside the crystal, which is useful in revealing one's true soul. Housed at the Light temple of Azurite, it—

A knock came at the door to the Gray Wing just as Kira's heart leaped right out of her chest. She glanced up toward the door, then back down at the book.

Just as she decided to ignore the person knocking to continue reading, she remembered who it might be.

"Micah!" she gasped, tossing a scrap of ribbon into her place in the book and flinging it on top of the desk.

She ran her fingers through her hair and smoothed down her green belt sash before opening the door to the wing. Adrenaline still rushed through her veins at the discovery she had just made, but it would have to wait until later.

Micah stood in the doorway, black shining hair casually falling into his eyes. He wasn't wearing his apron and was holding out a tin of tea.

"Thought we could have some tea with lunch," he said with a smile.

"Oh, Micah, I'm so sorry. I completely forgot. I don't think we have much to eat except rice and... pears maybe. Jun's been eating all of our food, and I haven't had a chance to get anything else." She didn't mention she had missed dinner last night after her excursion up to the top of the Spire, and had no idea what Jun even ate.

He gave her a sly smile and produced a small bag he had been holding out of sight. "I brought us something from the market I always go to in the city."

"Really? All right, come on in. I'm really sorry I don't have anything here. Things have just been so..."

"I get it. And don't worry. I've got the tea, I've got the lunch, all you have to do is enjoy it." He handed her the tin, and she opened it and sniffed.

"I don't think that will be a problem," she said. "Here, you can put that on the table, and I'll go get the tea things ready." She wasn't sure she wanted to be in such close quarters in the kitchen with Micah. Even just brushing his fingertips with her own as she handed back the tea sparked something that ran all the way up her arm and straight to her core. She flicked a look at his green eyes and away. *Wow*, she thought.

As Kira busied about the kitchen gathering tea cups and heating the kettle to a boil, her mind was whirring about what she had read in the *Alternative Magicks* book. *If there's a crystal that can help reveal my true soul, I can fix it and get my magic back*, she thought.

But as she loaded everything onto a black lacquered tray she had found in one of the cabinets, her stomach sank. The book has said it was at Azurite. And everyone knew Azurite had been destroyed when an unknown mage moved the waterfall beside it.

The crystal was surely as destroyed as the temple. Her shoulders drooped as she brought the tray out to the common room. But as she spotted Micah settling onto a floor cushion and peering inside the bag he brought, she felt herself smiling again.

Really, she was in the same place she had been in an hour ago—no plan, and no Shadow magic. She would just have to keep fighting.

She glanced nervously at Micah. "So, how's Spectra?" she asked, seizing the first topic that came to mind.

"Oh, she's all right. The extra hours do get to her though. She needs a lot of time to unwind and relax and get her thoughts in order."

"Mmm," Kira agreed. "I know what you mean."

Micah looked up at her. Every part of her body tingled as if suffused with magic when she met eyes with him. She focused on not dropping the tray as she set it down. Micah got to work making the tea. When he opened the tin, he held it out for her to smell. It was earthy and green, but with a strange, toasted scent. She looked inside the tin and saw little brown kernels.

"Toasted rice," he explained. "It enhances the flavor."

"Oh," Kira said as he scooped some into the strainer of the pot. She watched the steam rising in swirls from the pot lid while they waited for it to steep. She wasn't really sure what to say now that she and Micah were finally able to spend some time together. *All alone*, she thought with a jolt to her stomach. Sure, she was alone in the wing with Jun all the time, but he was like her brother.

"You know, I'm really glad you came to the Spire," Micah said before the silence grew too awkward.

"Me too," she said, meaning it. "I wish we had more time to spend together. My training hasn't been exactly fun so far," she muttered.

"I'm sorry, my work schedule has been so busy."

"It's nothing to be sorry about! You have your work, and I have my—my training," she said.

He reached out and covered her hand with his. It was so warm. A shiver ran up Kira's spine and she realized her heart was thudding so forcefully in her chest it was a wonder they couldn't hear it.

"I just don't want you to think I don't still like you," he said, looking up at her with those green eyes under dark lashes.

Her throat constricted, and a sudden urge to lean forward overcame all her doubtful thoughts. Elbows on the table, she leaned toward him, not thinking about anything—just those green eyes and the warm feeling radiating from her heart. It felt like it might burst with warmth.

He was staring right back at her; she suddenly found herself melting toward his mouth, and their lips met with almost an electric shock.

Her eyes had closed, but she flung them back open when she heard a rustle outside from the balcony.

She whirled around, drawing out the steel dagger she kept at her side at all times.

But it was just Thistle. *I really wish he would stop doing that*, she thought, her heart beating even faster inside her chest now.

Thistle swooped inside, floating down onto Kira's outstretched arm as gently as a falling leaf.

"Thistle! How did it go? Is Zowan back already?" She couldn't wait to discuss her theories about the Lord of Between with him, and pick his brain as to whether the Tiger's Eye Crystal at Azurite had been destroyed or not.

Thistle shifted from paw to paw on her wrist, his eyes darting all around. "No, he's not back yet."

"Then what happened?" Sudden panic gripped her at his nervous state.

"It's not them!" Thistle said. "The raiders aren't from the Stone Mountains. Zowan met with Lady Madora and she didn't know anything about it."

Chapter 23

An Act of Aggression

"*What?*" she demanded, finally dropping her other arm holding the dagger. "What do you mean?"

At that moment, the doors of the Gray Wing burst open.

Kira whipped around, half hoping to see Zowan striding through so she could demand to know what was going on. But it was the Spirekeeper, Kusari. Kira had forgotten how tall the short-haired woman was. Kira shrank a little, glanced at Micah, and blushed; but now wasn't the time to be embarrassed. Something was *off*. Something was wrong.

"Lady Starwind," Kusari said, "your presence is requested immediately by Commander Aita." Kusari crossed her arms over her chest as she noted Micah sitting at the table, but didn't comment on his presence.

"Oh, okay," Kira said. She looked at Micah again and winced. "I'm so sorry," she muttered. "Maybe we can have tea and lunch tomorrow?"

He touched his lips then gave her a sad smile. "Maybe."

Kusari called over to Micah, "You may go. Lady Starwind has duties to attend to."

Micah obeyed, turning his back on Kira after giving her a wave goodbye. Her insides writhed in a mixture of regret and excitement. She would get to spend more time with Micah another day, she was sure. *But first things first*, she thought. *I need to figure out what's going on*.

Kira followed Kusari out of the wing, Thistle still on her arm. "Well, where's Zowan then?" Kira hissed to him as they passed through the Jade Foyer.

"I left after I heard him speak with the Lady. I thought you should know right away. It seems like it could be a trick of some kind."

"Yes, it does."

She realized Kusari was leading her to Raiden's study. "We'll tell Raiden," she whispered to Thistle. "He needs to know, and alert the palace and the Gray Knights and everything. It could be some trick of the Lord of Between." *Oh, and I need to ask him about that Kage person too*, she thought. *And the crystal, maybe he knows.* She picked up the pace, her wide-legged trousers whipping around her legs as they entered the study.

Commander Aita stood in front of Raiden's desk, her arms clasped behind her back, swords at her waist, their hilts jutting forward. She studied Kira seriously as she walked in. Raiden sat grimly at his desk, his fingers tented up under his chin.

Kira's pace slowed.

"What's wrong?" she demanded. *Had they already heard the same news Thistle had brought?*

"There's been an attack," Commander Aita said briskly. "You and Lord Kosumoso are returning to Gekkō-ji at once."

"What?" Kira burst, all thoughts of anything else flitting from her head. "But we're safe here!"

"I'm afraid not," Aita said, wrinkling her tiny nose. "The raiders have captured Lord Zowan and the rest of the envoy. Now that they are in possession of one of the most powerful mages in the realm... If Lady Madora forces the Storm King's nephew to do anything, well, it's just not safe here for you right now."

Thistle squeaked from where he perched on Kira's arm, and she blurted, "But the raiders aren't being sent from the Stone Mountains, Thistle followed Zowan into Madora's stronghold. I think it's some kind of trick." She glanced quickly between the two of them.

A look of annoyance crossed Aita's face, and she shifted her stance.

Raiden's face was creased in worry. "I'm sorry Kira, b ut... we received this," he held out a scrap of paper with a slightly shaking hand.

Kira looked at him again and only just now registered the fear in his eyes. If Zowan really had been taken... But what about what Thistle had said?

She glanced down at the note, but her eyes became blurry at the familiar handwriting.

Raiders in SM—dangerous. Protect Kira.

"We have to go after him!" Kira said, blinking away the budding tears. "I can't go back to Gekkō-ji now!"

Raiden shook his head. "I know you're worried for him, but we both know he can handle himself. And besides, this time, not all of our best mages are incapacitated. I'll send a fully equipped Shadow Guard after him—I'll send three."

"But won't that look like an act of aggression to Lady Madora?" Kira asked, forehead creased in worry. If Lady Madora *hadn't* sent the raiders, and three contingents of Shadow Guards stormed in there...

A rumble of thunder murmured above their heads and Kira shrank back, pressing her lips into a thin line.

Raiden turned to Aita. "Take Kira and Jun if you must, but once this is over, they'll return here to finish their training."

Aita frowned. "Not if you're at war with the Stone Mountains. The Empress won't endanger the first new Gray Knights in two decades like that. Honestly, I don't think she even wanted them to come here in the first place, the peace being so new and all. That's why she sent us," she reminded them.

Raiden slammed his fist on his desk, and this time, a burst of thunder sounded from outside the windows. The sky was beginning to grow dark. Gray storm clouds appeared out of nowhere.

"Come, Kira," Aita said, ignoring Raiden's brewing anger. "We must get going before it gets dark. I'll gather the rest of the Commonality; you don't need to worry, there will be plenty of soldiers to protect you."

Dumbstruck, her mind reeling, Kira allowed Aita to lead her from the study. The Spirekeeper joined them in the hallway and followed like a tall shadow.

When they got to the Gray Wing, Jun was already there, packing. He was bringing a small bag into the common room when they entered.

"Jun, I—" Kira began.

"Hurry, Lady Starwind," Aita demanded. "We don't have a lot of time. If Madora's people use the Storm King's nephew to infiltrate the Spire, or to bargain for a trade, I don't want to be here when it happens. Pack only a little; we'll send someone later for the rest of your things if we can."

Kira stumbled into her quarters and fumbled in her trunk for a satchel. She began stuffing things in at random.

What had happened to Zowan? When would she get to come back to the Spire? She hadn't even been able to see Ryn to apologize to him...

In her study, she crammed *Alternative Magicks* into her bag since she hadn't had the chance to put it away properly before Micah had come for tea.

Micah... The memory of him walking away from her would be the last time she saw him. When would she return?

As she returned to the common room, she spotted the undrunk tea on the table, and tears welled up in her eyes. Her fingers grew cold as they remembered his warm touch.

Commander Aita had gone, to rouse the rest of the Commonality no doubt. Under the watchful eyes of Kusari and the two soldiers that normally stood guard outside the wing, Kira hesitated in the middle of the common room open-mouthed at the thought of leaving.

Then Anzu burst into the wing, her eyes blazing. She spotted Kira and marched over. "Is it true? They want you to go back to Gekkō-ji? I was in the stables and they were getting your horses—"

"Anzu, thank goodness you're here," Kira gushed, grabbing the knight's arm and dragging her over by the balcony, out of earshot of Kusari and the soldiers.

"Something weird is going on," Kira said. "Raiden got a message from Zowan saying the raiders had attacked him or something—"

Anzu stiffened.

"—but Thistle told me that the raiders weren't really coming from the Stone Mountains; Lady Madora said she didn't know anything about it—"

Anzu drew up her shoulders, an intimidating move with her spiked leather pauldrons. "But she could have been lying. Everyone knows she's got it in for Raiden, and that he's got a soft spot for Zowan. She could very well have taken him."

"I suppose they could have attacked him after I left," Thistle surmised.

But something didn't seem right. Kira just couldn't figure it out. Anzu was shifting her weight from foot to foot. And then Kira realized. "Go. Go look for Zowan."

Anzu looked down, blushing—to Kira's amazement. "No, my job is to protect you. I should go with you and Jun, get you to safety."

Kira glanced at Jun, who was watching them with a hollow look of disappointment on his face. She wasn't even sure he was really listening to them. "Jun and I can protect ourselves just fine."

Anzu smiled, placing a hand on Kira's shoulder. "You're right. You are as fierce and brave as any knight."

Through a watery smile, Kira said, "Go find him. Take Thistle, he can help you."

Anzu nodded and left, the flying squirrel perched on one of her pauldrons.

It wasn't long after that Aita returned. "Are you ready?" the diminutive woman demanded, hands on her hips.

Kira's eyes went to the tea tray on the table and she picked up the small tin Micah had brought. She opened her satchel and shifted the *Alternative Magicks* book side to make room for it.

"I guess," she muttered, really hoping she would be able to return soon, but if she couldn't, at least she would have the tea Micah had gifted her. Her heart began to ache at the thought of leaving behind her father's quarters and all his journals, but there hadn't been any time—or privacy—to get into his secret cache. *I'll be back*, she said. *Somehow. Sometime.*

Chapter 24

Illusionwork

Her head still spinning, she could hardly believe it when she mounted Naga and rode off into the temple grounds, Jun at her side. He hadn't said anything at all since they left the Gray Wing. He looked just as shocked as she felt. On the surface, Kira was hoping this was all a big deal over nothing, and Raiden would call them back at any moment. But deep down, a rising fear for Zowan's safety began to take hold of her.

As they left the stables, Kira spotted Ryn walking along the garden path where they had once sat together. She waved at him, forlornly thinking maybe she should send him a letter to apologize when she got back to Gekkō-ji. He just stared after her, eyebrows creased. Her heart sank.

After that she glared down at her saddle, wishing she had asked Thistle to stay with her. But he was needed for Anzu to track down Zowan, and that was the most pressing matter at the moment.

She turned around in her saddle as they crossed out of the temple grounds, gazing up at the Spire and already missing the place. *At least Micah and I were having a nice time before they made me leave*, she reflected, biting the inside of her cheek.

The walk through the city was a disappointing blur.

Outside the gates, the mounting fear began to impress upon her nerves. Zowan was missing, possibly in danger. She didn't know whether Raiden was going to try to send a Shadow Guard after Zowan, sparking a conflict between the Shadow and Stone Mountain regions. Would it cause another feud? All over another misunderstanding?

At least it's not the Lord of Between again, she thought with a shudder. She was almost glad it was the Stone Mountains.

She just wished Commander Aita wasn't treating her and Jun like children, hurrying them away at the slightest sign of danger. She could handle herself—she was a squire and almost a Gray Knight for goodness' sake!

Half an hour outside of Heliodor, Kira finally surfaced from her brooding thoughts and noticed they weren't taking the same stretch of the Kaidō road they had used to get to the city. She looked over at Jun; he was staring down at his reins in disbelief, obviously just as disappointed as Kira at leaving.

"This isn't the way to Gekkō-ji," she called to the commander, who rode in front of them.

"I know," the woman replied over her shoulder. "I'm taking you two to Meridian. That's where the Empress set up the base for the Commonality. We wouldn't be able to protect you as effectively at Gekkō-ji."

Kira looked at Jun again; he hadn't even lifted his head. She nudged Naga toward him. "This isn't right. We shouldn't be going to Meridian."

He finally perked up. "What? Meridian?"

"Yeah, weren't you listening? We're not on the road to Gekkō-ji."

Eyes wary, he finally looked around. "I don't want to go to Meridian."

"Me either," she said. "They'll probably stuff us somewhere where we can't even get any training done. But what are we going to do about it? This is ridiculous."

They both glanced around at the two dozen soldiers flanking them. Kira hadn't realized until now how many Commonality soldiers there were.

Jun's eyes lit up. "I have an idea," he muttered.

"One of your pet mage projects?" Kira hissed, her heart leaping.

A wily grin spread across his face. "The best one. But I haven't had a chance to see if I can do it yet. From the results of my Scrying, I think I should be able to."

"Elaborate, will you?"

He shook his head. "Give me some time. I don't know if I can do it. I need to focus."

Kira huffed and stared ahead, wondering if they'd be all the way to Meridian by the time Jun told her what he was even trying to attempt.

If they could break free of the Commonality soldiers, they could ride back to Heliodor. Getting sent back to Gekkō-ji was one thing, but what would they do with themselves in Meridian? Who knew how long it would take to rid the countryside of the raiders, or to rescue Zowan?

And if the Commonality followed them back to the Spire… well, then Kira would demand to stay this time. She was a Gray trainee after all. They had just caught them off guard. This time she would stand up for herself and Jun.

Regretting again that she'd sent Thistle with Anzu, she settled into her saddle with unease, letting her mind wander as she waited for Jun to do whatever it was he was trying to do. She didn't even know where she would send the little spirit, but his presence would have been helpful.

She sighed, looking out at the fields they were passing. She was surprised at how much she already missed the Spire, with the prospect of not returning anytime soon looming over her if they couldn't get away from these overprotective soldiers. The Gray Wing had become like another home, and even though she had spent a lot of her time in sleepless nights and melancholy days, the people were what she would miss the most, especially Micah.

A thrill ran through her as she thought back to their kiss. *If only I had more time with him*, she thought. *I know my training comes first, but how am I supposed to have a relationship with* anyone *when my life is like this?*

She shook her head, sneaking a glance at Jun to see if he had made any progress on his mysterious magic.

But there was no one sitting on his horse.

She blinked. "Jun!" she gasped, blinking some more as she realized her eyes must have been playing tricks on her, because there he was.

He was grinning at her. He said quietly, "Now I just need to try to make it so it works on you and the horses too."

Her mouth wide open, she just stared at him. "Were you—invisible? *You were invisible!"* she hissed, keeping her voice low so the soldiers on either side couldn't hear over the sound of all the hooves on the road.

"It's illusionwork," he said just as quietly. "You'll never guess who taught me!"

At her questioning look, he replied, "Ayana! From the Third Guard?"

"Oh," Kira said, cocking her head. "Oh! That would explain how she kept sneaking in and out of Gekkō-ji last year during the Storm King's visit. I kept wondering how she was getting in. So she taught you how?"

"Yeah, sort of. I've mostly been talking to mages just to get an idea of the scope of Shadow magic—there's so many possibilities. I mean with Light magic—"

"Jun," she warned. "Shouldn't you be focusing on something?"

"Oh, right." He stopped talking, and a blank look came over his face, his eyes out of focus, lids half-closed. She suspected he was doing some sort of meditation, though how he could concentrate on a moving horse, she had no clue. She studied him out of the corner of her eye, waiting for it to happen again. But she knew this type of magic must require a lot of training, especially to use it on such a large scale for two people and two horses.

Her stomach began to ache with worry. He wouldn't have enough time to make it work. They were going to get stuck going to Meridian, and get trapped in the niceties of the palace, being served tea and conversation instead of focusing on their training.

She had already grown tired of sneaking glances at Jun before she caught him at it again. They had been riding for a few hours now. Anxiety welled in Kira's chest the further they got from the Spire. She couldn't believe Aita was taking them to Meridian. When she saw Jun fade, and then his horse, she gasped again.

A moment later, and he was back.

"I probably shouldn't keep doing that," he said, glancing around at the soldiers on either side. "Not until we're ready anyway. Are we ready?"

"I don't know," she muttered. "Do you think we could really just slip away? Can you even use the illusionwork on me and Naga yet?"

"Yeah, I already did."

"What?" She looked down at herself but didn't notice anything unusual.

"You were looking at me," he said, shrugging.

"Okay," she said slowly, the idea that she had been invisible and hadn't even known about it rolling about in her head. "Well, do we wait for a distraction or something?"

"What kind of distraction?" Jun said, looking around. They were surrounded by flat farmland, only the wide dirt track of the Kaidō road before and behind them. "Look, no one's behind us, I'll just cast the illusion, and we'll slow the horses. No one will notice."

"All right, I guess," she said warily. It was as good a plan as any.

Kira waited. Seconds ticked on, the horses clopped on down the road, and it felt like hours passed. *Any minute now...* Finally, Jun and his horse disappeared. She looked down at her lap, but she didn't have a lap, or a horse, for that matter. But she could feel Naga beneath her legs, feel the reins in her hands. She loosened her reins, easing her speed.

How am I supposed to know where Jun is? she thought desperately, though a thrill of excitement was ringing through her. She was invisible!

Don't worry about Jun, she told herself, *just worry about slipping past these soldiers.*

She held her breath as Naga plodded on slower and slower, and finally she brought her horse to a halt and watched the soldiers marching their mounts onward down the road. She sat there in her saddle feeling silly, unable to see herself, unable to see Jun. An itch crept up her spine, like the feeling that someone was watching her. She glanced around wildly, but the farmland around them was still rather unoccupied.

Then, as the Commonality continued marching on obliviously, Jun reappeared, a few paces in front of her. He pulled his horse around to meet her, a huge grin on his face.

"Wow," she said. "They really weren't paying that close attention to us, were they?"

"Well, they were protecting us, not imprisoning us."

Her stomach squirmed, but she refused to feel guilty about it. Aita and the Commonality were too overprotective.

"You'll have to teach me that one when I get my magic back."

"Anytime. I think it's my favorite magic so far. Though my father hasn't ever told me about this one, so not everyone can do it."

"Back to the Spire?" she said.

Jun looked back at the way they had come, frowning. "Once they realize we're missing, don't you think they'll follow us back there first? I think we should maybe head to Gekkō-ji. I mean, once we're surrounded by the masters and knights, who are they to tell us what to do?"

Kira thought it over for a minute. "I suppose. But won't we have to get off the Kaidō road to get there? It's either that or follow it to Meridian so we can go northwest. And we're *not* going near Meridian."

"Yeah, you're right, we'll have to travel off the road," Jun agreed. "But these lands aren't too wild in between. It's mostly farms like these."

Kira stiffened, spotting a figure moving on the road back the way to Heliodor. "We should have gotten off the road sooner," she hissed.

It turned out to be two figures on horses. One tall and one short, both riding fast down the dirt track.

For a moment, Kira wondered if the Spire was sending someone from Heliodor to call them back—perhaps all of the confusion over Zowan had been solved, and everything was fine between the raiders and the Stone Mountains.

And then Kira recognized the riders. "Ryn? *Yuki?*" she called in disbelief.

Ryn and Yuki urged their mounts faster to reach them. Naga danced on the spot as the two horses and riders joined them, a cloud of dirt rising up to greet Kira and Jun.

"What's going on?" Kira asked. "Why did you follow us?"

Ryn's gaze searched her face. "What happened to the commander and the soldiers?" he demanded.

"We—uh, sort of ditched them," Kira said.

Ryn let out an exaggerated sigh. "Thank Kamellia. When I saw you leaving, I noticed something strange about the commander's aura. Something that wasn't there before."

A chill ran down Kira's spine. "And...?"

"Her aura was an entirely different set of colors," he explained. "And she had magic."

CHAPTER 25

THE WRONG AURA

"*What?*" Kira said, "You're saying she suddenly has magic now? I thought you read her aura before?"

"I did, thoroughly," Ryn assured her. "But the aura of the Aita who left the Spire with you a few hours ago, and the Aita who has been stomping importantly around the temple for the past week wasn't the same."

Kira and Jun looked at each other, horrified.

"And Yuki could tell too," Ryn said, glancing at the acolyte.

The girl cringed then nodded. "It's not the same person," she said. "I assist the Spirekeeper sometimes for my chores and so I've been around the commander a lot recently. And today—that wasn't her. And then I found out from Ryn you two had gone..."

"It's them," Kira whispered. "We need to get off the road, right now."

She pulled Naga around, pointing her toward the trees to the eastern side of the field. The others followed, and Kira tried to keep to the edge of the field where the ground was more solid and would show fewer hoofprints should they be followed, something she had learned from her lessons at Gekkō-ji.

Her stomach began to ache with fear, and she gripped her reins tighter. She was just glad she and Jun had decided to escape the commander's company—but if it really was the Lord of Between... An unpleasant tingle ran up her spine. She hoped it wasn't because they were being watched.

Finally, they reached the windbreak line of trees. It was only two or three trees wide at most so it didn't offer much protection from view, but it was better than standing out in the open road.

"Let's follow this until we can get to that hill," Kira told the others. They agreed, Yuki looking more than a little terrified. Kira was still surprised the acolyte was there, and a little touched that the girl had been that worried for them.

Leading at a fast trot, Kira beelined for the shadow of the hill that rose up on the edges of the fields, the tree line providing a straight path.

Where can we go? What do we do? Fear began to wrap its cold fingers around her mind, and she clenched her teeth, trying to will it away. It wouldn't do to lose her head, not right now.

"So, Commander Aita," Jun gasped when they all reached the woods at the base of the hill. "—was *the Lord of Between*?"

"Not this whole time," Kira said, looking at Ryn as he pulled up his horse.

Ryn nodded. "Right, she *was* common. Her aura was very purple—pride—and with slivers of gold, for bravery and proving herself. But when I saw you leaving the Spire, it was different. A *lot* different. Red—anger. And yellow—triumph. And some sickly turquoise I haven't seen before. But what drew my eye was a lot of black, which is unusual. And a rather thick haze all around it radiating with magic."

Taking a second to appreciate the thought Ryn put into reading the aura colors, Kira bit the inside of her lip. "So that's the Lord of Between right now. I bet they staged the raiders and sent Zowan into the Stone Mountains on that fake envoy mission." She gasped. "Zowan went with Commonality soldiers to see Lady Madora. You don't think he was actually attacked, do you?" she asked Jun.

He let out a breath through his nose. "Well, there's nothing you or I can do about it right now. We have no idea where he is. Anzu and Thistle will find him. I'm more worried about us." He gave Kira a look. "Where are we going to go? Gekkō-ji still? Or back to the Spire? I know Raiden will back us up against the Lord of Between—even if they're parading as Aita—he's got all of the mages at his disposal."

Ryn shook his head. "I wouldn't. There's still some Commonality soldiers there, they didn't all go with fake-Aita. And if you can't trust Aita anymore, I don't think you can trust any of the soldiers."

"How long do you think they've been pretending to be her?" Kira asked, and then quieter, "What do you think happened to the real Aita?"

"I don't know," Ryn said with a sigh. He glanced at Yuki, who grimaced.

"I don't think it's been very long," Yuki said in a small voice, clasping her fingers together.

"How do you know for sure?" Jun asked, his eyes narrowed slightly.

"I uh—" she began.

"It's fine," Ryn urged the acolyte. "They won't care. Really."

Kira looked closer at Yuki. She had wondered what the girl's proficiency was. It seemed like people avoided her because of it.

"I..." she began, staring down at her horse's mane. "I can read... thoughts."

Kira's chest tightened, and a prickle of fear began in her heart as she thought back to the two sisters, Nia Mari and Nikoletta, who had been able to manipulate minds. But that was different... Right?

Yuki hadn't seen the fear in her eyes, and she kept going. "Aita's thoughts are normally focused on security; I get snatches of it whenever I pass her in the corridors. She's very loud," she added with the barest hint of amusement. "Normally I try not to hear others, but when a person has such strong thoughts I can't help but hear them. But then I caught something unusual when I was in the stables this afternoon—I saw Aita before I heard the thoughts, and it was just wrong. I couldn't actually understand them—" Yuki said in answer to Kira's questioning look— "but the thought pattern was intense enough that I could hear it, like discordant music, and it was all wrong. And then I bumped into Ryn later and he was thinking about you two leaving with an Aita who had magic..." she trailed off, looking at her clasped fingers which she had been wringing.

Kira noticed her mouth was open in surprise, and she slowly closed it. She had had no idea Yuki could read thoughts like this. *Well, that would explain why the other acolytes seem to avoid her. But she seems pretty harmless.* "All right, so this seems like a recent development then. Thanks for that."

Yuki raised her eyes and then looked away again.

"We still need somewhere to go," Jun said, his gaze darting all around the field in front of the woods. "We can't just stay here; the Commonality could come back. I'm surprised fake-Aita wasn't keeping a better eye on us. But maybe they didn't want to tip us off."

Wracking her brain, Kira thought of places the Commonality and the Lord of Between would be unlikely to find them, but if the Lord of Between had been shifting forms and infiltrating as deep as the inside of the Spire, there was nowhere she knew that would be safe. Except...

"Azurite," she said. "We're near there, aren't we?"

The three of them gave her blank looks, a hint of worry on Jun's face. "Kira..." he began.

"No, listen. I know it was destroyed years ago. So it would be the perfect place to hide. And there's something there I want to look for."

She told them all she knew about the Tiger's Eye Crystal and how it could help reveal her soul, and about the connection her father's journal had uncovered about the Lord of Between.

"So you think this Kage person is their real identity?" Ryn said, rubbing his chin.

"It sounds like it," Kira said. "How many mages go bad and want to experiment with souls? He's certainly been working on it for a while."

"Well, regardless of who he may or may not be," Jun said. "Are we decided? Is that the plan?"

Kira nodded, then turned toward Ryn and Yuki. "You two should go back to the Spire. It's not like he's coming after you. You'll be safe there."

Ryn gave her a patronizing look. "Honey, I'm coming with you. Obviously, you can't tell the difference between a benign yet self-important commander, and a mad person, so I think you might need me."

"And I want to come too," Yuki said, sticking out her chin. "My proficiency might not make me a lot of friend s... or be good in a fight, but maybe I can help."

"Are you sure?" Kira asked.

"I'm sure they're sure," Jun said impatiently. "They just said so, didn't they? Look, let's stop wasting time and get going. We need to get away from the Kaidō road."

So they followed the curve of the hill for a little while until Jun got his bearings. Having grown up studying maps of Camellia during his history lessons before even arriving at Gekkō-ji, he knew the land off the top of his head. *He's better than GPS*, Kira thought with a giggle.

He gave her an odd look as she did so. She decided to explain it to him later when they weren't in danger. He normally got a kick out of her stories about the Starless Realm, but now really wasn't the time.

Jun led the way, guiding them over footbridges, down narrow dirt roads that were only wide enough for one horse abreast, and around the outskirts of a small village. Kira constantly kept watch behind them, but so far, they hadn't been followed.

When they were passing through a forest of old black pines, Kira pulled her horse up next to Ryn's. The way behind them was clear, and she felt like it might be now or never to speak with him.

"Listen, Ryn, I'm really sorry about what I said yesterday," she began. "I haven't been feeling myself lately. I just feel horrible all the time, like I can't even control my own emotions, let alone my magic." The words tumbled out, not quite what she had rehearsed in her head over the past hour, but it was close.

"I understand," he said. "No really, I do. And you shouldn't feel bad about it. It happens. And it definitely happens to people who've had their soul damaged."

"But that's not an excuse for what I said."

"I forgive you then."

She gave him a watery smile. "You're a great friend, you know that, right?"

"The greatest of friends," he said grandly. "Got it."

Kira chuckled. Then she remembered something. "You'll never guess who I met at the top of the Spire..."

When she finished telling Ryn about her meeting with Kamellia—while Jun and Yuki listened with rapt attention from behind them—the forest around them grew sparse. Kira soon became aware of a shushing sound far up ahead.

"So you need to *reveal* your true soul," Ryn mused. "And this Tiger's Eye Crystal can do that?"

Kira nodded. "That Kage person had this book," she said, slipping it out of her satchel to show the others the cover. "And my father confiscated it when they were there to kick him out of the temple. But it's not all bad magic," she said quickly. "It mentions the Dragon Crystal too."

"Was there anything in there about what they tried to do to you?" Jun asked. "To your soul I mean?"

"Well, maybe," Kira said. "I skimmed the whole book for anything to do with soul magic, and I think they were pulling out souls to use for magic, like we pull on Light and Shadow essence for magic. I think... I think that's why they've been able to summon portals to the Starless Realm, and shapeshift and everything, they've been stealing soul magic and using its essence this whole time."

Jun agreed uneasily. Ryn shuddered, his shoulders arching up towards his ears.

The woods through which they walked was an old forest, the trees larger than many Kira had seen in Camellia. Slowly, everything was becoming greener and greener, with moss covering every surface. The sound of gushing water grew louder and louder though they still couldn't see its source. A hum of anticipation ran through Kira, growing stronger as they approached.

They all stopped talking, as if they were entering a sacred temple, the peace of the forest and the hush of the water settling over them.

And then they came to an opening in the trees at the top of a ridge, and the waterfall came into view.

For a moment, it washed every anxiety from Kira's mind, her heart soaring at the sight of it. The great water fell from a high outcrop on the other side of the valley they now stood at the edge of. The entire valley was an explosion of green. In the shadow of the falls, Kira spotted vague shapes of rock and moss. A dead tree stuck up from the place nearest the falls at an odd angle.

They dismounted and led their horses into the valley, still in silent awe, with Kira and Jun at the front. As the horses picked their way over the mossy slope, Kira glanced over at Jun. He was staring at the place where the rocks stood, his eyes crinkled, his mouth pressed into a thin line.

As they approached, Kira looked more closely at the scene, and it was then that she realized what she thought was a dead tree near the base of the falls was really a wooden point attached to a long-destroyed building. The tip of a pavilion.

They were looking at the ruins of Azurite.

CHAPTER 26

THE RUINS OF AZURITE

Their silence persisted as they reached the former site of the Light temple. What Kira had thought were boulders were really stones from the foundations of old buildings, and the destroyed wall that had circled the temple. Kira had never really thought the ruins of Azurite would look like this. But after a glance back up at the roaring falls, it was no wonder the temple had been so thoroughly destroyed.

And it was no wonder the Light region reacted so strongly when they thought Raiden was responsible for the tragedy.

When they reached the toppled pavilion, Kira finally broke the silence.

"There's no way the Tiger's Eye Crystal survived this. I had no idea it was like this..."

Jun was shaking his head. "Me either."

Ryn went over to sit on a rock along the side of the ridge leading up to the falls. He drew up his long legs and rested his head on his knees, his eyes squeezed shut. A pang went through Kira's heart. She went over to him and rested a hand on his shoulder.

He jerked away, his eyes flashing open.

"Sorry," Kira said. "I just—are you okay?"

He shook his head, shrugging. "It's... I'm fine."

Yuki glanced between Ryn and Kira, frowning.

"Are you sure?" Kira said. "Do you want to leave?"

"I'm fine!" Ryn snapped, launching himself off the ledge and stalking away a few places, staring up at the falls with his hands on his hips.

Kira and Jun traded bewildered looks. "Do you know. ..?" she asked Yuki.

The shorter girl nodded, but with half a shrug said, "It's not my place to say."

"I understand," Kira said, watching Ryn's back. *We'll just give him some time, I guess*, she thought, *I wonder if he knew people who hadn't made it out of the temple or something?* But it was a Light temple, and the Shadow delegation that Raiden had brought here had all been outside when the falls had moved in and destroyed everything.

"Maybe we shouldn't have come here," she said to Jun quietly.

He put a hand on the sword at his belt, glancing around the lush valley. “We didn’t have any other plan. I say we look around anyway for this crystal of yours. It could still be here. If we’re on the run from the Lord of Between now, it might be good for you to have your Shadow magic back again.”

Kira nodded. “That might be ideal, if we can even find it and figure out what to do with it. All right. But some of us should keep watch at the top of the ridge, and the place where we came in. We’re pretty exposed if anyone comes in that way.”

“I’ll keep watch,” Jun volunteered, looking up at the falls.

“I will too,” Ryn said, his back still to them.

“Are you sure?” Kira asked.

“No offense,” Jun started, “but... are you any good at fighting?"

Ryn turned around, his eyes rimmed in red. “I am,” he said, in a voice unlike his own. “I’m quite good. I just don’t like to... I don’t really like to use it. But if I have to I will.”

“Are you sure?” Kira asked again, softer this time.

He nodded, his eyes flicked over the ruins of Azurite and back to Kira. “I wasn’t here for the destruction of the temple or anything,” he said in a clipped voice. “But I’ve seen plenty of battlefields and broken homes and villages to feel the pain all over again. I—I never told you this," he said to Kira, "but after I completed my training at the Spire I joined the Shadow Guard. I fought for Shadow, knowing that the Light region was trying to eradicate us.

"And I was good at it. Really good. My aura magic helped me fight. But whenever we would clash with the Light Knights, I could see their pain. All of it. I couldn't take it anymore.

"So I had to leave the Guard. I went back home after. I've never been able to forget the pain we inflicted. Whenever I see—I can't get it out of my head. I just—" his voice broke, and he turned away.

Kira went over and put her arms around him, and he let her. He was so tall that he could rest his head on top of hers.

"Oh, Ryn. I'm so sorry."

"It's not your fault,' he sniffed. "And we'd likely still be feuding if it weren't for you."

"You really don't have to do this," she said. "You don't even have to stay. You could go back to the Spire, or home even—"

He pulled away. "I'm doing this," he told her firmly. "I said I'd help you fix your soul damage and I will. Besides," he gave a weak chuckle, "I want to do this. For you. What kind of friend would I be if I didn't stay?"

"A happier one? Ryn, I don't want to torture you like this. You don't need to do this for me."

"It's not torture. I'll be fine, really. And besides, I don't have to hurt anyone. I'll go easy. I often did scouting missions because of my proficiency. The auras are visible at a distance, even when a person is hidden."

She raised an eyebrow but didn't comment. He must have been some fighter.

"I'll need a weapon though. A sword like yours," Ryn said to Jun.

Jun obliged him and summoned a beautiful blade from Light magic and handed it over. Ryn admired it with a professional eye.

"Wow," he said, drawing it halfway out of the scabbard and studying the blade. "This will work."

He loped back over to the ridge where they had come in, stationing himself there, poised and ready, scanning the lush green woods. Jun headed in the opposite direction, climbing the steep incline up towards the top of the falls. He positioned himself on a ledge about halfway up, where he had a clear view of the whole valley.

"Well," Kira said to Yuki, "I guess you and I are looking for the crystal then."

They began picking their way delicately through the ruins. But they soon found out that everything that wasn't stone had been completely destroyed. They shifted aside a few rocks only to reveal the dark earth beneath. Nothing else had survived. Kira brushed moss from every stone that looked a likely candidate for the crystal, but only found dark gray stones, damp from the ever-present mist coming from the falls. She was sure the Tiger's Eye Crystal would be clearly identifiable if they happened upon it.

After an hour of searching the ruins, Kira started losing hope. What were they doing here? The Lord of Between could easily have followed them; why was she endangering her friends with this pointless search? They should find somewhere safe to hide until they could figure out what was going on, and make a plan.

Just as she was about to call everyone over to tell them they should all go, Jun gave a short whistle. Kira looked up and around, her heart thudding. But the valley was just as peaceful as it was a moment ago.

She turned to stare at Jun. He had moved from his post and had taken to bounding from ledge to ledge along the ridge that led up to the falls. He had gotten rather close to the edge where the water gushed past not ten feet away from him. He jerked his thumb toward the waterfall. Kira cocked her head, sure he wouldn't be able to hear her if she tried to yell. He motioned again, so she and Yuki went to get closer.

They had to scale a few ledges until they could get within earshot. "What?" Kira demanded. "Did you find something?"

Jun nodded eagerly, then pointed to a crevice in the rock beside him. Kira levered herself up onto the ledge on which he stood, then inched over to where he was pointing. He scooted over so she could put her eye to the crevice.

Inside was a cave, and from the soaking wet floor, she figured it was behind the waterfall. In the center stood a stone podium, and on top, a brilliant sphere with brown-gold hues nearly dancing on its surface.

Chapter 27

Behind the Falls

Kira turned to Jun, her eyes wide. "But how do we get in there?"

Jun just stared at the rushing water.

"Any of your pet mage projects cover this sort of thing?"

He shook his head. "No. And I wouldn't want to risk trying to use Shadow wind to fly myself in there. Not with the falls right there. I haven't had enough practice yet."

Kira looked around the verdant valley as if it might hold an answer. The horses grazed peacefully beside the ruins, Ryn stood sentry at the edge of the forest, and Yuki remained below at the bottom of the rock wall.

Jun was still peering through the crevice at the crystal.

"How can we....?" Kira edged closer to the waterfall, her hair gathering mist like dew on grass. "Do you think we could make a platform out of Light or something to get around this corner?" she practically yelled over the constant rushing water.

Jun eyed the distance between the ledge on which they stood and the falling water. They couldn't see the entrance to the cave from this side.

He shook his head, shrugging. "I don't know," he yelled back.

Kira squared her shoulders and took a deep breath, pulling on the Light magic in the world around her, gathering it up into her core. A heady rush washed over her at the magic running through her.

She studied the cliff she needed to traverse. A platform would need to be supported from underneath, and nothing she summoned would stick to the rock face unless she pushed it with something. And she wasn't about to risk passing out performing Shadow magic while clinging to this cliff.

"What if I summon steps and you push them into the rock with Shadow magic?" she shouted to Jun.

He nodded once, then planted his feet, his palms up.

She unspindled some of the Light magic from her core and pushed it back out into the world, shaped sort of like a flower petal—with the sharp skinny end for jamming into the rock, and the flat wide end for stepping on.

Before Jun could summon wind to jam it in, gravity took it, and it floated down towards the crushing waters below.

"Sorry," he shouted. "Maybe I should just do both."

Before Kira could respond, a flash of light caught her eye across the valley.

It was the sword Jun had conjured for Ryn, glinting in the light of the setting sun as he drew it from its scabbard.

A gasp that no one heard escaped her mouth as she spotted figures moving in the trees. Ryn held his ground as the first of them came running at him, clad in dark green, swords held high.

Ryn was fast. Faster than fast. It was as if he could predict the swordsman's movements. And then Kira realized—maybe he could. Maybe his aura magic was what gave him the fighting edge.

She turned to Jun, seeing the panic in his eyes. "The Commonality," she said. "The Lord of Between."

"What are we going to do?" he shouted.

Kira glanced down. Yuki was trying to climb up to reach them—she would get pinned against the cliff wall if the soldiers got this far. But she was having trouble climbing. Without thinking, Kira conjured a rope and lowered it down to assist her up. Kira dug her heels into the ledge while Yuki grabbed the rope thankfully and used it to pull herself up the first ledge.

Then Kira had an idea.

"Jun, look inside the cave and see if there's anything at the edge—anything a hook might latch onto!"

Seconds ticked by as she watched more soldiers come out of the woods, all the while Kira stood still, holding the rope as Yuki climbed.

"There's a few rocks jutting out of the front of the cave, but I don't know—"

Ryn was falling back. Four green-clad soldiers were on the ground, but Kira could see they were still moving. Dozens more were appearing out of the woods, advancing on their lone sentry.

"Here, take this!" She checked Yuki's progress and carefully handed over the rope to let Jun take over.

With the Light energy spindled in her core, she quickly conjured a throwing knife into her right hand. Drawing it back, she flung it as hard as she could toward the ridge. It landed at the feet of a soldier, who looked down, then up, spotting them on the cliff.

Kira already had another throwing knife in her hand. She threw knife after knife, but the distance was too great for any accuracy—they dodged them easily. But it provided a distraction for Ryn, who turned and fell back for the cliff. Kira kept up with the throwing knives as Yuki finally joined them on the ledge, and then Jun joined her in the defense. He was more skilled with hand-to-hand combat, but the blades they summoned were enough of a deterrent to slow some of the soldiers down as Ryn reached the base of the cliff.

It was easy for him to scale it with his height, and he was soon panting next to Yuki on the ledge.

Kira threw him a grateful glance. He nodded at her, his lips pressed into a line. "What now?" he asked.

"We've gotta get in there." Kira pointed to the crevice, and he and Yuki peered inside.

"I have an idea." She sent more Light energy through her fingertips to produce more rope, but this time she also summoned a big three-pointed grappling hook at the end.

The Commonality soldiers were crossing the ruins now, and it would only be moments before they reached the bottom of the rock wall. They were so close now that Kira could see the grim looks on their faces. *What in the world had Commander Aita—or the Lord of Between, rather—told them to make them want to come at us like this?*

She didn't see Aita anywhere, but she wasn't surprised. She had no idea which face the Lord of Between would be wearing.

Jun summoned a large shield to protect them—the soldiers with bows had finally gotten to the front of the line.

Kira lowered the grappling hook she had summoned and swung it back and forth a few times, gaining force.

Finally, she flung it around the corner of the cliff, seeking out a ledge she couldn't even see.

"Close!" Ryn called, his eye to the crevice. "Try again!"

She felt the hook scrape rock, then come falling down. She swung again, and again. Then—*clank!* It stuck on something. She yanked on the rope to secure the hook, but with an unpleasant give, the hook came loose, swinging into view again. "Argh!" she groaned, glancing below. And then she spotted the false Commander Aita.

Kira's chest tightened. The face of Aita was gazing up the cliff with a supremely smug look on her face, yet with coldness in her eyes. How could Kira have mistaken the person who stood below her for the real Aita?

She swung again, throwing everything she had into it. With a satisfying *clank*, she knew it landed securely. She yanked on it, and this time it held. Turning back to Jun, she saw him mouth, "Go!"

Unwisely, she glanced down at the crashing waters below. The bottom dropped out of her stomach.

Jun elbowed her in the back. "Go!" he shouted in her ear.

So she went. She stepped off the cliff and her insides froze. Clinging to the rope for dear life, she swung around the rock face. When she reached the apex of her swing, she tightened her core, throwing her feet out to scrape against the cliff.

The rope hanging in a straight line above her now, she climbed hand over hand, praying the hook would continue to hold.

Her feet scraped against the rock wall, slipping, unable to find purchase. Finally, she got near the top but froze—how was she going to get over the water-soaked edge? The falls gushing behind her, blood rushing in her ears, she closed her eyes for a second, thinking. She tried to take a clean breath in and out, and somehow, it worked. She opened her eyes, and she knew what she had to do.

With a burst of brightness, she summoned a Light dagger into her left hand. Only holding the rope with one hand, she plunged the dagger into the edge above, willing the magic to be strong enough. It didn't pierce the rock ledge much, but it was enough. Between the dagger and the rope, she scrambled her way up and over, scraping along inch after inch, her muscles straining in ways she never imagined. Finally, she levered herself onto the wet ledge.

She lay there panting for a second, then remembered her friends' immediate danger. She raced over to where she thought the crevice was, for a second completely ignoring the Tiger's Eye Crystal inside the cave with her. Pressing her face to the crevice, she spotted Ryn nearby.

"I'm going to throw another rope around; catch it and anchor it to something!"

"All right!"

She raced back over to the edge and summoned a nice long rope coiled in her hands, careful to focus her will on coiling the magic into strong fibers. This sort of thing had taken her a long time to perfect, and they couldn't afford any defects. Not now.

She held onto one end and swung the coil around, hoping they would catch it—she felt a tug and she knew they had. Next, she secured her end around one of the rocks her hook had anchored around.

She put her hand on the taut rope and took a deep breath, pulling in some more Light magic from her surroundings. She barely noticed it tingling through her consciousness as she pulled it in. As she exhaled, she closed her eyes and willed more Light magic into the taut rope, adding short vertical ropes coming off it, and another long rope at the bottom. She pictured a horizontal ladder—and when she opened her eyes, that's what she saw.

"All right!" she said, dancing away from the edge when she immediately felt pressure on the rope ladder.

As she waited for her friends to edge around the cliff, she went over to the crystal, eager to figure out its secrets. She brushed aside the feeling of being trapped—for now. Once she got rid of the rope ladder, they would be secure in here, for a time.

The podium on which the crystal stood was carved out of stone, in the shape of a water geyser. "Fitting," she muttered, reaching toward the golden-brown crystal. But she held her fingers back, not sure how it worked and not wanting to risk anything just yet.

Ryn was the first to arrive in the cave. He came around the bend, his hair plastered to his forehead from the spray. Kira thought he was striding over toward her, but he went to the crevice first and pressed his face against the opening, and yelled, "It worked! Go now!"

He turned and grinned at Kira. "That Light magic is rather convenient."

She laughed, a crazed, exhausted laugh. "And so is your Shadow magic. That was some fighting. Thank you for that," she put a hand on his arm, trying to put more meaning into the gesture than her words. She knew it had been hard for him to pick up a sword again after all he had been through.

"Of course. That's what friends do. They keep each other alive from insane shapeshifters controlling imperial soldiers meant to protect them."

Another crazed chuckle escaped Kira, just as Yuki rounded the corner.

"Jun's coming now," she panted, her eyes wide. "He wanted to leave a trap or something I think."

Kira gazed through the crevice but her friend was out of sight. She turned back to face the others. "Well, let's figure this thing out, shall we?"

CHAPTER 28

PUSH AND PULL

They quickly found out that the *Alternative Magicks* book held no more answers. Kira slammed it back in her bag after rereading the brief mention of the crystal a few times, but it only mentioned its whereabouts and purpose, and not how to use it.

Jun stood sentry at the crevice, a bow made from Light in his hands, drawn, with an arrow ready to shoot through the small opening.

They had gotten rid of the rope ladder. With a touch, Kira had dispersed the magic back into the world. There was no way for the Commonality soldiers to follow them.

But that didn't mean they had a lot of time. If the Lord of Between really was this Kage person, then they now knew he had Shadow magic in addition to his abhorrent soul magic. They didn't know what he was capable of.

Kira and Ryn stood across from each other on either side of the crystal.

"Any ideas?" Kira asked him after they stared at it for several minutes, the deafening sound of the falls the only sound.

"Quiet, I'm thinking," he yelled over the noise.

Kira dug her fingernails into her palms, clenching her fists. She watched anxiously as Ryn held one hand up to the crystal, hovering it an inch or so away, doing something Kira couldn't see. After a few minutes he stopped, then returned to staring at it.

Tapping her foot, she let out a huff. They needed to figure this out and get out of here. The soldiers were probably getting Aita-turned-Kage, who could no doubt access this cave easily with his magic.

"We're running out of time!" Kira shouted. "I shouldn't have dragged you all in here on the slim chance of getting my magic back!"

Jun shook his head at her. "We're here, and we're doing this."

"You should take Yuki and go," Kira told him.

The acolyte planted her feet firmly on the wet stone.

"Let's all just go before it's too late. We'll never get this stupid crystal to do anything—!" Then she reached for the crystal, intending on smacking it with the back of her hand.

And everything shifted.

Kira felt as if her damp hair were floating, like she had just touched a tesla coil. Her fingers felt warm, but not in a bad way. She looked up at Ryn.

"I can see..." he began, his eyes wide, "I can see another aura on top of yours, but it's much brighter. I think it's your true aura, the way it should be."

"Really?" Her heart leaped into her throat. "I mean, that's what Kamellia said, we needed to reveal my true soul because it was deformed or something."

He turned his head this way and that, studying her aura. "So, if that's the projection of your true soul, then we revealed it, right? Do you feel any better?"

Kira grimaced. "Should I try some Shadow magic?"

He scrunched up his face. "No, let me look deeper first. Here, take my hand, I'll try to do a soul reading like we did before."

She took his hand with her free one and immediately felt the familiar feverish sensation at the back of her neck.

"Um, Ryn?"

"What?"

"Can we try and do this faster? I really don't want to pass out behind a waterfall with soldiers at our backs."

"I'm doing my best. It's not like I know how to use this thing." He squeezed her hand, then he placed his other hand on the crystal.

The sensation at her neck spread, tingling unpleasantly down her spine now. Her vision swam, and black spots bloomed at the edges of her sight. *No!* she thought. *Not yet.*

"All right," Ryn said, and she looked up at him. "I can see your true soul wavering on top, the colors that should be where the black spot is. But my magic can't affect it, I can't shift it or anything. I'm so sorry, Kira."

A jolt ran through her. How was she supposed to get her magic back? How could she fix her own soul? Blackness that had nothing to do with her broken magic descended on her. They couldn't do it. She had led them here for nothing.

She swallowed, her gaze going blank. *This can't be it. I have to do something. I have to keep fighting!*

After a shaky breath, she let go of Ryn's hand. "Let me try. I need to try."

He backed away and she placed both hands on the golden crystal, closing her eyes. The sound of the rushing falls was the loudest white noise she could possibly imagine, and it easily blocked out all her other thoughts. She breathed in and out, focusing on the sound of the falls, and her breath. She willed herself to focus only on her breath, to calm the storm of emotions welling up inside her. With each breath, a clean energy stole over her, settling her rattled thoughts.

When she opened her eyes again, the cave was filled with a rainbow of light. Not Light magic. She could tell this was something different.

Ryn, who was closest, was surrounded by a dark blue glow, which floated around him in a gentle haze. A darker glittering light danced over the edges of the blue. Jun, his back to her as he watched through the crevice, his arm pulled back drawing an arrow, was surrounded by a blinding gold light with slivers of black and white sparkles and green shimmers. And Yuki, standing against the far wall, was a beacon of buttery orange.

Kira's mouth dropped open in surprise. Were these auras? Is this what Ryn saw all the time?

Ryn and Yuki were staring at her. She took another deep breath to maintain her calm. *Ok*, she thought. *If auras are a projection of the soul, can I see my own aura?*

She looked down at her hands, spread across the crystal. All around her fingertips she could see a haze of blue-silver light. Her breath caught in her throat. She could see it shifting and licking at her fingers like flames. But it also seemed to be getting drawn into the golden crystal. She stared at it, wondering if a little push from her Shadow magic would be needed, just like with her Scrying. She glanced around at the others, then decided.

With another deep breath, she reached out to the Shadow energy in the orb and pulled.

It pulled back.

Her aura stretched out towards the orb, and a tingling sensation cut across her whole body.

So far, the achy feeling in her neck was absent. *Good*. She pulled again. The crystal pulled back, stronger this time. Each time, her aura snapped right back, but that was the only thing that seemed to be happening.

So she pushed instead.

She pushed and her aura went into the orb, flowing through her fingertips. Her heart racing, terrified at what she was doing, she looked down and realized that a black haze seemed to be traveling out of her body now.

That's it! It's working!

She kept pushing her aura into the stone, and the black haze went with it, and disappeared. The stone glowed with her aura now. She felt dizzy, but she had never had her aura outside of her body before. *Now the crystal has my aura, it must have filtered out the wrong part, the disconnected part.*

Now I just have to take it back.

Just then, a figure appeared in the waterfall. Kira blinked hard. There was a figure *in* the waterfall, a black haze all around him.

Chapter 29

The Falls of Azurite

Inside a parting of the water floated a man, one who looked vaguely familiar, though Kira knew exactly who it must be. He stood atop a wave of water inside the rushing falls, the water parting neatly above his head.

Her heart beating in her chest like a frightened rabbit's, she didn't let go of the crystal—*her aura was still in there!* Quickly she began trying to pull it back out, but it was like trying to drink molasses with a straw. As it trickled back in through her fingers, a wave of chills ran over her.

"I see you've found the Tiger's Eye Crystal," the man said, somehow lowering himself to the edge of the cave on his personal wave. He stepped onto the rock and flicked the water from himself in a burst of shadow magic.

Kira shuddered, the chills running up and down her spine from her lack of aura, her skin beginning to burn in cold pain, as if her body had been flayed and wind pushed at her. The longer she stood there auraless, the worse it got.

She needed to keep fighting through it. Was the pain getting better already? She couldn't tell, the fear rising up beginning to drive away the sensation.

Jun abandoned his post by the crevice and came to stand next to Yuki and Ryn, who were falling back by Kira. Jun's arrow pointed straight at the man's heart.

"What do you want?" she demanded belligerently, trying to distract him while she got her aura back.

The man just laughed. "The answer to that question is rather long, Starless girl, and I don't think I'll let you stall that long while you are auraless and powerless. But for now, I'll settle for you and your friend here," he nodded at Jun.

"What for?" Jun demanded.

The man cocked his head. "For keeping you out of my way. And for other... powerful reasons."

Kira swallowed hard. A flash of memory blinded her. Her, chained to the ground, her soul being pulled from her body. He had been stealing the souls of powerful knights and mages. And nothing in this realm was more powerful than a Gray Knight.

Nothing.

A sudden warmth spread over her stinging skin, as the thought of her father stole over her. Not exactly a memory—she didn't have any of him—but the feeling of him.

The words and feelings he had committed to his journals, the stroke of his brush on his paintings. His self. His soul.

Strength returned to Kira's voice. "No. Leave us. You and your vile soul-stealing magic are not wanted anywhere in Camellia, *Kage*."

He bristled a little at the name.

"Who are you, really?" She could feel her aura returning. But she had no idea how much was left. Could she do Shadow magic yet?

Kage brought his hands together to crack a few knuckles, and Kira saw it.

The two missing fingers.

The fingers that she had found beside a portal to the Starless Realm ages ago. It was definitely him, the man who had started all of this horrible magic with portals that didn't belong, that had ripped her family apart—but she wouldn't let him rip her soul apart too.

She yanked on the crystal, but the magic only continued to seep out at the same infuriating speed.

Now he surveyed her with narrowed eyes. "You know nothing about me nor what I'm capable of. Do you think knowing an old name of mine has power over me? I am he and a million others."

"No, but I know you've been practicing vile soul-stealing magic since your Spire days, since my father and Sir

Jovan helped remove you from the temple," she spat at him, seconds still ticking by until she would have her aura back.

"That's enough," he said and gestured at her and Jun.

In a rush, she was yanked from the crystal, propelled toward the edge of the cliff. A wave of chills rolled over her. She felt naked, exposed, raw. She must still be missing some aura. She stumbled next to Jun, only a few feet away from where Kage stood.

But she could still see everyone's aura, including his. Kage's was disturbingly black in most parts, but she wasn't surprised. Was she still siphoning her aura back? She felt a warm sensation in her fingertips and tried pulling on the crystal.

"You know, I was going to take you with me," he said, pacing around them, making them inch further toward the waterfall. "But you've been much too much trouble. And that business with your fathers... well, I'd say it's not personal, but it is. It's all personal.

"They thought they could forbid me from practicing magic? Stunt my powers, my growth by cutting me off?" He scoffed. "It's a shame to waste yours when I know Gray magic is so strong a force. But I can't do it here. So we might as well just—"

With a gesture, Yuki and Ryn skidded toward the edge too, joining Kira and Jun. Their backs to the falls as Kage advanced on them.

"Wait!" Kira cried, panic seizing her. "Stop. Don't hurt anyone. Please, we'll go with you."

He appeared to consider it for a moment. Then he shook his head. "No, it will be best to have the realm's newest most influential magic users out of the way—the age of the Commonality is set to begin. There will be no need for all this Light and Shadow magic, wielded only by a select few.

"And I just can't risk transporting you to Meridian right now to take your souls." He frowned in mock concern. "It's a shame you left the protection of the Commonality soldiers, only to fall victim to those dreadful raiders from the Stone Mountains."

He raised his hands.

"No, stop!" Kira pleaded, taking a step forward. She was feeling stronger now; she must have most of her aura back by now, right?

What did she have to lose?

"Why are you doing this?" she couldn't help but ask. "Because the Spire kicked you out?"

He ran his hand down the front of his robes. Then he rolled his eyes. "The temples are stagnant, their practitioners coddled and spoiled. Gray ones especially. I'm simply looking to level the balance in the realm."

"Then why open the portals?" she asked. "You upset the balance by driving the spirits insane. The spirits told me to fix the balance."

She could feel power gathering at her fingertips. But when she looked at the crystal, it still glowed blue with her aura. But how much was there?

Kage glanced at the crystal and then back at Kira. She wondered if he could see it too.

He reached out, and in an instant, Kira was lifted off the ground, a pressure seizing her throat. She kicked out her legs and reached up to claw at the force at her throat, but there was nothing there to touch. *Shadow magic.*

A scuffle sounded behind her, and she saw Jun and Ryn attempt to reach her. But something invisible flew through the air, binding them somehow.

Her throat closing up, her eyes popping, she watched as Kage strolled over to the crystal.

"Since you've already done me the favor of siphoning your soul's energy into the crystal, perhaps I can take it from here. Before you all tragically fall to your demise in the falls."

He touched the crystal. Kira expected to feel something, but the choking hold at her throat was all she could feel. Was he stealing her soul's energy from the crystal?

He looked up, annoyed. "Come here," he said, and with a wave of his hand, she flew through the air, the force at her throat dragging her like a pair of hands. Another invisible force grabbed one of her hands that was still clawing at her throat and brought her palm to the crystal.

A jolt went through her, and perhaps it was because she was near to suffocating, or perhaps it was because he was trying to connect to her aura instead of merely looking at it—she saw something shift in the world again. It was as if everything was overlaid with an exact duplicate of itself. The cave walls were blurry, the crystal itself doubled around its edges, and the form of Kage, outlined in a blurry black aura still, was overlaid with an image of another man.

One Kira knew quite well.

"You!" she gasped, the word barely audible.

But he looked up. The face of the most powerful person at the Imperial palace beside the Empress shadowed over his face. That of Tigran Tashjian, the grand steward.

He narrowed his eyes at her from across the crystal, and then she fell to the ground.

Coughing and spluttering, she grasped her throat with one hand and tried to scramble away from him with her other hand, slipping and skidding on the wet cave floor. Her double vision was gone, and she was left looking at the face of the man who had entered the cave.

"Yes," he drawled. "Me." And a change came over his face, revealing Tigran's appearance.

That must be his true face.

"You have caused me enough trouble, *Starwind*," he spat, advancing on her. "I won't even take your aura yet. First, I want to dispose of all your friends while you watch, so I can see how it rends your aura each time. I've had enough of you."

"No!" Kira shouted, scrambling to her feet in front of the others, who still stood bound at the cave entrance, the falls gushing behind them. They all seemed to have their limbs bound to their sides with invisible bonds. She flung out her hands in front of them.

She saw Tigran take a quick breath in, and felt a drop in the energy all around her.

He's going to push them over. The falls will kill them. I can't let him!

Without caring that she probably only had half her aura, she yanked on as much Shadow magic as she could find, pulling it from as far as she could. She swayed, her blood pounding painfully through her veins. But she stood firm.

The moment Tigran reached out to push her friends over the falls, she let out a burst of energy, throwing her hands forward. She ignored the tingle at the back of her neck, it was barely even there anymore.

The two forces met midway, and gusts of undirected Shadow wind spun around the cave, throwing Kira off balance. But he kept pushing; she could feel the air moving when she reached out her thoughts to touch it. Jun, Ryn, and Yuki were sliding closer to the edge of the cliff, helpless.

No, Kira thought, pushing the air currents in the other direction. *No!*

But Tigran's magic was too strong. Despite having never completed his training at the Spire—and perhaps because of his despicable soul magic, he was winning. They were going to go over.

Wild ideas ran through her brain in the time it took her to blink—could she conjure a net from Light magic? How would she attach it to anything? Wouldn't the rushing water just sweep it away? The fall into the pool probably wouldn't kill them, if not for the rocks at the bottom of the violently crashing water.

That's it. The water.

She didn't care if she couldn't do it. She *would* do it. She had no choice.

While Tigran was busy pushing air currents out of the cave to shove them off the cliff, Kira kept him occupied with an opposing force. But in the back of her mind, her thoughts were busy reaching out to another element that her Shadow magic could touch. The water.

As the back of her neck began to ache again, she sent her thoughts to the water and found its path along the ridge. She dove into the rapids, cataloging and touching it all with her mind. Without realizing it, her breathing settled into a rhythmic pattern. And with one hand blasting air currents away, she reached the other out to the water above, and shifted it.

Nothing happened at first. She glanced back to see Jun nearest the edge of the cliff, his heels inches away from the edge.

A deep breath, and she shifted the waters again. She only needed the falls to move out of the way of the pool below, so her friends wouldn't be crushed when Tigran finally won their battle over the wind.

He flung something at her, but she whisked it away. She couldn't let him bind her, not like the others. Then all would be lost.

She sunk to one knee, the ache in her neck rolling down her spine now. But she hadn't passed out yet. That was good, right? She had no idea how much of her aura she had taken back, but it seemed like enough. In the back of her mind, a spark of joy zinged through her. She was doing it! She could touch Shadow magic again!

Focusing again on the task at hand, she narrowed her thoughts back to the water. Pushing and pushing, she rode the water molecules with her mind, shifting them, nudging them in a different direction—*only temporarily*, she told them.

And then the sound outside the cave began to change.

Despite Jun's trap left on the ledge outside, there must have been some soldiers there attempting to get in, because they began yelling in surprise on the other side of the rock.

The sound of the falls changed. Kira didn't look, but the noise of the crashing water had shifted drastically in pitch.

She was doing it. She was moving the falls.

Tigran's eyes widened in momentary fear and he gazed at her for a long moment while she struggled to hold the magic. Then a nasty grin came over his face.

"So, you're after my other legacy, too?"

"What?" she ground out; her teeth clenched as she fought to keep both magics moving. Her feet had begun to slip, forcing her back toward her friends as he pushed.

"The Fall of Azurite," Tigran said simply, still not breaking a sweat from the force of his magic. "You had to go and fix all that, too, didn't you? Raiden's downfall... for a time. Until you came along."

"*You* moved the falls?" she gasped, her voice shrill. "You destroyed Azurite and started the feud?"

She almost lost her concentration, and her foot slipped again. But the water was her main focus. It slid across her thoughts, the Shadow magic present in the water slippery and hard to move. But she pushed. With all of her might, she pushed.

"Again, the surprise," Tigran said. "Of course it was me. Not even Raiden is as powerful as I, though I'll admit it was infuriating to lay the claim at his feet. But the reward was worth it."

"*Reward?* Starting the feud, you mean? Why on earth would you want to do that?" Rage filled her. How many lives had been lost because of the decades-long feud? She pushed a blast of energy out toward him, shoving it from her fingertips and renewing her attack.

Tigran stumbled backward but came back harder than before. Kira shifted her main focus back to the water.

The pitch had changed entirely. But she couldn't tell where the water was. Had she made the drop safe enough? Could they just fall into the pool of water below?

If he shoved them off the cliff, she hoped the falls wouldn't crush them—as long as she held on to her magic.

She pictured the falls slipping over the ridge, down the cliff, and into the moss-covered ruins instead of the pool below. Right now, she had no sympathy for the Commonality soldiers gathered there; they would see it coming, and they had chased them into this cave, battling Ryn on their way—it was clear these soldiers were in league with Tigran's more sinister plans. Was that the case for the entire Commonality? She had no way of knowing.

A wave of dizziness crashed over her, and she swayed on the spot. But she couldn't stop now. The waterfall would just go back to its original path if she let go. She had to defeat Tigran, or he would throw them off the cliff to their deaths just to get rid of them.

Tigran's Shadow magic was strong. Kira was sliding toward the edge from the force of it.

Would they even make it if they fell safely into the pool below? Would the soldiers just capture them when they landed in the water? She didn't know if moving the falls had done anything—the soldiers probably ran for the high ground where they had left their horses.

She looked back at Jun, Ryn, and Yuki, and saw the fear in their eyes. She wished Ryn and Yuki had never come.

A jolt of adrenaline rushed through her, and she forced herself to take a quick clean breath and focus. All those hours meditating had to be worth something, right?

She locked eyes with Tigran, and he gave her a knowing smile. She was failing. Her magic wasn't strong enough.

But then she remembered her father's favorite book of poems.

Even the fiercest sink into darkest despair

Only to rise brighter than all the stars combined.

She couldn't let her friends die, just for helping her. And she wasn't going to go down without pushing herself to her limit. She and Jun didn't deserve to die just for being Gray, and getting in Tigran's way.

The waterfall was putting an enormous strain on her magic, her temples throbbing, not to mention the back of her neck aching something fierce. So she let it go.

Tigran grinned, thinking her defeated.

She continued blasting Tigran with Shadow wind while she pulled more Light and Shadow from all around her. After letting go of the waterfall, it was easy. She could pull it in quicker than breathing.

And then she let it all out in a burst of calculated power.

With her right hand, she shot a force toward Tigran, while with her left, she used both Light and Shadow to encapsulate her and her friends.

It wrapped around them in a bubble of twisting magic, the two forces knit together in a barrier as strong as her will. With her blast combined with Tigran's assault, their

Light and Shadow capsule shot from the cave like a bullet, breaking through the barrier of water and sailing through the air.

The force knocked them all together. Elbows and knees sticking into her back, Kira tried to focus on willing the capsule not to break. Whether they would land in water or on land, she didn't know. But they were away—away from Tigran—or Kage—or whoever he was.

She flung her hands out, touching the sides of the capsule, which were nothing more than a thick cushion of air surrounded by a pulsing barrier of light magic.

In the next instant, they crashed.

Her temples throbbed alarmingly, and she felt the barriers go down.

And then everything went black.

Chapter 30

Allies

The scent of spiced orange incense filtered in through her subconscious, and she woke with a jolt.

Somehow, she was back in her room in the Gray Wing.

Thinking she must be dreaming, she scrambled to her feet, her head swimming. She put a hand to her throbbing temples as she emerged into her study and then out into the common room. It didn't feel like a dream. The lamps were lit, and it was dark outside, but everything was bathed in the dim glow of Light magic. Where was everyone? How did she even get here?

Soft voices filtered inside from the balcony, half of the paper-paneled doors open to let in the summer night. The smell of food wafting from the kitchen made her mouth water, but she continued stumbling toward the balcony, her heart thudding.

"Starless girl, you're awake?"

It was Zowan.

She crashed into him, throwing her arms around his torso. "You're okay!" she cried.

"Of course I am," he said, pulling away and looking at her, one hand on her shoulder. "Are you?"

She tucked a strand of hair behind her ear, looking around the balcony. Anzu was close by, still in full armor as always, standing nearest the railing. Jun, Yuki, and Ryn were grouped around a small table that held tea and an assortment of food. They were all looking up at her.

"I'll survive," she said. "What about Tigran—Kage, whatever? What happened? We have to warn the Empress, and tell everyone—"

"Sit down, why don't you?" Jun said, coming over and shoving a warm pastry into her hand. "Eat something. You really drained yourself with that magic. The Gray Knights are on their way here to help us take care of the situation, and Zowan sent a letter on the wind to the palace."

"Really?"

"Really. Now, eat something. Anzu brought all this from the tavern where she's lodging, so we have some proper food and meat."

She allowed Jun to steer her over to the table and into a cushioned stool that he must have summoned with Light magic. She bit into the pastry but didn't taste it she ate it so fast. He handed her another, looking concerned at her drooping eyelids. She tried sitting up straighter. She didn't care if she was tired. She needed some answers.

"Well, what happened?" she demanded between bites.

Ryn chuckled, and then his face turned serious. "After you got us out of the cave, we couldn't wake you up. Jun did some Shadow magic on the four of us so the soldiers wouldn't see us."

"Then I summoned a sled to carry you," Jun continued. "And we found the horses away from the ruins; they must have fled when the water moved. And we rode back to the Spire."

"But what about the soldiers? And Tigran?"

"We watched for a little while to see if they were going to go to the Spire to look for us, but they didn't. They packed up and left. I didn't see Tigran, or Kage, or whoever he is anywhere. He probably changed form after coming out from the waterfall."

The waterfall. Kira's face went blank.

Had she really moved it?

The silence from the others confirmed it. She stared at her hands in shock. All that power that had gone through them. She had no idea she was capable of something like that. And that was only with part of her aura restored.

She lifted her hand, wondering.

"It's healed," Ryn said in answer to her silent question. "Or reconnected, as the spirit said. After you sent it into the crystal and your complete soul was revealed, your aura began to return, filling in the pieces that were covered in black."

"But I didn't take it all back from the crystal; is it still there? Did Tigran...?"

"Your aura is full. It's generated by your soul, so even if you left some behind, it would come back to you anyway. I think he needs a lot more magic and a specific setup to take a soul—that's why he wanted to take you with him, right?"

"Oh. Yeah."

Jun pushed a plate her way with more food. She ate a steamed bun in silence, savoring the meat inside.

Then she voiced a question that had begun to weigh heavily on her ever since she moved the falls.

"The soldiers at the waterfall—I didn't—did I...?"

"I don't think you killed anyone," Jun said bluntly. "From what it looked like, they all left on their own two feet. And the ruins were already ruins." He held a note of respect in his voice she hadn't heard addressed to her before.

"But what about Tigran?" she repeated. "We have to go to the palace and warn the Empress."

Zowan cleared his throat and said, "We're working on it. Like Jun said, the Gray Knights are on their way here. We can't just go marching into the palace and accuse the grand steward of the highest treason. Especially a man that powerful. I sent a letter to Advisor Goten; he's trustworthy and can alert the Empress and the other advisors without tipping off Tigran—if he even shows his face there after all of this."

Kira thought that over, relaxing her shoulders a little. "Well, that seems like a good course of action. How long until the Gray Knights get here?"

Jun glanced over the balcony northward, where rolling hills hid the landscape. "Hours yet still. They were spread really thin because of the raiders—just what Tigran wanted, I'm sure—but my father was closest, hopefully he gets here soon."

Kira eyed the tea on the table, and Yuki poured her a cup without her asking. Kira took it gratefully.

Zowan was shaking his head. "I can't believe he's the reason for the feud. Destroying Azurite..." His eyes went blank, no doubt recalling the destruction. After all, he had been there.

"Where's Raiden?" Kira asked suddenly. "What does he think of all this?"

"He and Commander Aita went to the Stone Mountains," Zowan said.

"He *what?* With *Aita?*" Kira asked, nearly toppling off her stool.

Zowan shook his head. "I couldn't believe it either. But it might be worth it. They were fairly amenable when I went to inquire about the raiders, considering I was accusing them of attacking us. He wanted to reach out for an ally now that we know Tigran is our enemy."

"I guess knowing who framed him for the fall of Azurite gave him some incentive to reach out to Lady Madora?" Kira mused. "And Aita wanted to go? What for?"

"After you all came back," Zowan explained, "Aita was found unconscious in her study. After what happened with the Lord of Between—Tigran, I should say—Aita wanted nothing to do with the palace or the Commonality anymore, not knowing who she could trust. So she volunteered to go with him to see Lady Madora. After quitting the Commonality she might not be too welcome in Meridian anymore."

"Wow," Kira said. A silence descended on the balcony, as everything they had told her sunk in.

Thistle soared down from where he had been hiding in a nearby tree and landed on Kira's knee, making her almost spill her cup of tea. "I hear that was some fine magic you did out there," he squeaked.

Kira's face warmed as she realized everyone else was looking at her. "I—well, I didn't know how else we were all going to get out of there."

"You moved the whole waterfall," Jun said with a grin. "You don't have to be modest."

Kira didn't know what to say to that. She took another sip of her tea, which had gone cold during the conversation. Anzu put a hand on her shoulder.

"You did well," the knight said.

"Thanks, Anzu."

"I think you should all try to rest more while we wait for Jovan and the Gray Knights," Anzu said. "Do you think the traditions of the Spire could be waived for one night?" she directed at a puzzled Zowan. "I'd like all of us to stay in the Gray Wing," she clarified with a hint of a smile.

Zowan and Jun chuckled.

Kira said, "If the Spirekeeper comes to yell at us, it's not my problem."

Chapter 31

Approach with Strength

Kira was shaken awake in the early hours of the morning by Anzu. It felt as if she had only been asleep for a few minutes; they had stayed up as late as they could, waiting for the Gray Knights to arrive.

"They're here," Anzu told her. "Outside the city's gate. Jovan's sent word."

In less than ten minutes, the whole lot of them were striding down the Hall of Spirits to meet up with Yuki and Ryn, who had gone ahead and readied all of their horses.

They rode through the predawn city streets in silence, fresh adrenaline surging through Kira's veins. Finally, they would clear all of this up, finally, they knew who the Lord of Between really was.

She had no idea if Tigran would try to return to the palace now that his identity had been revealed, or if he would retreat with his beaten soldiers, readying for another attack, another assault on the balance of Camellia.

Thistle perched atop Naga, clutching her mane for balance. Kira patted the mare gratefully as they passed through Heliodor's gate. She was glad her friends had been able to recover the horses after the incident at the waterfall. She had almost lost Naga once before, she didn't want to lose her again.

Silhouetted against the dawn, six mounted figures stood just outside the gate.

Sir Jovan dismounted at the sight of them, his diamond-patterned chainmail draped across his shoulders and chest, clinking against his shoulder pauldrons. He strode over to Jun, who had dismounted as soon as he saw his father. Jovan drew his son into a hug, clapping him on the back.

"Well, it looks like we missed the fight," Jovan said almost wistfully as he pulled away, eyeing Kira. She blushed and gave him a stiff smile. "We'll ride for Meridian straight away. I wouldn't put it past Tigran to return to the palace—the Empress could be in danger, but it's best we approach with strength and care. You sent a message warning them, correct?" he asked Zowan.

He nodded swiftly. "I sent a note to the advisors; they should be able to enable the safeguards for the Empress without alerting Tigran, if he dared return."

"Let's hope they received it," Jovan said darkly. Then he turned his gaze on Jun and Kira. "We need to get you two trained properly so you can officially join us. With skills like yours Kira, you'll be a knight in no time. But it's no wonder, you being Rokuro's daughter."

Her face burning even harder, she gave him a slight bow from her saddle. She couldn't even imagine joining their ranks yet.

"We better get going," Jovan said, mounting his white gelding. "Like I said, I doubt Tigran would return to the palace after you discovered him, but the Empress needs to know; we should inform her in person. Tigran has been grand steward almost her entire reign. And if he is there, well, we need to approach the situation delicately."

Jovan turned his gelding north on the Kaidō road, and clicked his tongue, urging his mount to speed. Kira and the others followed, with the other five Gray Knights flanking them.

They followed the Kaidō road as the sun rose, cantering when they could, eating up the countryside with their long strides.

Kira's mind was refreshingly calm considering everything that had happened in the last twenty-four hours. But despite the worry over Tigran still being at large, the knowledge that her soul was intact filled her with joy. She could reach out with her mind and touch the Shadow magic in the world around her, and not even a hint of the ache in her neck threatened. She was healed. She had done it.

And it had been worth the fight. They had discovered the Lord of Between's true identity, and even though at the time she had thought she and her friends weren't going to survive the encounter behind the waterfall, she had performed powerful gray magic.

For once she felt like she was following in her father's footsteps.

It wasn't until after dark that they reached the city of Meridian.

The city was awash with lantern light, and Kira could see everything outlined in the delicate glow of Light magic. They rode in through the main gate and up the streets to the imperial palace, Kira's nerves jangling. Where was Tigran? Would they need to defend the Empress?

When they reached the bridge leading over the moat that surrounded the palace, they were stopped briefly by the palace guards. So far, Kira hadn't seen a single Commonality soldier. *Tigran and the soldiers must be in hiding,* she thought. *I can't believe he convinced all those commoners to follow him. Well, it's not like he hasn't done it before, turning them against magic.*

After a hurried conversation with the guard, Jovan led them all inside the palace grounds, passing through a large wooden gate, and following a wide white stone path to the side of the palace. They quickly left their horses with the stable hands and headed inside.

Kira hadn't been at the palace since last year when the Empress had been keen on inviting her for formal teas after they had found out she had lived in the Starless Realm. But after the debacle at the spring festival, Master Ichiro had pleaded on her behalf that she needed to focus on her training and should stay at the temple.

The corridors were exactly as she remembered, and the dark wooden boards chirped under their feet. Beautiful paintings and wall hangings decorated the walls, gilt accents glittering in the lantern light, among decorative vases and statues at regular intervals.

A palace guard led them to a room Kira hadn't been in before. He swung open a set of wide double doors, revealing a rectangular room, with an ornate throne facing them on the opposite side. The throne itself was a gold and turquoise lacquered affair, with ornate carvings of chrysanthemums and leaves along the wall behind it. Above, a small awning covered the area, carved and colored in the same style.

The Empress surveyed them as they walked in, her dark brows pinched in worry. Her curly hair was styled atop her head, with a simple silver and sapphire tiara sticking out of a fold in her hair. She wore a beautiful gown of matching sapphire, with white and black flowers boldly depicted across the fabric.

Seats at the other side of the room were filled with the palace advisors, many of whom bowed in their seats to Kira and the Gray Knights as they walked past. Tigran Tashjian was nowhere to be seen, nor any of his Commonality soldiers. Kira breathed a sigh of relief, her shoulders relaxing slightly.

Sir Jovan matched Kira's strides, and soon the two of them stood in front of the Empress. They both bowed deeply, and when they straightened, Empress Mei gave them a slight nod of acknowledgment, her forehead creased in worry. Kira looked at Jovan, and he held his hand out for her to speak.

Her stomach writhed as she licked her lips, wondering where she should start, and why she of all of them had to do it. The Empress did favor her, she knew, but couldn't Jovan do it? *But I was there. And if I'm to be a Gray Knight, I'll need to take the lead in times like these, I suppose.*

"Your Majesty... I—we—have come here with an important discovery. You see, yesterday we discovered the identity of the Lord of Between, and coincidentally, he's the same person who is responsible for the Fall of Azurite." She glanced at Jovan, who gave her an encouraging nod.

"Since he can shapeshift, it was difficult to figure out his identity, but I used the Tiger's Eye Crystal at Azurite to see through it and—well, the Lord of Between is—"

The double doors burst open, and there stood Tigran Tashjian.

Chapter 32

Protect the Realm

"Good, you're here," Tigran said swiftly, sweeping into the throne room. He was as polished as ever, a thigh-length surcoat fastened with ornately carved wood buttons running down the front, the fabric giving off a subtle twinkle from the black gems embedded in the fabric.

Kira's jaw dropped. He was here? And acting so calmly? A cold panic seized her, and her breathing became shallow as she watched a dozen or so Commonality soldiers in forest green uniforms follow him into the throne room, falling into a line behind him.

"Your Majesty," Tigran said to the Empress with a bow, "it appears the Starless girl was healthy enough to apprehend the Lord of Between after all; you need not have worried."

"I—wait—*what*?" Kira stuttered.

"Take them," Tigran instructed, pointing at Sir Jovan and the Gray Knights.

Kira remained motionless as half of the soldiers marched over, each holding an unusually delicate set of manacles. They placed the delicate silver manacles on all six of the Gray Knights. Kira felt a strange change in the energy around her, as if more magic were in the air.

"Do not worry," Tigran went on, addressing the Empress and the advisors at the back of the receiving room, "they can do no harm with these new manacles the Commonality was able to create. They're able to remove any magic from a person once encircled around their wrists."

Kira thought back to a moment in the rain, when she knelt in a circle of silver, her powers being stripped from her. "But—!"

Tigran was pacing in front of them and now stood directly in front of Kira. As he leaned over to check on Jovan's manacles, he whispered to her, "I would keep your mouth shut if I were you, Starless girl," he said, his lip curling in an unpleasant smirk. "Unless you want to go with them. The Empress likes you. You want to keep it that way, hmm?"

She stared wordlessly at him as he turned his back on her. She looked over at the others who thankfully remained unharmed. Jun was struggling to stand still,

Zowan and Anzu holding him back; perhaps they had heard Tigran's words too. A terrible ache settled in her stomach, bile roiling around and making her feel sick.

Ryn stood stock still, though she noticed his right arm hung awkwardly at his side, his fingers clenching and unclenching, as if wishing he had a sword. Yuki was staring at the Empress. Kira wished she could ask what in the world they all were thinking.

"But the Gray Knights—" Kira blurted, unable to help herself.

"We are all disappointed," Tigran said in a serious tone as if agreeing with her. "But after that display of power yesterday at the ruins of Azurite, just to intimidate the Commonality soldiers, well I'm not surprised Sir Jovan turned out to be this nefarious Lord of Between person. Clearly, they all have a disdain for the common people, seeking only to further magic. Just another reason the Commonality is needed to protect the realm."

"But Sir Jovan isn't—"

"And to think Jovan started the feud in the first place by crushing Azurite." He shook his head, *tsking*. "Clearly the Gray Knights wanted to cripple the realm so they could rise to the highest power, making us rely only on magic. But thanks to the Empress' clever appointment of the Commonality, we can once again have balance in the realm. An even field for all."

Kira couldn't think anymore. Couldn't come up with anything to say. If she disagreed with Tigran, she would look like she was making it up, and he would just toss her in manacles too for siding with Jovan. Why hadn't she just gone out and said it was Tigran? Hadn't the palace gotten their message?

Clearly, it had been intercepted; Tigran must have returned here right away to lay his trap and secure his innocence. Kira quickly scanned the row of chairs where the advisors sat. Goten was not among them. She bit her lip, hoping the kind advisor was all right. He was the only advisor with Light magic. Dread boiled in her stomach as she wondered if Tigran would attempt his soul-stealing magic on the kindly advisor.

As the Commonality led the Gray Knights away, Kira swallowed hard. She met Jun's eyes; his face was contorted with rage, and his eyes pleaded with her to do something.

But what could she do?

She opened her mouth, but nothing came out. And then the Empress spoke.

"I am disappointed in our knights," Empress Mei said sadly, her long lashes brushing her cheeks as she watched the last of them as they were led out the doors. They have been protectors of the realm for longer than my reign. However, with the accounts from Tigran and at least a dozen soldiers, the facts cannot be denied. The Fall of Azurite was a great tragedy that sparked twenty years of violence, and those responsible for it cannot be allowed to walk free. The activities of the mage known as the Lord of Between have upset the balance of the realm even further, creating chaos among spirits and hatred among people."

The Empress turned to Kira and beckoned her forward. Her legs felt numb, but somehow she propelled herself a few feet ahead. What should she do? The Empress favored her, like Tigran said, so she would believe what Kira said, right? Or would the Empress just be disappointed in her too, for siding with Jovan? Her stomach twisted as she tried to come up with something—anything to say that would fix this.

"Lady Starwind," the Empress said, "I thank you for your service to the realm once again. With you at our side, and our new Commonality, we will find peace and equality for everyone. I'll be looking forward to hearing more about your training. After you helped uncover the Lord of Between, I expect even more great things of you."

Kira's mouth was dry now, but she had nothing to say. Numb, she just bowed and then fled to stand beside

Zowan, shaking. It was over. It was too late. Tigran had the upper hand.

The Empress stood, and everyone bowed. Before Kira even straightened again the Empress was on her way out of the room. It was all moving too fast. What could she do?

Nothing if she was put in a cell, with no access to magic. She glared at Tigran, who was giving her a polite smile. But she could see the malice and trickery behind those cold dark eyes.

Tigran followed the Empress out the doors, his surcoat furling as he went, his stride sure. He had beaten them again. Had struck a blow so hard she had no idea how they would recover.

As soon as they were gone, the advisors began leaving their seats. Not wanting to get caught in conversation with them right now, Kira grabbed Zowan's arm and pushed Jun and the others from the room.

"Let's get out of here," she growled. "Before Tigran changes his mind and has us arrested too."

The chirping boards underfoot sounded far less cheerful as they fled to the stables, now six people short.

"We have to go back in there!" Jun burst as soon as they were out of earshot of any of the guards. Kira noticed a set of Commonality soldiers posted at the stables who hadn't been there when they came in. *It was a trap. He knew we would come, and he was ready to scapegoat Sir Jovan.*

"We can't," Kira said, grabbing Jun's shoulders. "I'm sorry. Tigran will arrest all of us—and what then? How will we do anything to fight against him?"

He shook his head violently. "He has my father!"

Zowan stepped in. "Your father wouldn't want you risking your life too. We need to stay smart in order to have any chance of rescuing them or convincing the Empress of the truth. Kira's right, if we're all locked up, we'll have let him win, and we won't be able to take any action at all."

Jun stared at him mutinously, but he said nothing.

They found their horses as quickly as they could. Kira felt as if the Commonality soldiers watching them might try to stop them at any moment, and when she found Naga, she ran up to the mare, her eyes stinging with tears.

Jun led his father's horse out beside his own and attached his reins to his saddle. No one said anything.

Five minutes later, the six of them were mounted and making their way toward the bridge that led out of the palace grounds over the small moat. Kira stared at the opening in the wall, willing the guards and soldiers to remain where they were, to let them pass.

She let out an immense sigh as they passed over the bridge, and into the main street.

"It's a good thing Empress Mei likes me," Kira said in a hollow voice as soon as they were out of earshot of the guards, "Otherwise I think Tigran would have included us in his treachery."

"We should ride for Gekkō-ji right away," Anzu said, flinging her long braid over her shoulder and summoning a tall polearm now they were out of the palace grounds. "We need to alert Mistress Nari and Master Starwind."

"And Raiden," Zowan said, adjusting the swords at his hip. "We can't trust this information to messages. Tigran obviously has ways of intercepting them. We should have ridden for the palace straight away once we knew it was him," he said a little too loudly.

"It probably would have been too late already," Anzu said quietly. "By then he would have returned with his soldiers—and he probably would have accused *you*."

Zowan grumbled something, then said, "I'll go alert Raiden. It's a good thing he was already seeking an ally. We're going to need them."

Kira sniffed. "And it was probably a good thing he wasn't here for this."

Zowan and Jun muttered their agreements. A display of irrational storm magic in front of the Empress wouldn't have helped anyone—except Tigran perhaps.

"Well, we're lucky Tigran hasn't outlawed Shadow and Light magic," Zowan said in disgust as they all headed through the city.

Kira shuddered. "Yeah, he's only got a non-magic army ready for when he does though."

"We won't let it come to that," Anzu said.

Kira felt a pricking sensation at the back of her neck that had nothing to do with her soul, and everything to do with the handful of Commonality soldiers they spotted along the streets. She wasn't sure if they were following them, or if there were somehow so many that they were posted throughout the city. Kira and the others moved fast, feeling that Tigran and the Commonality might change their minds at any moment and arrest them.

Once they rode through the gate out of the city, the lantern light subsided, and Kira found herself staring at the star-filled sky above a dark plain. The stars seemed to press down upon her, a heavy weight on her heart.

They tore down the Kaidō road, a cloud of dust at their heels. They summoned balls of flame to act as lanterns, so that their horses—and the Shadow mages—could see, the orbs floating above their heads as they galloped on in the night. When they reached a fork in the road, they came to a halt. Kira patted Naga as she stared up at the star-strewn sky, still feeling a little lost.

Ryn and Yuki had pointed their horses to the path to the left toward the Spire. But Zowan was still next to Anzu in the center of the fork.

"Well, Starless girl?" Zowan said. "Which way are you heading?"

With one last glance up at the stars, she sighed. "I don't know what we need to do to defeat Tigran anymore. But I know I definitely need to work on my Shadow magic to be of any use. Which is why I was going to ask you if I could be your squire."

Zowan's mouth dropped open and beside him, Anzu smiled.

"I told you," Anzu said, nudging his leg with her own.

Looking more than a little flustered, Zowan squeezed Anzu's leg, saying, "I guess I owe you dinner then."

Kira couldn't keep the smirk off her face as she traded amused looks with Jun. *Zowan and Anzu?*

"Well I should head on to Gekkō-ji," Anzu said. "I don't think you need extra protection in Heliodor anymore Kira; you'll be in good hands with Zowan."

"I'll go with you," Jun told the knight. "I'd like to speak with Master Starwind and Mistress Nari myself, too. And—well, if you'll have me, Lady Anzu, I'd like to be your squire," he said with a small bow of his head.

Her face lit up briefly. "I'd be honored, Kosumoso. We all need to stick together now. We can't know who else Tigran has in his pocket. I still can't believe he convinced the Empress..."

"I'll go with you too," Thistle chimed in. "I need to report this to Gekkō. He's not going to be happy, but maybe he can help you, now that we know who's responsible for driving all those spirits to ruin." He glided over to Jun's shoulder, who stood up straighter with a shadow of a smile at his lips.

"We'll head for the Spire then," Kira said, nodding at Zowan. "And south if we have to, to find Raiden."

"*I'll* go to the Stone Mountains if anyone has to," Zowan growled. "You're going back to the Spire. Now that you have your Shadow magic back, you need to learn how to control it."

She lowered her chin and looked up at him. "What? Right now? We can start later, what with Tigran and the Commonality—"

"Even the Empress expects you to keep training," Anzu reminded her. "Both of you," she looked at Jun. "We mustn't give the palace any reason to be suspicious. You'll both continue training while we figure this out."

"All right," Kira sighed. "But Tigran is even more dangerous now that we know who he is. And with the Commonality at his beck and call—"

"We'll handle it," Anzu said. "Somehow."

"Together," Zowan added.

Kira nodded and looked down the road that led to the Spire. So she was finally to begin her Shadow training, after all this. She shook her head. Part of her almost wished her soul was still damaged and everything was normal.

But things wouldn't really be *normal* until they removed Tigran as a threat to the realm. And he was growing more and more powerful by the day.

A guilty thought occurred to her as she realized with a hint of excitement that she would get to go back and learn Shadow magic, begin assisting Zowan as his squire, and even pick up where she left off with Micah—provided Tigran and the Commonality didn't start another feud or anything.

She took a deep cleansing breath. It was her duty as a future Gray Knight to protect the realm. She would have to do whatever it took to get Jun's father back, and to stop Tigran and the Commonality. "We've got to do this. We've got to fight."

They said their goodbyes, and Kira tried not to let the tears in her eyes spill over while anyone could see.

She and the others rode on into the night, the blanket of stars illuminating the skies as her Light magic illuminated the earth.

About the Author

Liz Delton writes and lives in New England, with her husband and sons. She studied Theater Management at the University of the Arts in Philly, always having enjoyed the backstage life of storytelling.

World-building is her favorite part of writing, and she is always dreaming up new fantastic places.

She loves drinking tea and traveling. When she's not writing or reading, you can find her baking in the kitchen, out in the garden, or narrating books on her podcast, Fictional Bookshop.

Visit her website at **LizDelton.com**

Also by Liz Delton

REALM OF CAMELLIA

The Starless Girl

The Storm King

The Gray Mage

The Starlight Dragon

The Fall of Azurite

SEASONS OF SOLDARK

Spectacle of the Spring Queen

The Mechanical Masquerade

All Hallows Airship

The Clockwork Ice Dragon

EVERTURN CHRONICLES

The Alchemyst's Mirror

FOUR CITIES OF ARCERA

Meadowcity

The Fifth City

A Rift Between Cities

Sylvia in the Wilds

WRITER'S NOTEBOOKS

Writer's Notebook

Teen Writer's Notebook

Guided Writer's Notebook

Made in the USA
Las Vegas, NV
05 September 2024